FELICITY CARROL
AND THE
PERILOUS PURSUIT

FELICITY CARROL

AND THE

PERILOUS PURSUIT

A MYSTERY

Patricia Marcantonio

CROOKED
LANE

NEW YORK

Published in the United States by Crooked Lane Books, an imprint of The Quick Brown Fox & Company LLC.

Crooked Lane Books and its logo are trademarks of The Quick Brown Fox & Company LLC.

Library of Congress Catalog-in-Publication data available upon request.

ISBN (hardcover): 978-1-68331-896-5
ISBN (ePub): 978-1-68331-897-2
ISBN (ePDF): 978-1-68331-898-9

Cover design by Melanie Sun
Book design by Jennifer Canzone

Printed in the United States.

www.crookedlanebooks.com

Crooked Lane Books
34 West 27th St., 10th Floor
New York, NY 10001

First Edition: February 2019

10 9 8 7 6 5 4 3 2 1

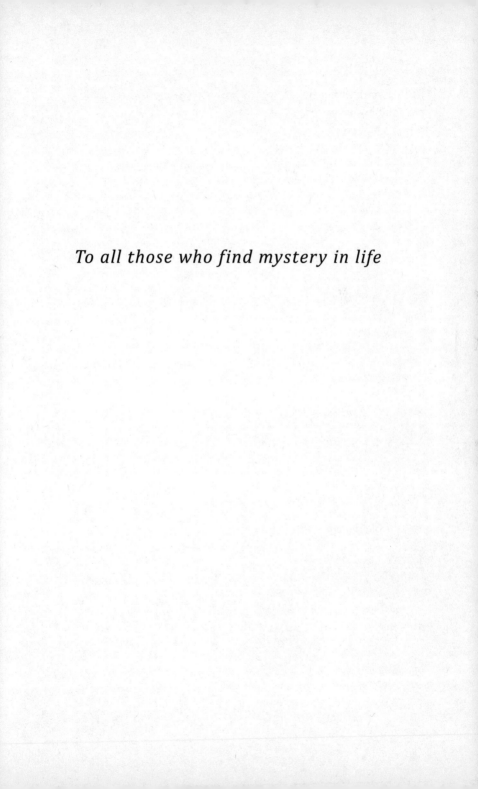

To all those who find mystery in life

There she weaves by night and day
A magic web with colours gay.
She has heard a whisper say,
A curse is on her if she stay
To look down to Camelot.

—Alfred, Lord Tennyson

CHAPTER 1

Surrey, England
1887

"Everyone, please take shelter behind the hedges," Felicity Carrol announced.

Her homemade bomb was about to explode.

The dozen servants obeyed without hesitation. It was nearly ten at night, and they had already rescued what furniture and art they could from the east wing before Felicity told them to leave the rest to the flames. With help, she had first rescued the chemicals and scientific equipment from her laboratory, which was the source of the fire currently consuming the house.

When Felicity had determined that the blaze could not be contained and would spread, she had come up with a plan to save the rest of Carrol Manor. In the kitchen, she had combined the perfect amounts of glycerin with nitric and sulfuric acids. She added torn paper and porridge oats to absorb the unstable mixture. With cautious movements, she packed the volatile paste into an Italian ceramic urn she had always disliked. As she did so, she reviewed the formula in her mind. Many times, pride in her knowledge and abilities suppressed any doubt about her experiments. She loathed that aspect of her personality—taking pleasure in what she could accomplish. For instance, she would have bet no other young woman in England—well, in all of Surrey anyway—was capable of constructing a bomb in her kitchen. Despite the delicate work, Felicity wanted to laugh. Besides her, what young woman would even want to pack an urn with dynamite?

Still, better to be careful in case she did not know as much as she thought she did about bomb making. Although confident in her chemistry, she didn't want anyone harmed if something went wrong. And plenty had already gone wrong this evening. The fire was proof of that. So she had asked the servants to leave while she created the explosive.

Aided by John Ryan, the affable Irishman in charge of the grounds, she had carried the dynamite-filled urn outside. Together, they had placed it in the middle of the long hallway connecting the east wing to the rest of the manor.

After glancing back to make sure everyone was protected, Felicity lit a match to a line of gun powder Ryan had supplied. Spitting sparks, the powder burned toward her handmade explosive.

"Time to run," she told Ryan.

"As you say, Miss Carrol."

She picked up her skirt for an unfettered escape. Ryan ran alongside her.

Behind the hedge, they all waited. The air pounded. The ground tremored, and glass shattered. A burning timber flew over their heads, eliciting gasps from the female servants.

Felicity peeked around the hedge. A good thirty-foot chunk of the hallway had been blasted away. Her explosion had contained the fire to the east wing. The main house had suffered some shattered windows but was otherwise safe.

"You did it, Miss Felicity. No doubt they heard your bomb clear to Guildford," Ryan said in his comfortable brogue.

"How much simpler if we'd had a stick of dynamite. But one must make do, thanks all the same to Mr. Alfred Nobel." She did not want to appear too pleased with herself.

The remaining fire spit and hissed.

"What in heaven will your father say to all this?" Ryan shoved his hands in his pockets.

How would her father react? She knew very well. Samuel Carrol would only squint his eyes, let out a billow of annoyance at his daughter's actions, and hole himself up in his den with cigars and brandy. He had scarcely visited the manor since she had returned home from the university eight months ago. She didn't expect him to rush back because she had accidentally torched part of the house.

Felicity wiped ash from her forehead. Her throat dried from more than the smoke in the air. She wished her father would yell. Better yet, she wished he would sit her down and talk about how she had been careless and tell her to be more careful next time. Ask whether she had been injured during the course of the evening. Did she need to see a doctor?

But all those conversations with her father would never happen. For they would mean actually talking *with* her and not around her or through her, as was her father's way.

"Although the fire did start in my laboratory, we did manage to save the rest of the manor. Perhaps the explosion will amount to a point in my favor," she told Ryan.

"Let's hope so, Miss." Ryan bowed. "Excuse me, I'm going to have the men soak the hallway nearest the house so the blaze won't jump the fine new gulf you created."

He ran off to join others hauling buckets of water drawn from one of the wells on the estate.

Ash scattered onto their heads as Felicity and the other servants watched the fire broaden its reach into the east wing. The flames resembled orange ribbons waving destruction. The servants' faces were red from the heat and smeared with cinders. With recognizable annoyance, Horace Wilkins shrunk his eyes down to nothing and gripped his braces when three windows blew out in the flaming building.

"What do you estimate we lost, Mr. Wilkins?" Felicity said.

"Several of your father's paintings from Russia, and maybe a tapestry or three." The head butler's stiff politeness stung with accusation.

"I must admit I did find the Russian artwork utterly depressing, Mr. Wilkins." She loved to tug at the servant's dour demeanor. She also admitted her behavior to be childish beyond words, especially when watching a section of her home burn.

"All a matter of taste, Miss Carrol." Wilkins did not flinch.

"My experiment with a voltaic pile got away from me." She brushed long reddish-brown hair away from her eyes. "Thankfully, no injuries except to my ego. It is terribly bruised."

She had been creating an electrical battery similar to the one invented by Alessandro Volta in 1800 and trying to improve on it. Following his plan, she had alternated copper and zinc discs with cloths soaked in diluted sulfuric acid in between to boost the conductivity. She had succeeded in sparking a current through the voltaic pile when she linked the bottom and top contacts with a wire. But lace curtains had hung too close and a spark had caught them alight.

"Pardon me, Miss. I shall see to the work inside the part of the house not on fire," Wilkins said, and bowed.

Without an acknowledgment, he passed his sister, Helen, who was Felicity's former nanny and now her personal maid and friend. A marked contrast to her older brother, Helen was big-boned and benevolent. Horace Wilkins came in thinner and efficiently grim.

"You were very fortunate tonight, Miss Felicity," Helen said. "You could have been burned alive."

"Better than being burned dead, Hellie."

Helen gave a laugh. "Nor that." But her laughter stopped abruptly.

"What is it?" Felicity said.

"I hope your gown doesn't stink like smoke. You have to attend the ball at the Wheaton house tomorrow night. Your father's orders."

Felicity hated that word—*orders*. "It's too bad *that* ballroom didn't burn down."

"Miss Felicity, really."

Felicity put her hand on Helen's. "A joke. A weak one, Hellie, but a joke."

"Yes, a weak one." Helen smiled.

"Don't fret. Smoky gown or not, I shall go and dance in my father's hope that I attract a suitable mate." At that moment, Felicity had the urge to walk into the flames consuming the east wing. She shook away the negativity.

She would also do something positive.

Walking in front of the servants also watching the fire, Felicity motioned for them to quiet down for her announcement. "Thank you all for your help tonight. I believe a bonus is in order for your extraordinary service."

The male servants bowed their heads while the women curtsied.

Felicity spun at the sound of the bells from the fire brigade wagon rushing up the road. "At last."

At the onset of the fire, Felicity had asked a servant to summon the brigade in Guildford, a village located nine miles away. In sunlight and good weather, the distance could be covered in one hour with steady horses. Since it was near eleven at night, the brigade had needed to travel slower but had managed exceptional time to the manor. When the wagon pulled up, the firefighters bolted off the engine and toward the blaze.

Felicity noticed the steam-powered pump on the wagon. "Very progressive," she pronounced, and would have liked a closer inspection of the machine, but this was not the time.

Soon after the fire brigade arrived, the roof of the east wing collapsed with a whoosh and another spray of ashes. At midnight, the brigade commander ruled the fire out but the structure lost. While the men gathered hoses and ladders, Felicity asked the cook to prepare eggs, bacon, and bread to serve them in the large dining room. She requested Horace Wilkins to open several bottles of French wine from the cellar. He was the only person with the key. At his elevated eyebrows, Felicity remarked how bravery should always be rewarded. The brigade men ate and toasted her with a "Hip, hip, hooray."

"No, gentlemen. You deserved that toast for your work tonight." She raised her glass to them. She admired their courage.

The house finally settled at almost two in the morning. In her chamber on the second floor, Felicity relished the breeze from the open window. An occasional stink of torched and wet lumber from the other side of the house drifted through. Although fatigued, she could not sleep. There had been too much excitement. Experiments. Fire. A bomb.

How could anyone close their eyes after that?

Putting on slippers and a white dressing gown, Felicity lit a candle to guide her way along the blackness of the hallway. She had suggested that her father install electricity in the house, but he abhorred the thought of artificial light.

As a child, she had been just as restless. Often sneaking out of the nursery, she had roamed the many halls and rooms of the manor, searching for the ghost of her mother. She imagined finding the ghost sitting in a chair in the library. The apparition would open her translucent arms when she saw Felicity and enfold her in them. Felicity had lived for such an encounter.

Descending the wide front staircase, Felicity supposed she must presently resemble a spirit roaming the house. Perhaps the ghost of her mother. Solitary. Forever young. Forever waiting to be discovered by her child.

Her grandfather Anthony Carrol had built Carrol Manor. Adept at making money, he had proved less so at architecture. Gothic, medieval, and Palladian styles clashed throughout the home. To Felicity, the result was gauche rather than grandiose. No matter the design, the house was never so large and oppressive as at that time of night. She might as well have been carrying all the Italian marble fireplaces and stone columns square on her shoulders. Once she was old enough, she had come to understand that the burden had been a constant all her life. The weighty price of privilege and having more than enough money.

She tried to make sure she didn't pay the price with her soul. The only way she had found to resist the pressure of all that stone and marble was through knowledge. Through education, she would become more than a young lady of society. In a few hours, she would have to resist again. Felicity's father rarely asked her to do anything, but he had launched a campaign to put her in the way of bachelors of means ever since she had returned from her studies at the University of London. Through Helen, her father had commanded Felicity's attendance at the Wheaton ball. Felicity would rather remain home, reading and pondering and redoing her voltaic pile experiment. But she would be a good daughter and follow her father's dictate. Nonetheless, she couldn't help hating herself for it.

On the main floor of the manor, servants had nailed boards across the doors leading to the burned-out east wing. She went outside through the wide front doors. In the moonlight, the bones of the burnt wood took on the form of a prehistoric creature. Tendrils of smoke rose as if the earth still cooled. Horace Wilkins had been correct about the losses. Several of her father's beloved Russian paintings had burned, as well as two tapestries once belonging to the Borgias. Anyway, the artwork was insured, so her father would make out financially, as was his talent.

Although artwork covered their house, Samuel Carrol had constructed the east wing to display his favorite treasures. As a child, Felicity had often followed him as he observed each item in his personal art gallery. Pretending it a game, she had kept out of sight by ducking behind chairs and curtains. Although her father must have memorized every stroke and stitch, he had smiled with admiration and contentment at his belongings. But his smile dwindled when he spotted her. After that, she had stopped following him.

Wrapping the dressing gown tighter around her, Felicity headed back inside. The destruction of the Russian paintings and Borgia tapestries was the best birthday gift she had ever received.

CHAPTER 2

A fire and a ball within forty-right hours. Felicity believed she must have set some sort of record in Great Britain. If not, she certainly should have.

As the orchestra played, gowns whirled around her. Gowns of lace, silk, satin, muslin, and tarlatan twirled like bright umbrellas across the parquet dance floor of Wheaton House. Bodices were pulled tight as torture devices from the Spanish Inquisition, and Felicity wondered how the women could breathe, much less move. While conservative fashion of the day demanded concealment of a female's body, the décolletages on display hinted of outrage.

The men, meanwhile, were stiff in black dress coats and white shirts and vests that directly contrasted the ruffles and flounce of their partners. In regimental colors of red and black, military officers maintained rigidity as if a ball were merely another maneuver. As they danced, males held onto the tiny waists of females. Their white kid gloves intertwined. The faces of the young women opened like flowers, their curls springing as they moved. On their feet were satin slippers that could not be heard above the rustle of swishing fabric.

Couples swayed to music customarily played at such events. Waltzes, slow polkas, quadrilles. The air thickened with ladies' scents and burning candles everywhere, which added to the stifling atmosphere. Servants dressed in spiffy black outfits carried silver trays of punch, wine, and biscuits to and from refreshment tables.

At these events, upper-class young ladies met upper-class young men in the hopes of matrimony and producing upper-class children. At the mere thought of it all, Felicity almost choked on her punch. She estimated there were two hundred people who actually wanted to be there, unlike her.

The ball was taking place in the opulent home of Mr. and Mrs. Lindsay Wheaton, an estate or three removed from the larger Carrol Manor. The Wheatons were a pale and punctual bunch, the only noticeable traits Felicity could discern about them. Mother, father, son, and daughter also shared red hair and expressions never straying far from reserve.

"Your father has high hopes for Lindsay Wheaton Junior's pursuit of you," Helen had told Felicity when they arrived at the ball. "He says you would be a lucky woman to have such a young man."

That was the way Felicity learned about her father's intentions— through Helen. Felicity and Helen were mistress and servant in name only. Helen had raised Felicity after her mother died. Cared for her through sickness, read her bedtime stories, kissed her good-night, and talked with her about thousands of things important only to a child. Helen used to play the inventive games Felicity made up, such as knight and damsel in distress. Felicity always played the knight, saving Helen, who wailed and cried for help with such enthusiasm that Felicity hugged her in appreciation when the game ended. Helen's attention went well beyond salary or the assigned duties of nanny or personal maid.

Felicity could not conceive of a life without her friend. Her surrogate mother, whose love and support had seen Felicity through the death of her mother and brother and the neglect of her father.

Such was Helen's love that Felicity had the feeling the older woman would have stayed with her, wage or not.

At the ball, Helen sat with a collection of other chaperones and governesses on one side of the ballroom. Felicity looked over at her friend in the gallery of black silk dresses, which they all wore. The older woman pushed her lips up into a smile to encourage Felicity to do the same. Felicity did so, if only to please Helen.

With the forced smile, Felicity turned to watch the crowd. She observed, as she always did at similar activities. She was an outsider of her own making, and she would have it no other way. Besides, the view from the periphery proved infinitely better than from the center. She listened in on conversations among the young women. Too bad they consisted mostly of gossip and how to win the man of their dreams. The girls all seemed to share the dream of the same prince who showed up in every Grimm fairy tale. The shining knight who would carry them away, and they didn't appear to care where he took them.

"Don't you want to marry?" Helen had asked Felicity on the way to Wheaton House.

"I must first fall in love." Felicity sat back in the carriage and closed her eyes. "And he would have to be something special. He must be intelligent and accepting of who I am."

"That's a start."

Felicity had caught herself sounding as daft as the silly girls she detested. She sat up and opened her eyes. "That kind of romantic love can wait for the time being. There is much more to learn about life."

"Such as, Miss Felicity?"

"That is what I am hoping to find out, Hellie."

"Mark my word, young lady, one day Cupid's arrow will hit you," Helen said.

"Not if I duck," she had replied.

As the ball twirled and eddied around her, Felicity glanced at her watch. She had been there for an hour, but the time had dragged on for what felt like a millennium. Then she spotted a young man talking with a group of men and women. Wavy brown hair was swept over a face solid with poise and promise. She guessed him to be in his late twenties. From his comportment, this man was a titled noble. She would wager her father's money on it. Straight back. Expensive clothing. Taller than the rest of the men in his party, as if he ruled over them. He could have posed for one of those familiar portraits she had seen in many an art gallery. A painting of a young king, vying for greatness, even Arthur himself. All right, yes, he was striking. Never had she witnessed such confidence in a person.

Standing near her, a group of young women also watched the young man. Their faces reminded Felicity of lionesses hunting a gazelle.

"He *is* a catch. Handsome. Rich. Everything a lady requires in a husband, and much more," said a young woman with a massive pile of curls atop her head.

"One of England's most desired bachelors," remarked another, fiercely fanning herself.

"Yes, indeed he is, but who will catch him?" said another young woman.

"I hope it's me," one of their companions added, inciting giggles from all of them.

The young man took up the hand of a lovely girl in his party and danced away. Not surprisingly, he was an excellent dancer.

"Goodbye, Prince Charming," Felicity whispered to herself, and laughed.

"Miss Carrol."

Felicity spun about. Lindsay Wheaton Junior stood in front of her. The young man was slender like his father, with wide-set eyes behind round spectacles. She had met him several times at teas, hunts, and other societal functions. Felicity inwardly moaned whenever she saw him. Compared to Lindsay Junior, a lazy Sunday afternoon in the country was downright thrilling. She suspected his only interest in her arose from the sizable dowry her father would pay. The Wheatons were wealthy but not as wealthy as her father.

"How lovely to see you again." He kissed her hand.

She was happy she had worn gloves.

Young Wheaton started in on the only topic he liked to talk about—his horses. He called science a threat to civilization, novels a waste of paper and ink, and history a dead subject. He read only sporting magazines and business journals. That alone would have been reason enough for Felicity to avoid him.

"Let's go look at the garden, shall we? It is spectacular this time of year." He held out his arm for her to take.

Although she didn't consider herself much of a romantic, this man exuded as much ardor as a greasy piece of mutton. Wheaton Junior led her to the balcony and relative quiet away from the ball. The garden turned out to be more humdrum than impressive. Possibly it looked better in the day, Felicity thought, giving him the benefit of the doubt.

"I am mindful we have only met a few times and at social events, but I feel you would make me a superlative wife," Wheaton said.

"What did you say?"

"Our marriage. Your father and my family have entered into discussions."

Felicity bit her lip and tasted blood.

He patted her hand. "Sometime next spring. Spring weddings are always nice."

Her ears roared like the ocean battering the coast. "Marriage is simply impossible. Not in the spring. Not ever." Her jaw was clutched so tight in anger she was surprised she could speak.

His familial reserve didn't change. "Many marriages are made from less."

"We have less than nothing. Nothing at all in common. Let me amend my statement. The only thing we have in common is residing on the same island."

He flicked a hint of lint off his lapel. "We could learn affection. Many couples do. The advantages outweigh the emotion."

She licked her lips. Her hands became silk-covered fists. "What do you even like about me other than my sure-to-be-huge dowry?" She gave the sweetest of smiles.

"You are very beautiful and clever, from what I have observed."

Her mouth dried from the shame.

"Anything wrong, my dear?"

"Only that I have allowed myself to be put on display again. Like a heifer at a county fair for auction to the highest bidder."

"A heifer?" Young Wheaton's face hardened with puzzlement.

"Yes, a heifer with a price tag. I am leaving, Mr. Wheaton. Thank you for the trifling evening, and one more word."

"Yes?"

"Moooo." Her imitation was a good one.

On their way back to Carrol Manor, Helen did not talk, which was another reason Felicity loved her. Helen let Felicity be silent when she wanted to be. Besides, Helen had probably already guessed how the evening had turned out when Felicity found her sitting with the other chaperones. Felicity had announced, "Time to go home" in the manner of a person who wanted to escape Hades.

Halfway to the manor, Felicity did tell Helen what had transpired with Wheaton Junior.

"I had no idea about the marriage discussion, Miss, honestly I didn't," Helen said, panic wavering her voice.

"I believe you, Hellie. My father doesn't discuss business deals with anyone but his solicitor. Both of us were left out of those talks."

At the manor, Felicity told Helen she was going to take a walk.
"So late, Miss?"

"I have much to think about."

Helen nodded and went into the house.

Wearing her ball gown, Felicity ambled along the pasture and through meadows and the thick woods on the estate. The resplendent full moon escorted her and lit her way, although she knew every step. Above in the branches, fat olive-colored willow warblers blew their short bursts of whistles.

She ended up at her most treasured spot on the estate. A large, oval-shaped lake two miles from the house. Maples and elms encircled the lake, giving the setting immeasurable peace. In the middle of the lake was a small island with a wooden pavilion and, under that, a stone bench. Around the pavilion and bordered by a line of stones were wildflowers that returned each spring and summer with regularity. Gooseberry bushes reaching up to her waist dotted the island. They offered delicious berries once she got past the sharp spines. Fairies and magic dwelled among the foliage and hid behind the pavilion, or so she had believed when she was young.

Felicity stood alone on the shore of the lake. Much of her childhood had been spent alone. No siblings, no mother, and a father who barely spoke to her. In their place were tutors, maids, a governess, and Helen Wilkins. With Carrol Manor several miles from any neighbors, Felicity had had no young playmates. By nine years old, she had counted as her friends the characters in the books in the manor's massive library. She could rely on them to never change or desert her. Tales of adventure and wonder were her favorites. She would row out to the island with a pocketful of biscuits and an armful of books to charge her imagination. After reading tales by Jules Verne, she would glance up and wish she was heading to the moon, circling the globe in a balloon, or leagues under the sea with Captain Nemo. Other times, she envisioned herself hunting treasure with Tom Sawyer and Huckleberry Finn.

She loved the tales of King Arthur and his knights fighting for good against evil. She would always study the surface of the water in hopes of seeing the Lady of the Lake holding up Excalibur for Arthur. In her childhood visions, the Lady had long flowing yellow hair and wide blue eyes. A small faultless smile in a face like a lily, always blooming. The vision was much like that of her mother in the portrait hanging in the library. Felicity wanted to believe that her late mother hadn't gone to heaven at all but rather had transformed into a spirit living deep in the water. Her own Lady of the Lake to send her on to her destiny as Nimue did young Arthur. Perhaps not with the gift of Excalibur, but with bravery and endurance.

Now, as an adult, Felicity studied the lake, which was fluid gold in the moonlight. She had not been bothered by her loneliness for a long time. Until tonight. The downheartedness had nothing at all to do with lack of a husband or dispatching the advances of young Lindsay Wheaton. In fact, she was especially joyful about the latter. Mostly, Felicity felt distanced from the world of Carrol Manor, her father's world, and his expectations for her.

The water lapped at the hem of her gown as rhythmically as a heartbeat. The lake's waves resembled undulating black fabric. She smiled and narrowed her eyes, seeking a sword to appear out of the water, or at the very least, for some magic in a world with very little.

When none appeared, Felicity tapped the mud from her black ball slippers and headed back to the house.

★   ★   ★

At eight the next morning, Felicity and John Ryan stood in front of the burnt skeleton of the east wing. Unlike her feelings for

Horace Wilkins, who supervised the domestic staff, Felicity enjoyed Ryan's company. With a sense of humor robust as his frame and thick white hair, he had a habit of hiking up his pants as if he had someplace to go.

"Miss Felicity, you probably should leave science to Thomas Edison," Ryan said.

"Are you suggesting I take up needlepoint, Mr. Ryan?"

"Aye."

She laughed. "I'm sure even Mr. Edison had a few mishaps when he started out."

"Like burning down his laboratory?" Ryan said.

"Perhaps not. But what say we build my new laboratory a distance from the house in case any of my science goes awry. My father can decide whether he wants to rebuild the wing. Maybe he will collect French art this time."

"I'm sure he will. By the way, happy birthday, Miss Felicity."

She scratched her chin. "Twenty years of age. Anywhere in the British Empire, I would be declared an official spinster."

"Begging your pardon, Miss, but if you're a spinster, I'm the king of Sweden." He bowed and went about his duties.

In one of the smaller dining rooms, Wilkins supervised preparations for her breakfast. Standing near the door, he motioned for another servant to spoon out poached eggs from a silver serving dish on the sideboard and serve them to Felicity, who sat at the head of a long table. Fruit and toast had already been placed in front of her, along with an ironed copy of *The Times*.

Wilkins approached the table. "Everything satisfactory, Miss?"

"Up to your outstanding standards, Mr. Wilkins."

The head butler returned to his place by the door, every movement performed with self-possession. Complete with a facade of metal, he was a tin soldier who treated her with respectful disdain even though she was the only child of his employer. At a younger age, Felicity had been terrified of Wilkins and had run in the opposite direction at the sound of his clipped footsteps. These days, she and the head butler lived in a state of mutual tolerance, and not by her choice.

Before eating, she placed her hands on the table. "Mr. Wilkins, about last night."

"Miss?"

"I did not mean to take lightly the destruction of my father's artwork. I realize what they meant to him and in what high regard you hold my father."

His nod was imperceptible. "Anything else you require, Miss?"

She was a child once again. "No, thank you."

He bowed and left without a hitch in his crisp manner. Felicity sighed at the snubbing of her olive branch.

Starting in on her eggs, she opened the *Times*. Assimilating information like a dry cloth thrown into water, she recalled whatever she read, and she read a lot. At one time, she had believed this ability cast her as even more of an outsider in society, until she had accepted that it was, in fact, a gift. The words she read came to her when she needed them. She would pick facts and details like daisies in an abundant garden. Politics, economics, science, business, world events, crime. Felicity took satisfaction in her interest in everything except being a proper young lady of English society. She didn't tap her accumulated information at the social functions she attended at her father's request. The conversations of the young women there always centered—as they had at the ball the previous evening—on the latest fashion and empty gossip. When she attempted to join the more stimulating chat of the gentlemen, the men spread out as if she carried the plague on her white gloves.

As she cut a piece of ham with a knife, her eyes were drawn to an item on the front page.

EARL WILLIAM KENT KILLED DURING
ROBBERY AT MUSEUM

The body of Earl William Kent was found by a guard early Sunday morning at the British Museum in Bloomsbury, London. Guard Macintosh Leary was making his rounds when he came across his lordship's body in the new King Arthur exhibit.

The late Lord Kent had suffered a fatal wound to his chest. Scotland Yard inspector Jackson Griggs Davies relayed that police could not locate the murder weapon in the museum or nearby. The police could not even say what kind of weapon had been used in the attack. The unknown killer remains at large following the terrible crime against his late lordship, who was a relation to Queen Victoria.

Stolen was a copy of a valuable and ancient manuscript Lord Kent had loaned to the museum for the exhibition, "The Legend of King Arthur." No other items, including the sizeable amount of pound sterling on the victim's person and other treasured antiquities at the museum, were taken in the ghastly incident.

Earlier in the evening, Lord Kent had attended an exclusive reception celebrating the opening of the exhibit. After the event ended and all the guests departed, Mr. Leary witnessed Lord Kent walking around the museum, but this was his lordship's habit, said the guard. On the night of the murder, Leary saw no one else. Inspector Davies postulated that his lordship had returned to the exhibition, surprised a robber during his criminal act of theft, and been killed.

Museum curator Mr. Robert Foxborough reported that Lord Kent had been a generous patron of the museum and spent much time there. The curator also called Lord Kent's death a great loss to society.

Lord Kent was sixty years old. He was preceded in death by his wife, Lady Marcia Kent. He left no survivors.

The article went on about Kent's own extensive collection of art and antiquities.

While reading, Felicity absently clutched the knife's blade with her left hand. With each word, her fist tightened. When she had finished the article, she regarded her hand. The knife had slashed into her palm. Blood stained the white linen on the table, but Felicity felt no pain.

CHAPTER 3

With a bandaged hand on her lap, Felicity watched the world tremble past. Helen sat across the carriage, but Felicity didn't feel the presence of her friend as they headed to London. Since Felicity had read the news about William Kent, she had eaten little and suffered a thirst no amount of water would satisfy. Her very blood ached as it flowed through her veins. Rubbing a circle at her right temple, she hoped the muted pain would diminish. She seemed to succeed only in pushing it to the left side of her head. Felicity squeezed her injured hand. The throb from the cut echoed hurt, as if it came from far away. Her whole being was deadened and vacant like she had beaten her soon-to-be buried friend and mentor to the grave.

She was grieving, and this was a new experience for her.

Her mother had died when she was six months old, and her older brother Christopher had passed at the age of seven when Felicity was but five. She had been too young to mourn them. But she wept for William Kent. She mourned him. Ironically, she had known him longer than both of her deceased family members.

During her first year at the University of London, she had signed on for one of Kent's courses on the history of England. Even though the institution had been the first in England to admit women to work toward degrees years before, many of the male students continued to gawk at Felicity's attendance. She might as well have been a woman of the streets who had dared breach their masculine territory. Whenever she entered a classroom, men puckered their lips as if she had personally insulted them. Maybe she had. She had started attending the university at age fifteen and could already outthink most of the male students in her classes. Being an outsider hadn't bothered her, though she would have liked to have a friend on the campus. Unexpectedly, she had found one wearing the dark billowy robes of a professor.

Young and admittedly a bit immature, she had walked into William Kent's classroom and guessed him to be nearly eighty due to his thick white hair and a countenance belonging to the ages. As if he had lived through all those historical eras he would discuss.

During his lectures, however, the past turned vibrant and relevant. His voice resonated with knowledge and a love for the times long ago. He presented history as a matter of cause and effect. Be it war, plague, or a new king, the effect of that occurrence rippled through time and created change, which in turn created more change. Until then, she had viewed the past only as a list of events to be memorized and tested on, like learning the names of all the English monarchs. Her enthusiasm about this revelation had resulted in lots of questions in his class.

After one session, Kent had asked her why she had signed up for the history course.

"What happened years ago influences present events and is a guide to the future, if we choose to take note. And I choose that very thing," she had replied.

"I could not have stated it better myself. Well, perhaps a little," he had said with a wink and a trace of a smile.

"I didn't appreciate such a notion until I took your class."

"I see." Disappointment had passed over his face.

"From your expression, Professor, you must think I'm trying to solicit high marks with the compliment. That is not possible, since I am already first in the class."

Kent had laughed his response. "So you are, Miss Carroll, so you are."

She went on to take all of the courses he taught. Most of her other instructors were crusty and rarely varied their tone in class. William Kent passed on his lessons with the warmth of a grandfather telling stories before a fire. Over the course of the four years she attended the university, they had become friends outside the staid classroom. At a nearby café, she and Kent had regularly met. In addition to the history of Great Britain and its place in the world, they had talked about present times. How theirs was an era of steam and invention, as Kent had called it. Between them rested a common love of education and a common hatred of the "Season," to which they had both been subjected since birth. From house parties to hunts to the Derby, they detested it all. The only ball he hadn't disliked was the one where he had met his wife, Marcia, Kent had said. After five years of marriage, Marcia had died of complications in childbirth along with their unborn daughter. He had never remarried.

Kent had often held discussion groups in his chambers. There Felicity and other students had debated and challenged each other and Kent. Per tradition, he was supposed to be addressed as Lord Kent. But he had asked her and the other students to call him William.

"Is that allowed? I understand you have royal blood," Felicity had said.

His grin bore irony and amusement. "I do, yes, Miss Carrol. But considering all of my other ancestors, I will probably end up just a footnote in history."

"I seriously doubt that, William," she had replied.

She and Kent also shared a love of Arthur lore, although his interest was far more intense and comprehensive than hers. Kent's chamber at the university even resembled a miniature King Arthur museum, with a remarkable collection of paintings and books. She had once suggested he charge admission. Kent could talk about the Arthur story for hours. To catch up, she quickly read several books on the subject to ensure she could add to the discussions.

One day, Kent had brought to class his most cherished and valuable possession from his personal and vast Arthurian collection. Slowly, he unwrapped the item from linen. "This is a rare and irreplaceable original manuscript of Sir Thomas Malory's *Le Morte d'Arthur*. It is more than four hundred years old." Pride and reverence mixed in his voice.

The students had collectively breathed out in admiration, Felicity included.

"Malory's writings retold the previous English and French versions of Arthurian lore. He also touched on the now familiar characters of Merlin, Lancelot, and Guinevere. But Malory added new stories to the tale to enrich it further," Kent had continued. "The manuscript is one of the cornerstones of the Arthur tale."

"Given that you teach history, why are you so attracted to this legend?" Felicity had asked. She hadn't meant to be rude.

His smile made him look years younger. "I suppose King Arthur has captured my imagination ever since I was a boy longing for chivalry and heroic deeds. In the stories, Arthur accomplished magnificent feats and had extraordinary hope. Camelot was a shimmering example of what Britain could be. But those dreams were foiled by human nature. By deceit and by corruption. And this is what makes Arthur so human and much loved. We can all relate because of our own hopes and failures." He straightened his robe. "Of course, you students must realize that Arthur and company are only folklore. Marvelous and inspiring, but only what Miss Carrol has pointed out—legend."

As she neared the end of her university studies, Kent had

informed her that he needed to quit teaching to attend to family business after the death of his older brother.

"That will be a loss to education," she had told him.

His head had bowed in thanks for the praise. "And what will you do with *your* education once you leave the university?"

Her cheeks were singed with embarrassment. She hadn't thought of what she was going to do. "Whatever the direction, I hope to make good use of all that I learned," she had answered.

"You have a quick mind, Miss Carrol. But take heed, my girl. Employ that mind before you're absorbed into society and it's lost forever. You do not want to end up an automaton in silks and satins—aimless and blank." Such had been Kent's regular advice to her.

During the years they were acquainted, he had appreciated, encouraged, and accepted her passion for knowledge. She had held William Kent in such high regard that she sometimes imagined what her life would have been like if *he* had been her father. What animated discussions they would have had over dinner or in the library! Traveling together to old lands made new with their examinations. He would not have forced her to go to balls or teas. He would not have urged her to marry for wealth or position. He would have let her become what she was meant to be, even though she was not sure what that was. These musings had become her own kind of fairy story, especially at night when they lulled her to sleep. Kent was fond of her, she was sure. No matter he didn't share her feelings or look upon her as a daughter. She loved him for the respect and support he had shown her. She loved him for the possibilities of happiness.

Since her graduation from the university months prior, she had not seen William Kent. She had planned to visit London and invite him to tea. Now it was too late. Instead, she was heading to London to attend his funeral. She should have told him how much he meant to her. How much she treasured his friendship.

"Too late, too late," Felicity said.

Helen roused from a nap in the rocking carriage. "What, Miss?"

"Nothing, Hellie."

"You all right, Miss Felicity?"

"I'm fine."

"When will we reach London, do you think?" Helen said, and then yawned.

"Not long."

"Good." Helen closed her eyes again.

The carriage swayed and Felicity should have dosed, but another emotion kept her alert. Another emotion encroached on her grief.

Earl William Kent had been murdered, and she was angry. Unwrapping the bandage from her cut, she again squeezed, and this time felt pain.

★   ★   ★

A wreath of dried laurel tied with black ribbon hung on the door. Ebony crepe draped from the doorknob. A sure sign death had come and taken William Kent with it.

With no other immediate family surviving, Kent's creaking great-uncle and great-aunt greeted Felicity when she arrived at Kent House to offer condolences. Earlier that morning, the body of her friend had been interred in the cemetery on the estate. Not being a family member or business acquaintance, Felicity had received no personal written invitation to attend the burial, as was the custom. But she deemed it unthinkable to send only a note of sympathy at his passing. She wanted to honor him and was not alone in that intention. Fine carriages lined up along the road to the Yorkshire mansion.

Wearing her best mourning dress, Felicity introduced herself to Kent's remaining family. "This is a terrible event."

"The Queen herself sent a special representative to the intern- ment. Such an honor for William," the great-aunt wheezed.

"Deservedly so," Felicity said.

"And how were you acquainted with Lord Kent?" Checking his watch and tapping his feet, the great-uncle appeared put out rather than grieving.

"I met him at the University of London. He was one of my instructors."

"You attended university?" the great-aunt added in shock, as if Felicity and Kent had been cell mates at the infamous Tower of London.

"I was a student, yes, ma'am." Felicity imagined Helen rolling her eyes at the admission. The older couple did exchange alarmed glances. "May I ask if his murderer has been apprehended? The newspaper reported nothing about the status of the investigation."

The great-aunt and great-uncle swapped another stare of alarm.

"This is no place to discuss such crudities." The old man's lip stiffened to the consistency of pine.

"Quite right. Forgive me." Felicity bowed her head.

"Thank you for your condolences, Miss. If you please." The old woman motioned Felicity into the house with a reedy hand.

Kent House was larger and grander than Carrol Manor, as befit- ting an earl of the realm. Crowning the top of a resplendent marble staircase was a stained-glass window depicting a knight holding his mighty sword aloft to heaven. At the knight's feet lay the body of a red dragon. The window's colors encased the room in subtle and warm hues. Given Kent's love of medieval times, the theme was not surprising.

Mirrors in the Kent House had been covered with a black cloth. This funeral custom had arisen from a superstition that when the soul left the body at death, it could become trapped in a mirror and taken away by the devil. All this Felicity had learned from

Helen. Like a bank held on to notes, Helen held on to folklore and old wives' tales. Felicity thought the funeral rituals the worst kind of balderdash. Solely to prove them nonsense, all the mirrors would remain uncovered at her funeral, Felicity told Helen, and she would even stipulate that in her will.

Yet the black cloths over the mirrors at Kent House were an ominous reminder of a firm truth. Her friend and mentor had been slain in cold blood.

A large painting of Earl William Kent sat on a golden stand at the foot of the staircase. He had posed in his university professor robes, hands crossed in dignity on his lap. His white hair offset the black of his clothes. The artist had faithfully caught his intelligence and compassion. Felicity also saw a hint of amusement in the eyes, which truly captured the man's personality. She reached out to touch the painting.

Where was the man who loved to discuss history but respected her study of the sciences? The man who saw not a well-off heiress but an independent soul? The man who laughed without constriction and treated her with absolute kindness and respect? The man who kindled her desire for education? Where was he?

Gone.

She withdrew her hand from the painting.

Tea, port, biscuits, and cakes were served in the sizable library at Kent House. The black crepe and silk dresses of the female mourners rustled in the room like a horde of butterflies with hardened wings. Men in long black coats clustered in groups, talking in the deferential voices of funeral-goers. Among the men, Felicity recognized several instructors from the university.

Gazing at the substantial walls of books, Felicity was heartbroken her friend was not there to converse with her about them. Displayed about the library were also samples of the art collection the newspaper article had mentioned. Fine paintings by masters and talented newcomers. Sculpture both exquisite and experimental. Of course, the centerpiece of his collection dealt with the King Arthur legend. A tapestry of the mythical Camelot took up the length of one wall. The plains, streams, and mighty castle on a hill had been rendered in silken and metal threads. A topography of fiber. Felicity ran her gloved fingers along a row of books containing tales of the mythic king, including the twelfth-century writings of Geoffrey of Monmouth's *History of the Kings of Britain* and Alfred, Lord Tennyson's *Idylls of the King*, among many, many others. A painting of a young Arthur listening to the wise Merlin in the midst of a shrouded forest hung above the fireplace.

"Poor William," she said to herself.

"Yes, poor William." A young man stood next to her. "I don't believe I have had the pleasure." His bow was practiced and natural at the same time.

"Felicity Carrol." She curtsied to the young man she had seen at the Wheaton ball. The man who'd had several young women near swooning. Up close, he was even more perfect.

"How did you know Lord Kent?" the young man asked.

After explaining how she and Kent had met, Felicity waited for him to make a polite excuse not to talk with a woman who favored knowledge instead of nuptials. But he didn't move away and even smiled.

"Both beautiful and intelligent," he said.

Felicity disliked compliments about her appearance. Despite that, she was intrigued by this man who didn't recoil at her educational accomplishments. "And you are?" she said.

"Duke Philip Chaucer." He gently took her hand and kissed it. On a finger of his right hand was a ring bearing the likeness of an eagle holding a shield.

She sank deeper in her curtsy to the duke. She had read that was the proper greeting when meeting someone of his rank. Rising, she looked right at him. "I saw you at the Wheaton Ball and guessed you were royalty." She was somewhat gratified about her accuracy.

"How could you tell?"

"You appeared to command without even saying a word, as if standing on an invisible pedestal above everyone." She tried to sound as logical as she could. God knows she wasn't flirting with the man. It was just an observation, though it did smack of flattery.

Chaucer scrutinized her as if he had just noticed her presence in the room full of people. His focus amounted to a sunbeam fixed through a magnifying glass on the hottest of days. When she had first met him, his eyes had been light blue. They had now deepened to the color of a volatile sky.

"I am a fool," he said.

"Pardon me?"

"I am a fool for not noticing you at the ball."

She changed the subject to divert his focus and avoid another compliment. "Is that your family crest on the ring?" Heraldry usually bored her.

"Regrettably. So predictable and dreary."

She noticed a lighter band of skin around the ring, as if he normally wore another, larger one. "Many a family would love to have *any* coat of arms. My father included." She didn't mean for the tartness to enter her voice, but it did when she spoke of him.

"I am very familiar, Miss Carroll, with the space between how your parents envision you and who you really are," the Duke said, regret shading his voice.

"Yes, the space can be vast." Such as the one between her and her father. A distance from the earth to the moon.

"Then we share that."

He *was* fascinating and unexpected. He radiated a smooth detachment, as if nothing and no one could touch him. Felicity chalked it up to his being royalty and hundreds of years of privilege. "Were you related to William, I mean, Lord Kent?"

"A cousin."

Kent must have been a very distant one. Chaucer's handsome face was not drawn down by mourning. His voice was unaffected by grief. Then again, men rarely revealed true emotion. At least the ones she knew. She was curious about their relationship because Chaucer might have information about Kent's murder. "Were you two close?"

"Not as family should have been. But I suppose that does rely on how one defines family."

"In some cases, it's just a word."

"Precisely. But I was fond of William. He was quite brilliant."

"I greatly admired him."

He nodded as if knighting her.

"Do you know whether Lord Kent's murderer has been apprehended yet? The *Times* reported that his killer was at large."

"Not that I have heard. I know only what I have read in the newspaper."

"Until the murderer is caught, William will have no justice." She could have sworn the duke's stare intensified further. If it had been a knife, she would have been sliced to the marrow.

"The thief not only took his life but absconded with the *Le Morte d'Arthur* manuscript," he said.

"So that was the item stolen. I suspected as much." She didn't mean to sound so excited and quickly toned down her voice.

"How did you know about it?"

"Lord Kent brought the manuscript to class once day. He called it his most treasured possession."

"My compliments on your knowledge." He presented her with a light bow in salute.

"The pages almost shone with history. It is superb. Priceless."

"An accurate description, Miss Carrol."

"And what a discriminating thief to steal that item in particular from all the other valuable antiquities in the museum. Not to mention leaving behind the pounds and coin in Lord Kent's pockets." In her grief, she had not registered this fact until she said it out loud. Now the detail jabbed at her like a stick in her ribs.

"As you said, a discriminating thief," the duke said.

"A mystery." She scanned the room with its other Arthurian treasures and took a step closer to the Camelot tapestry. With wide eyes and a smile, Chaucer also appeared to admire the artwork.

"Your Grace, I can see that you, too, are an admirer of the Arthur story," she said.

"Who wouldn't be? It's a pillar of English culture. So, Miss Carrol, what else interests you besides history?"

"Everything. I believe we are on this earth to learn." *Quit showing off, Felicity*, she chided herself.

"A grand pursuit, especially for a female."

"For all, Your Grace, for all."

After checking a fine timepiece on a chain, he said he had to leave and kissed her hand. "I am sure we will meet again, Felicity Carrol." With a bow, he departed.

She watched Duke Philip Chaucer walk out of the library with his proud and assured stride, on a mission only he knew. He had charm by the ton. If her father's shipping line could have exported that charm, his company would have trebled its profits.

CHAPTER 4

The fork clinked against the dinner plate. In the hour since Felicity and her father had sat down to eat, the silverware against the china had been the only sound in the room. Muffled steps of the servants bringing out the courses broke up the quiet.

Clink. Clink. Clink. With each sound, Felicity's teeth gnashed—and not from the tough roast beef they had been served.

They ate in the dining room of their house on Grosvenor Square. By the time Felicity had reached the age of seventeen, she had regularly thought up excuses to stay away from their London place, mostly to avoid her father, who spent more time there than at Carrol Manor. His unspoken disapproval of her had thickened into a wall of impenetrable mortar. Her hands were bloodied from the attempts to break through. But because she had wanted to attend William Kent's funeral, she had decided to stay overnight in London and head back to Carrol Manor the next morning.

Two days before, her father had returned to the London house from one of his long business trips. She assumed they were for business, at any rate, since he never gave her any reason before departing. Before dinner that evening, she had gotten dressed in her room upstairs and cultivated the stamina she needed. *Go and talk to him,* she had told herself while brushing her hair, but she'd had to battle the temptation to climb out of her bedroom window.

In the dining room, they sat at each end of the table as they did whenever they were together, which was infrequent. At those times, Felicity would ask about his work or London politics, to which he would reply in succinct answers. She had even read books on business, hoping that might stir up the chat. It hadn't. He had told her the subject should be left to men. Her father would only ask her whether she had accepted invitations to social gatherings, and she made up excuses not to go whenever she could.

That evening, she studied him in the shallow radiance of the gaslights. Gray feathered the sides of his brown hair. He was a man of respectable deportment, slender and stately. A superior gentleman of society. Yet each year, his eyes grew emptier, like light receding down a tunnel.

Her father's gaze traveled from his wine glass to the portrait hung above the fireplace and back again. The painting showed her lovely mother sitting on a chair in the garden at Carrol Manor. Felicity had her mother's hair and eyes, but his resolve. As he regarded the painting, his durable visage dissolved into sadness, and she wanted to rush over and hug him so they could grieve together. The moment concluded quick as the dousing of a candle.

Felicity sucked in a breath for yet another try at communication. "Today I attended the funeral reception for Lord William Kent. He was murdered most brutally at the British Museum. He had been my mentor at the university."

His mouth turned downward at the word *university*.

"Did you ever meet him, Father?"

"No."

"Well, he was a fine, generous man and my friend."

Her father didn't answer.

She sighed. Conversation with him was akin to pulling gold

from the bottom of the Thames with her teeth. Still, she put her head down and smiled. Maybe her father was not going to mention the fire or what happened at the Wheaton ball. Maybe he had at last given up his efforts to secure a husband for her. Then again, maybe he had been waiting for the meat course.

"You are forbidden to perform any more of your ridiculous experiments at Carrol Manor," he said, staring down at his roast beef and not at her. His movements were precise as a surgeon's.

"They are not ridiculous, Father. They are important to my ongoing education."

"Education, ha." He pushed out a solid breath.

"I have asked John Ryan to see to the building of a new laboratory well away from the house. There will be no more accidents." She let out her own perturbed breath. Her chest constricted. She should not have taken such pleasure in the burning of his artwork. He *was* her father and the only family she had left. The same blood rolled in their veins. "Father . . ."

He did not look up at her.

"I do apologize for the destruction of your paintings and tapestries in the fire."

"Many of those pieces were irreplaceable, and you were irresponsible." *Clink. Clink. Clink.*

He brandished blame like a broadsword and without so much as a change in his voice. Over the years, she had attempted to build up an armor, but she remained vulnerable to the verbal blows.

"I am sorry," she said.

"I also had a most disturbing letter from Lindsay Wheaton Senior," he said.

"Oh."

"He complained you treated his son with the utmost disrespect. He said you acted like a person of common birth. In addition . . ." He set his fork down and threw her what she had termed his "half look," as if she could be seen only in his peripheral vision. "He claimed you mooed at young Wheaton like a barnyard animal."

"I am sure he deserved it." Really, the young man hadn't, and her cheeks heated from her treatment of him. She could have explained to her father the reason for the moo. How it symbolized her similarity to prized livestock up for sale, but she was sure her father wouldn't understand or laugh.

"Young Wheaton would have made a good husband."

"I was angry," she said.

"He did nothing to you."

"Father, I am cross and humiliated you didn't tell me you had entered into discussions with the Wheaton family about marriage."

"My business is none of your business."

"So am I a business deal instead of a daughter?" She was still surprised at the hurt he could cause her.

Clink. Clink. Clink. "There are plenty of eligible gentlemen who might forgive your loose tongue, although I may have to increase the amount of your dowry. At any rate, there is a house party next week at the Mannings. The family has twin sons, I believe. You will attend and you will behave."

His tone channeled indifference. Felicity had grown accustomed to it, but not that night.

Not that night.

Not after attending the funeral of her friend, the man she wished could have been her father.

The setting infuriated her. A family at dinner. Convivial candlelight in a well-decorated room. However, this was a charade of enormous proportions. She placed down her fork. "Father, I will not be going to the house party."

He concentrated on the pudding set before him and didn't ask why.

Folding her hands on her lap, she would explain anyway. "I no longer wish to be in the company of the foolish young people who populate those functions. The men are interested only in my face and fortune and not what's inside my head. And the women, ah, the women." She lifted her hands to make the point. "Porcelain dolls getting everything, except esteem as an individual."

"Nonsense." His eyes were on her at last. "I will not tolerate such indecent language. If you cannot be civil, do not speak." He displayed such bitterness she could taste it on her tongue like acid.

She lifted her chin. "I shall speak after our years of silence. So much silence it would pack cathedrals around the world."

Her constant hope was that they might become the kind of family she had read about in novels. Close and caring. Sharing and compassionate. But he had never hugged her. Never comforted her. Never laughed with her. A kind word from him would have had the impact of a comet striking the earth. On the other hand, he merely requested she attend those silly social events. Until lately, he had never ordered her to do anything. That left her to become independent and do what she desired. And what she desired was to learn. What she had sought was his love.

"Father, I only attended those functions to please you, but I can see nothing I do will ever please you. I cannot be what you want. My life will be what I make it. I hope you can accept me as I am and respect my wishes." Her heartbeat accelerated, but at the same time, she enjoyed the freedom that came with her overdue honesty. If she couldn't have his love, maybe she could gain his esteem.

"All this so-called education has done is render you unfit for society." His hands clenched. "You have proved yourself unfit as a wife or mother, even as a good companion. You are an anomaly. You might as well be a ghost in a Parisian frock."

"I am no ghost."

He folded his hands on the table. "Fine. Then, pray tell me, what *will* you do with your life?"

Felicity stood up. For a moment, she was unsure how to answer, and the uncertainty compressed her body like the tightest of corsets. The question coming from William Kent had embarrassed her. The same question from her father angered her. What *would* she do?

She could become an astronomer like Caroline Herschel, who had discovered several comets, or Mary Somerville, the first female member of the Royal Astronomical Society. Perhaps pursue botany like the American Jane Colden or take after paleontologist Mary Anning, whose discoveries had changed perceptions of prehistoric life. She might even become a physician, teacher, or patron of museums like her dead mentor William Kent. The opportunities excited her.

"Well?" he said.

She needed an answer and not only for her father.

"Whatever the course, I will strive to do my best. But it will be what I choose. Not society. Not you. My future will be my decision."

The air turned turbulent with their words. Her father stood up, knocking a wine glass to the floor. The glass shattered. Standing near the door, the servants did not move.

"I am going abroad for three months. When I return, I expect a substantial shift in your attitude. Either you will find a suitable man to marry or you shall attend a strict women's institute in Switzerland I have investigated. The institute will turn you into an acceptable young woman of society."

Her mind twisted like a leaf in an eddy from the amount of words her father had spoken to her—the most words ever passing between them in one instance. She balled up her hands to stop the spinning.

"Both of those alternatives sound equally disagreeable, Father. What if I don't marry or wish to attend the women's institute?"

"Then you may find yourself out on the street with nothing but your books and education. And since you are so fond of thinking, you have three months to think about *that*."

"Father, I will prove to you I can accomplish more than you ever thought possible. You will be proud of me, whether you want to be or not."

"I doubt it." Samuel Carrol threw down his napkin on the table and walked out of the dining room.

Felicity dropped back into her chair. Thunder in the spring did not compare to her crashing heartbeat. She was not worried about his threat. For the past twenty years, she had lived in the shade of her father's disregard. Compared to that, disinheritance would be a stroll along the Thames on a spring day. Rather, the pressure came from the test she had set for herself as well as for her father. A challenge to demonstrate that her life had reason and merit. A risky and reckless challenge, but that only made it more essential.

She would hunt down the killer of Lord William Kent.

From behind her came the lavender scent she had given Helen for Christmas.

"May I get you anything, Miss Felicity? A cup of tea? Warmed milk?" Helen said.

Felicity supposed one of the servants had told Helen about the battle going on in the dining room. "Hellie, I *would* like something."

"Anything, Miss."

"Please ask Matthew to get the carriage ready. I need to obtain as many past copies as I can of *The Illustrated Police News*." She dotted the napkin to her lips. "I shall be waiting outside."

"*Illustrated Police News*, Miss?"

"I have so much to learn. Oh, and when I return, I will have tea."

CHAPTER 5

The following morning, Felicity was about to step out the front door when Helen Watkins stopped her.

"Where are you off to, Miss?"

She wished Helen hadn't asked that. Felicity turned around. "To the British Museum?" She hadn't meant for it to be a question.

"Without a chaperone?"

From Helen's expression, Felicity could have been about to walk naked in Trafalgar Square, waving around the Union Jack and whistling "Ode to Joy."

"Young women don't go anywhere by themselves, Miss Felicity."

"They do when they want to get someplace," Felicity replied as a joke.

Helen didn't laugh. "You managed to sneak out before."

"But Hellie, I went to a funeral."

"Please wait until I get a shawl from my room."

Helen could be as rigid as her father in some circumstances, but mostly to protect her. "All right, off with you then. I'll wait in the carriage," Felicity said.

More than once Helen had told her she had learned which

battles she could win with her young mistress when it came to propriety, and which she could not. Felicity let her win this one.

The day following their disagreement in the dining room, her father had departed on his trip. For as long as she could remember, he had never bidden her goodbye when he left. He simply informed Helen or the other servants he was going. Normally, her father took his valet with him when he traveled, but this trip he had also asked Horace Wilkins to accompany him. Felicity was ecstatic. That gave her ninety days of freedom to conduct her investigation without Wilkins's scrutiny. Even if her father had remained in the city, he would not have cared where she went, but she didn't want to take the chance.

Helen Wilkins *did* care about where Felicity went.

"You are quite stubborn, Helen Wilkins," Felicity said as the carriage clopped along to the museum.

"I am when it comes to you, Miss. I won't have people talking bad about you, not if I can help it."

"I realize that and appreciate it."

"You can always fire me," Helen said with a playful sternness.

"I suppose so." Felicity returned the stern look. That would be tantamount to firing her own mother—if she had had one.

Helen sat back and smiled.

Felicity could not believe Helen and Horace Wilkins were related. Wilkins was closed as a coffin behind a cement mausoleum. His sister Helen was alive, full-bodied as a sun-filled morning after the rain. They must have had different fathers, Felicity surmised.

"Miss Felicity, I am glad you did not leave home. I feared you might." Helen put her head down as if she knew she had breached the wall between their stations.

Felicity reached over and patted Helen's hand. "I could never leave you." Felicity could accept the loss of all the money and property, but not of Helen's friendship and love. "I certainly cannot picture myself as Mrs. Wheaton Junior or twirling a parasol for the rest of my life. Nor will I attend a school that turns out society ladies like sausages. So when my father returns, I should have a bag packed for that day."

"I'm sure your father didn't mean those threats."

"But, Helen, that's exactly what they were."

"You're so young, Miss. Sometimes it takes time to understand who we are."

"And so it does."

The carriage rolled on, the wheels cracking against the cobblestones.

"Hellie, when we arrive at the museum, I ask you to give me leeway to walk around by myself. There are things I must do without question."

"I am rising above my post, but may I ask why you are doing all this, Miss Felicity?"

"Because someone has viciously killed my friend, and my goal is to discover the murderer."

"Shouldn't the police solve this crime?"

"They haven't found the killer. So what's the harm if I have a go at it?"

Helen nodded with faith. "I am always your servant, Miss Felicity."

"And I am always your friend." She took both of Helen's hands in hers. "One extra item, my dear. What you will hear me say and do at the museum or from here on out may seem quite extraordinary, but trust me. I am not going mad."

"I know you're not, Miss. I just like to think of you as eccentric."

Felicity threw herself back in the seat and laughed.

As they drew closer to the museum, Felicity prepared herself.

Time to start putting to use what she had learned. While Oxford and Cambridge universities allowed women students to sit for examinations, they did not award degrees to females. The University of London did bestow a few degrees to women. But for Felicity, the knowledge she gained was more important than a paper certificate to hang on a wall. When she had first informed her father she wanted to go to the university, he had asked why in a tone not unlike the one he used when inquiring why there were no eggs for breakfast. She told him she had acquired a desire to learn more about the world than she could from tutors.

"You don't need an education. You need to be married," he had replied, then left the room, and she hadn't seen him again for nine months.

Promptly, she had enrolled at the university. Her father had never attempted to stop her or even talk her out of it. He just didn't bother. Neglect did have its advantages. Nevertheless, she appreciated that her family's assets allowed her such an opportunity.

At the university, she had taken any class that interested her. And exactly as she had mentioned to Duke Philip Chaucer, *everything* interested her. For knowledge about the human body, she had attended classes at St. George Hospital Medical School. She wanted to understand what made the world work and took classes in chemistry, mathematics, and physics. She could not ignore the natural sciences and attended instruction in astronomy and history. The study of literature, philosophy, and Latin were essential because they were the heart of humanity. The more she learned, the more her mind expanded to learn.

Petite of form, Felicity had wanted to improve her body as well as her mind. She detested how women were often described as frail and delicate. So she took fencing lessons, although she did have to pay extra since she was a female. As in everything, she worked to excel in the sport. How she loved to guard and deflect blows with the rapier. The instructor, whose family had taught fencing for years, repeated how the weapon should become an extension of the arm. And she found that it did. One of grace and danger, tip or no on the end. The only aspect of fencing she disliked was the costume for females. The calf-length skirt and canvas shoes made her appear as if she had just stepped out of the nursery. She also rode horses and walked.

Near the university, she had rented a small house where she resided with Helen. Never had she been so content, despite the reception by others. As she was walking to a class one day, several male students called her a "bluestocking" as she passed. This was no compliment.

In the 1700s, women of the Blue Stocking Society had stressed education and met informally in England to discuss the arts and literature. Oddly, the name had come from a male participant who wore blue stockings because he said he couldn't afford black silk ones, or so the story went. But the term had taken on a negative meaning. Published years before in England, *The Popular Encyclopedia; or, Conversations Lexicon* defined a "blue-stocking" as "a pedantic female; one who sacrifices the characteristic excellencies of her sex to learning." A bluestocking was considered less than a female because she wanted to overtake man's hold on intelligence.

Felicity labeled the term rubbish.

After the taunts from the male students, Felicity began wearing blue stockings under her dresses and dared to show an ankle at the male students on occasion.

Few people ever let her forget her gender at the university. While dissecting a female cadaver, an anatomy professor remarked how the corpse's ovaries were tiny and shriveled.

"This woman must have been too educated. It has that effect." He spoke with the utmost resolution and stared at Felicity, the only female in the room.

"Professor, isn't it true the same will happen to a man's brain if he doesn't use it?" she asked.

A few of the male students did hide smirks. The professor puffed out his cheeks and didn't answer. He couldn't flunk her because she had the highest marks in the class.

Only a few men at the university treated her as an equal. One of them was William Kent.

So, my girl, Felicity told herself as the carriage pulled up to the museum, *here is the opportunity to use what you have acquired.*

CHAPTER 6

The last time Felicity had visited the British Museum, she had worn a short pink dress with an insufferable large white ribbon atop her curls. Felicity had begged Helen to take her to the new exhibition on the inventions of Leonardo da Vinci. On their visit, Felicity had walked through the display determined to soak up da Vinci's genius and creativity as if they were beams from the sun. An exasperatingly precocious child, she had infuriated everyone with a ceaseless line of questions, a habit she had found difficult to break as an adult.

At the da Vinci exhibit, Felicity had been especially captivated by his flying machine design. When she had returned home to Carrol Manor, she had drawn up her own plans based on that of the Renaissance genius. With help from the servants, she had started construction of her flying machine in the greenhouse. Making progress on the wood and linen machine, she had intended to make a trial run off the top of the greenhouse when it was finished. But Horace Wilkins had thwarted her plans when he told her father, and her father had ordered the device burned. She had been furious because she was convinced she would be able to fly.

The funny thing was, she still wanted to soar.

Heading to the King Arthur exhibition on the second floor,

Felicity set her shoulders back with another plan. This time, to obtain the information and access she needed to learn more about the terrible death of her friend. Helen followed behind, a little winded from the stairs.

"Miss Carrol?" The museum curator met them in front of the exhibition hall. A tall man, his eyes were small as beans, as if they had been permanently shriveled from reading ancient texts. Those or balance sheets. Earlier, she had sent a message to tell him of her impending arrival and a possible endowment to the museum.

"Mr. Foxborough, this is my companion, Helen Wilkins."

Helen gave her best curtsy.

"Helen wanted to visit the exhibition of Renaissance art on your main floor, so she will leave us as we visit." Felicity gave a slight nod of her head, and Helen picked up on it.

"So right, Miss Felicity. I do love the Resurgence," Helen said with a grin.

"Renaissance." Felicity smiled and turned to the curator. "She always gets that part confused."

In advance, Felicity had apologized to Helen. She might be some time at the museum and suggested that Helen have the carriage take her back to their house on Grosvenor Square. Felicity would take a cab home when she wrapped up her business. Stalwart as ever, Helen had responded that if need be, she would pop out for tea at the café next to the museum or remain in the carriage to wait for her young mistress. Either way, she was not going to desert Felicity.

Helen bowed again to Felicity and the curator and departed back down the stairs. She sneaked a wink at her young mistress as she left.

"We are so honored you are considering a gift to the museum." The curator glowed at the thought of her money.

"My pleasure, sir." Felicity did intend to make a donation, though the amount would not be as much as the curator probably envisioned or hoped for. Since she had turned fifteen years old, she had been allowed to draw out as many funds as she desired from her account at the Bank of London. Ironically, her father had informed her of this in a letter as if she were an employee at one of his companies. Before then, she had had to ask him for money—when she saw him—to spend on books, chemicals, or equipment for her laboratory. Her father had probably opened the bank account for her so he would not have to deal with the requests. Then again, he had never asked her to explain what she was buying.

"So gratifying to see a young person such as yourself take an interest in history," the curator remarked.

"I am *very* interested, particularly in your new King Arthur exhibit. Knights excite me so." She tried her best to twitter as if she didn't have a brain. It was difficult.

He lowered his voice. "I suppose you did hear about the recent unpleasantness in the exhibition hall?"

"Yes, yes, shocking. I was acquainted with Lord Kent."

The curator rubbed a hand over his baldness, and his small eyes flickered tears. "I looked upon him as a friend, and I believe he returned the affection." He dotted a handkerchief at his eyes. "His lordship used to joke that he gave so much money to the museum, we should set up a bed for him in the basement so he could visit anytime he liked."

That did sound like William Kent, she thought, and smiled.

"Such a blow to the museum and the Empire. His lordship was a good man," the curator said.

"He was that. I hoped a portion of my patronage would fund the new exhibit." She blended truth with exaggeration and was a little disturbed that it came so easily to her. "May I see it?"

"I was hoping to give you a tour of our Roman collection. The walls there do need refurbishing."

"How tragic. Let's save that for another time and endowment, shall we? I was so looking forward to seeing the King Arthur display."

"Very well, Miss Carrol."

Her breath seemed to rise from the bottom of her feet. She had entered the place where her friend had died. According to the latest article in *The Times*, a coroner inquest jury had ruled that Lord William Kent had been murdered by an unidentified assailant likely caught in the act of stealing the treasured document. The cause of death was massive bleeding from a chest wound. No murder weapon had been found at the scene. Additionally, no one had been seen leaving or entering the museum before or after the killing. At the time of Kent's death, two guards had been having tea in another part of the museum. From her remarkable memory, she had recalled all the details in the newspaper story.

A large hall had been devoted to the King Arthur exhibit. On the walls hung several paintings by various artists of the fabled king, his knights, the Holy Grail, Guinevere, Camelot, Lancelot, and other scenes and characters from the many Arthurian tales. Two sets of gleaming knight's armor stood like sentinels on both sides of the entrance. Behind glass lay an outstanding copy of *The History of the Britons*, an account of the British people written in 828 or thereabout. The pages were open to an entry about Arthur, which supposedly was the first mention of him anywhere. In the entry he was called not a king, but a *dux bellorum*, literally a Duke of Battles or war leader, in his campaigns against the Saxons.

"Magnificent display," Felicity told the curator, who smiled with gratification.

On top of a table sat a carving of an imagined Camelot so detailed Felicity expected to see knights rushing out to slay dragons. All scaled down, but regal nonetheless.

Above the castle rendering was a copper crest, a sword held in the claws of a golden chimera. Below was written:

BELIEVED TO BE THE CREST OF ARTHUR
BASED ON SEVERAL WRITINGS

A creature of Greek mythology, the chimera had the head and body of a lion and a goat's head rising out of its back with a serpent for a tail. The monster destroyed lands with its breath of fire until slain by the Greek hero Bellerophon as he rode the mighty Pegasus. In heraldry, it symbolized good over evil.

Directly across from the exhibit entrance was an empty space near the wall. Felicity walked to the spot. Speckles of broken glass lined the baseboard. She speculated that this was the location of the glass case that had held the stolen manuscript.

The curator's face inflamed. "His lordship was shot with some type of projectile. His body crashed into the glass case containing the irreplaceable document he had loaned to the museum."

"*Le Morte d'Arthur.*"

"Why, yes. *The Times* made no mention of the title."

"Just a guess. Was the manuscript opened to a certain page?"

He answered with a nod. "The one describing how Arthur had received the sword Excalibur from the Lady of the Lake."

William Kent had read that passage in class. He had told the students how the Lady of the Lake had captured his heart. Her presence was woven throughout not only Malory's writings but other previous tellings of the story. She gave Arthur Excalibur. Merlin loved her. She raised Lancelot after the death of his father, naming him Lancelot du Lac—of the lake. When Arthur was mortally wounded in battle, the Lady and her sisters carried him away to the mythical isle of Avalon and into fame. In the different tales of Arthur, she had many names, Nimue among them. She was portrayed as both an enchantress and a woman. To Kent she was one woman—all women. Spirit and flesh. He could not help but love the thought of her.

Felicity pushed down her sorrow. She needed more details. Glancing up at the curator, he appeared more confused than ever by her questions. His bewilderment pleased her. Normally men expected her to be a vacant female, but she loved to surprise them with what she knew. Pure vanity on her part, but pride in her mind was better than in her looks. At least, that was her justification.

Facing the entrance to the room, she estimated the distance at fifty feet. That would give the murderer a clear shot and cleaner getaway.

On the wall above hung a painting as tall as she. A black cloth had been draped over it. Moving away the cloth to look underneath, she saw an exquisite thirteenth-century painting of the Lady of the Lake handing Excalibur to Arthur. Unlike other paintings showing only the lady's hand rising out of the water, this one revealed a beautiful creature with wispy hair and serene beauty. When Arthur took the sword, he was really reaching for his destiny.

"We covered it out of respect for his lordship's passing," the curator said.

"Lord Kent loaned the painting to the museum so patrons *could* enjoy the work of art. Perhaps it is important they see the artwork to remember him and his love for King Arthur."

"That had not occurred to me. You might have a point." He nodded with decision. "I shall have the cloth removed."

"An excellent choice." She wanted a closer study of the crime scene without the curator watching. "Forgive me for taking up so much of your time, Mr. Foxborough. Please continue your work, and I will be in touch about the donation. You have been very generous with your attention. Before you leave, may I have a list of guests who attended the exhibit's reception?"

"For what reason?"

"As a remembrance of Lord Kent to place in a keepsake book." She batted her eyes in feminine innocence. "It would mean the world to me." More batting.

"Of course."

"By the way, did you know all the people in attendance that night?"

"Not all, but Lord Kent did. He helped prepare the list, in fact. I do look forward to hearing from you about your gift to the museum." He looked up at the veiled painting. "Everyone at the museum is devastated about his lordship's death. So horrific, especially the other thing."

"What other thing, sir?"

He leaned into her and whispered, "The word he wrote as he lay dying. Written in his own . . . blood."

This detail had not been mentioned in any newspaper story about Kent's murder, nor at the inquest. "What did he write?"

"Not a word really."

"Please spell it."

"M-e-d-r-a."

"Medra?"

"Police said his bloodied finger lay at the end of the 'a.' Dreadful, like out of a cheap penny dreadful novel."

"Mr. Foxborough, forgive my inquisitiveness, but one more question. Was his lordship wearing his hat and coat when he was killed?"

The curator's perplexity returned. "He must have been carrying them when he was attacked. They were on the floor beside him."

"Was there a coat room for the reception?"

"There." He pointed to a small door at the end of the exhibit hall.

Felicity tapped her foot at the revealing fact. William Kent had

had his hat and coat and was leaving the exhibition. *How could he have caught the thief in the act of stealing?*

She smiled at the curator. "Thank you again, sir, but you must have a lot of work to do."

"I could stay . . ."

She held up one of her gloved hands. "I wouldn't think of imposing myself on you any further. I will remain here and soak in all of this delightful Arthurian splendor. You will receive my donation soon."

He gave a slight bow and left.

Her veins pumped excitement at the prospect of searching the chaos for clues about who had killed William Kent. She had prepared for this moment. For the past two days, she had read many copies of *The Illustrated Police News, Law Courts and Weekly Record* to learn how the police investigated crimes. Frequently sporting lurid drawings on the cover, the penny newspaper reported details of murders and other wrongdoings and how they had been solved, if indeed they were. Granted, the reporting was sensationalized, but she considered the information comprehensive, helpful, and a bit depressing. She had truly lived a protected life behind her family's wealth. William Kent was the first person she knew who had died by someone else's hand.

Out of her bag, Felicity drew a magnifying glass to allow her to see what was hidden from the human eye. She also carried tweezers to pick up any evidence without touching it and envelopes in which to place the clues—if she discovered any, that is. She had read about using the glass and envelopes in various *Illustrated Police News* articles.

Through the magnifying glass, she examined the wall around and under the painting, inch by inch. Only an older couple was in the exhibition hall at the time, and they would probably attribute these odd actions to her being a zealous Arthur enthusiast. She hoped so, at least.

Just to the right of the painting was a square groove in the wall. Under her magnifying glass, blood spots spread out from the indentation. What did this evidence show? The projectile had gone through Kent's body with great force. This was indicated by the depth of the hole in the wall, and the blood spots shaped like rain smashing against a windowpane during a deluge. Museum staff had apparently tried to clean up the blood, but blood was difficult to remove because of the proteins that made it coagulate.

But why had the killer removed the projectile?

The mark in the wall was not a slit from an arrow nor round like a bullet hole. The square cavity measured about an inch on each side. She placed her little finger into the hole. The indentation went downward at what felt like a seventy-degree angle. Felicity straightened. In her stockings, she was a little over five feet. William Kent had stood only a few inches above her. The killer must have been taller than Kent, given the angle of the projectile's impact in the wall.

She pushed back her hat. Really, not much data for a start. A tall man who knew enough about the Arthur legend to steal the most valuable item in the room. She touched the mark in the wall again. The murderous object had had power enough to pierce a man's body, break the glass case holding the manuscript, and stick into the wall. All this at a relatively short distance. Only a few weapons were capable of that force and accuracy.

"Of course," she said out loud.

Felicity hurried out of the hall and found a guard. "Excuse me, do you have display of crossbows?"

He directed her to the exhibit of medieval weapons on the first floor of the museum. Old muskets, lances, javelins, daggers, swords, and really everything else that could kill a person had a place in the exhibit. On another wall was a copy of Leonard da Vinci's drawing of a crossbow from about 1500. A specimen dating back to fifth-century Greece lay under a glass case. The long wooden implement was elegant and deadly.

Various types of crossbows hung in a line on the back wall. Felicity checked out each of the historic weapons that had been mounted with hooks. A crossbow on one end of the display appeared slightly off-kilter, as if it had been put back in haste. The crossbow was the type where a lever pulled back the string to load the weapon.

In an open case below were a collection of bolts, the metal projectiles used in crossbows. The bolts came in shorter, thicker, and heavier than arrows.

With the magnifying glass, she studied each of the bolts. Even set on a bed of red velvet, they were violent-looking things, some with barbs at the end. They showed rust and age, all except the last bolt in the line. One end formed a square, and the tip came to a sharp point. The square appeared to match the dimensions of the hole in the hall upstairs. Dried blood streaked the body of the bolt and the velvet where it lay. Looking around to make sure no one watched, she picked up the bolt in her gloved hands for a closer examination in the sunlight coming from a large window overhead. Turning it around, she saw there were red streaks on it, as if the killer had attempted to wipe off the blood. Although the stains were mere traces, the bolt felt hefty in her hand. It had been used to kill. Her mind hummed with questions, but she did have one answer.

She, Felicity Margaret Carrol, had found the murder weapon.

CHAPTER 7

Helen stood by the door, her hands tangled together in nervousness.

"Don't be frightened, Hellie. The police aren't going to arrest *me*," Felicity said. "At least, I don't think they will."

"Oh, Miss Felicity." The tangle tightened.

After Felicity made her discovery, she had asked the museum curator to summon the Metropolitan Police. They arrived quicker than she had expected while she waited in the medieval weapons exhibition hall. She asked Helen to sit on a bench outside to rest.

A constable and a young man in respectable street clothes entered. Clad in a dark-blue, high-collared tunic and familiar helmet, the constable stopped and stood by the door. The other man continued on toward Felicity, staring straight at her with brown eyes and an expression that almost shouted that he was not happy to be there. His black hair wasn't as well-groomed as that of the rich young men she had met at those unbearable social events, but his suit was well cut and his shoes a shiny black. Six feet with muscles filling out his jacket, he was handsome in the way of a man who didn't care if he was or not. He had the square jaw of a Shakespearean actor. His eyes betrayed a concentrated intelligence with a hint of cheekiness.

"Inspector Jackson Griggs Davies, Criminal Investigation Department, Scotland Yard," he said, almost as if throwing down a verbal gauntlet.

She had read his name in the newspaper articles about Kent's murder, and she couldn't help but stare at him. He was the first Scotland Yard inspector she had ever seen. "That is quite a name and title."

Even his grimace was interesting.

"I meant it as a compliment, Inspector."

"Who are you?"

"Felicity Carrol."

The inspector did not greet her with the customary bow of a gentleman to a lady, and she found that incredibly refreshing. A curtsy had always made her feel more subservient than polite.

From his jacket, he took out a thick pencil and a notebook with a black cover and wrote down her name. The cover was worn and the pencil short, which told her he was a careful man who took lots of notes on his cases.

"The museum curator said you had new information on the murder of Lord William Kent."

"No mere information, Inspector. I have found the murder weapon," Felicity said with gravity, and then pointed to the deadly bolt she had replaced in the case.

Davies didn't even look at it. "Miss Carrol, many officers combed the museum inside and out for many days searching for the murder weapon. What makes you believe you have found the object that killed Lord Kent?"

Davies eyed her up and down, though not in a lascivious manner. She recognized lasciviousness because she *had* been stared at like that before. His scan was more one of exasperation at a woman who claimed to have accomplished what Scotland Yard could not.

The inspector leaned over her, no doubt to try to intimidate her because of his height and position, she guessed. She did take in a whiff of excessively ripe pipe tobacco.

"You some kind of female reporter?" he asked.

"If I may . . ."

"The *Morning Chronicle* had one about ten years ago."

"But . . ."

"If you are a reporter, this will be a totally different conversation."

"I'm no news reporter. I am a concerned citizen and a friend of the late Lord Kent."

"Oh, well, that explains everything then." He smiled with derision. "And let me tell you this, it will go down very hard on you, Miss Carrol, if you are wasting my time."

"Inspector . . ."

"I've got more important things to do than listen to a young girl's fantasies about being a detective."

He spoke with an East End accent, though it was a tad more refined. As was common with the speech pattern, he didn't drop the "h's" as much as let them dangle with menace. The glottal stops common in the East End style of speaking were more like pauses with the inspector.

Felicity held out her hand to him. "If you would please stop interrupting me, I will tell you about my find."

The constable standing near the door chuckled. The inspector turned and threw the officer a stare that could have melted pig iron.

Davies took a step back from Felicity and stretched out his large hands. "Go ahead, Miss Carrol. I'm all aquiver to hear your erudition in crime solving."

"This afternoon while inspecting the scene of the murder, I noticed an indentation in the wall above the spot where the body was found."

"We are well aware of the mark." He placed his hands behind his back. "We do our jobs."

"What did you think it was?"

His eyes searched the heavens with irritation. "A projectile of some sort fired by a weapon we have not yet uncovered." He took out a large scratched silver watch from his coat, checked the time, and tapped one of his feet.

"I deduced something other than an arrow was used."

"Deduced?"

"That means I came to the conclusion by reasoning."

"I'm quite familiar with the definition. Get on to your point."

"For a while I thought your head might come to a point, too, Inspector." Felicity's smile toyed with the tease.

He made a slight growling noise, so she thought she had better continue. "The mark in the wall was square, larger, and deeper than that an arrow would have made."

"I'm listening."

"The form and depth of the indentation in the wall and the distance between the killer and the victim led me to believe a crossbow was the murder weapon. I came down to the medieval weapons exhibition and noticed the last crossbow was crooked, as if it had been replaced in a hurry."

He examined the crossbow. "Maybe."

"What better way to hide a murder weapon than in the sight of the public?" Felicity said. "Given that the crossbow was the weapon used on his lordship, it was only logical to inspect the displayed bolts. That's when I spotted the one with streaks of blood."

"Maybe that's blood from an old battle," Davies replied, but immediately made a face signaling he realized at once the silliness of his remark. The inspector pushed his pencil down hard on his notebook.

Although she disliked his condescending treatment of her observations, Felicity did not want to embarrass the man in front of the constable in the room. She leaned closer to him and whispered, "Old blood would be a darker color, Inspector. In addition, there are smears on the velvet mat where the bolt was returned to the case."

"You know this how?" He did not whisper. "I mean about blood and all."

"From my medical studies through the University of London. But Inspector, the point is that a bolt of this type shot from a crossbow would have pierced the chainmail of a knight."

"That so?"

"I also studied history, among other subjects."

He picked up the bolt with his bare hands, and she clicked her tongue. "Aren't you worried about obliterating fingerprints of the killer, Inspector? When I touched it, I wore gloves." Felicity had made it a point to study not only current police procedures, which she found wanting scientifically, but also the newest methods of investigation, such as fingerprint comparisons.

"Fingerprints aren't used by police."

"They should be. Seven years ago, Scottish surgeon Henry Faulds published a paper about utilizing fingerprints for personal identification and how they could also help catch criminals."

"Never heard of no fingerprints solving a crime, Miss Carrol."

His smile irritated Felicity.

"May I bring to your attention that as early as 1879, Dr. Faulds actually solved a burglary in Japan by comparing the fingerprints of two suspects left at the crime scene."

"Japan? Faulds?"

"The prints on the bolt might give you a clue as to who shot the crossbow at William Kent." She grew irritated with herself for sounding a bit desperate. Trying to convince this man of anything was like attempting to move Windsor Castle with a silver pie server. She knew she had lost him when he replaced the notebook in his jacket pocket.

"Obviously, a robber stabbed Lord Kent with a sharp object," he announced.

"Excuse me." She took the bolt from him. "Let's see if this fits the bill, or rather the hole in the wall."

Felicity walked out of the weapons display room and upstairs. Davies and the constable followed. Felicity gave Helen a reassuring smile as she passed, though the two Scotland Yard officials were on her tail.

In the King Arthur exhibition hall, Felicity placed the bolt into the wall. The fit was perfect.

"Unless I am horribly wrong, which I doubt, you will find the bolt also matches the dimensions of the wound in Kent's chest," she said.

The inspector tried it himself, growled again, though quietly, and asked the constable to take the bolt as evidence. The officer grabbed it and placed the bolt in his pocket.

"All right, all right. So you may have discovered what killed Lord Kent," he said. "'Course, to be sure, we'll have to see if it *does* match the wound."

She tried not to smile with satisfaction.

"If you're not a reporter, you a scientist?" the inspector asked.

"I'm not Augusta Ada King-Noel, Countess of Lovelace, if that's what you mean."

He grimaced. "Who in the blazes is she, and what does she have to do with this investigation?"

Felicity needed a good strong cup of tea at this point. "I was merely saying that while I have studied science, I am not a scientist per se, nor do I make my living as one. And for your edification, the Countless of Lovelace was a mathematician who worked on the analytic machine."

"I'm not even going to ask about that."

"Good thing." She dared to smile.

"Why were you even here in the first place?"

"I am going to make a donation to the museum."

The curator, who had followed everyone into the exhibition hall, nodded his head in agreement.

"I also wanted to see where my good friend was murdered." Her voice snagged with emotion, but she couldn't let it deter her from the challenge she had set for herself.

"That sounds a little morbid to me," Inspector Davies said.

"I want to find the man who killed him."

"Scotland Yard wants the very same thing."

"Then don't you find it extremely strange, Inspector, that the person who killed William Kent stole only the *Le Morte d'Arthur*?"

"The what?"

"*The Death of Arthur*, a famous manuscript."

"Right."

"And nothing else, not even the gold in his pockets, according to what I read in the *Times*," she said.

"You can't believe everything you read in the newspaper, Miss."

"Oh, then did the killer steal William Kent's money?"

"No."

This time she smiled with triumph. "Tell me, Inspector Davies, what kind of thief leaves gold and other valuables lying around? What kind of thief steals just one unique historical document?"

"Some thieves do specialize in antiquities, Miss."

Her eyes brightened with the potential lead. "Really? I was not aware of that. I would like to talk to them."

"No, you wouldn't." The inspector frowned again, as if the

observation had not occurred to him until that moment. The moment passed. "We're done here. Where can we contact you if we have more questions?"

She gave them the address to the London house.

"Nice location, Miss."

"Not if you live there."

"What?"

"Never mind. See here, Inspector, there are a voluminous number of unanswered questions in the murder of William Kent, so many they would pack this museum." Her hands shot out, the left one striking him on the chest. "Sorry, Inspector, but you can see how passionate I am about this."

"That could amount to assaulting an officer."

She peered at his face. "I can't tell if you are joking."

One side of his mouth lifted in a smile and faded as quickly. "It would be my pleasure to arrest you another time, Miss Carrol. As for your many questions, only one counts." His accent thickened.

"Who killed him?"

"You are clever as well as nice to look at."

"And you cut a fine figure as well, but your flattery is unnecessary and unwanted."

He full-on smiled, but only for a moment. "Simply being honest, Miss."

She wondered if his smiles ever lasted more than a few seconds.

"From your self-proclaimed expertise about the crime scene, maybe you killed his lordship, Miss Carrol." He pointed the tip of his finger at her.

She could not tell if he was jesting or not again, and it bothered her that she could not read this man. "I was at my house in Surrey and have many witnesses to that fact. May I ask where *you* were on the night he was killed, Inspector Davies?"

"I have witnesses, too, Miss." He straightened so hard she thought his back might crack.

"Fine, we both have alibis, Inspector Davies. So what about the word the victim wrote in his own blood? Medra."

Davies turned his head toward the curator and shook it with displeasure. "We didn't want that particular item publicized because we considered the detail too sensational. A name in blood and all. Besides, Miss Carrol, who can tell what thoughts went through the mind of a dying man?"

"Maybe he was writing the name of the killer."

"Scotland Yard considered the possibility but could find no such man. We're still looking. So we're not as completely incompetent as you may think."

"I didn't say that, Inspector. I may have been thinking it, however."

"Thank you for your help, Miss Carrol, but the police will take over from here." He returned to his police manner, a mass of rules and no imagination.

"But . . ."

"Good day."

Felicity was shooed out of the room as she had been so many times by her father. She clinched her teeth and swiveled around but took on an unruffled demeanor. "Inspector Davies, the killer stood almost a head taller than the victim, gauging from the angle of the bolt mark in the wall. Most telling is that William Kent's hat and coat were found near his body, meaning he was going home when he was killed. If the culprit only wanted the *Le Morte d'Arthur* manuscript, he would have waited for Lord Kent to leave and then pilfered the item with no witnesses. Why would a thief kill a man if he didn't have to? Chew on that, Inspector." She gave an exaggerated curtsy and departed.

The inspector muttered behind her, "I'll be damned."

* * *

The grim reaper could have been waiting inside, enjoying a pint, and twiddling bony fingers until called upon. In other words, the building was dismal and efficient as death. The ideal location for the London coroner.

Felicity balled up her gloves with guilt. Back at the London house, she had lied to Helen. Specifically, Felicity had told her friend she was going to a dressmaker for the fitting of a new gown for a ball her father had coerced her into attending. Felicity's real destination would have caused the older woman much worry.

She had no time for guilt. Felicity took a few breaths and entered the coroner's building. Gaining the information she required might be a problem. She had no official title or authority.

"Oh well." Self-assurance and determination would have to do, as much as she could muster or fake them, at any rate.

Though grime rested in the corners, the office was tidy. Death, however, coated the walls like paint. An odor piercing and dull simultaneously. Felicity had gotten used to the smell of mortality while attending anatomy classes at the medical school in London. The corpses wheeled in for dissection had been kept cool to slow decomposition, but the stench lingered in her nose like a bad dream from which she couldn't wake. The bouquet of rot and finality, she called it. Chemically, the smell originated from the compounds putrescine and cadaverine, which were produced from decomposing amino acids in dead animals. Such was the scientific explanation, one she could even draw out on a blackboard in a chemical equation. Although she had to remain neutral about the bluish-white cadaver on the metal table in class, she still thought about how the decay had once been a human being. What was their life like before the end? What did they think and feel? But the essence of the person had left and all that remained was the putrefying shell.

A clerk with red cheeks and mousy, accusing eyes watched her every step as she approached his desk.

"Good morning," she said.

"Miss." His breath was that of a raw chicken left out in the sun.

Felicity attempted to sound capable but friendly. "I would like to read the coroner's report on the late Earl William Kent."

She wouldn't have believed it possible, but his eyes tightened. "Why?"

"That is no concern of yours, sir."

"You a suffragette?"

"No, are you?"

Why did everyone ask her if she was something other than what she was—a person who wanted to find out who had killed her friend?

"I need to check with my supervisor." The clerk sniffed and wiped at his nose with a dingy handkerchief. He walked into a small office, where an older man sat at a larger desk. They started talking—certainly about her request.

In her studies, Felicity had read many a medical book, but few about the impact of violence on the human body. That most certainly included murder. To fill the gap and ready herself for the investigation, she had stayed up nights to read the sixteenth-century work by French army surgeon Ambroise Paré, who had studied the effect of violent death on organs. She had also read *A Treatise on Forensic Medicine and Public Health* by French doctor Francois Emmanuel Fodéré, published in 1798. Fodéré had described forensic medicine as the art of applying medicine to the law, criminal and civil. She liked that explanation.

"Miss?"

She was startled back to the matter at hand in the coroner's office.

The supervisor stood in front of her. He had the face and

demeanor of sleet. He sniffed also. "My associate here says you want to read the coroner's report on a murder?"

"Yes, is there a problem?" Felicity channeled the voice of her father. The one she had observed him applying whenever he knew what he wanted—from the best table at a restaurant to ordering the servants about. She disliked using such an approach but tapped the tone in order to obtain the report.

The clerk and his superior eyeballed each other. The superior answered, "Other than police, elected officials, and newspaper reporters, no one else has ever asked to look at one."

"Then I shall be the first. It is public, is it not?"

"Why, yes," the supervisor said.

Both men sputtered like pots of tea ready to boil over.

"The information would be very disturbing to a young woman." The supervisor sniffed again. The building was damp, so Felicity could not blame them for having perpetually fluid noses.

"Very disturbing," the younger clerk emphasized.

"I assure you I shall not faint. Is there a fee to examine the report?" She prepared to open her beaded purse.

"No, Miss."

"May I have it, please?"

The men whispered to each other. The supervisor said, "You cannot remove the document from this office, Miss."

"Then I shall read it here."

"One moment," the supervisor announced.

The men retreated to another room.

The supervisor returned and held out two pieces of paper. "The report on Earl William Kent. You may use my office to read it."

She followed him. Her bedroom at Carrol Manor was five times larger than the office, which humbled her.

"You may sit at my desk," the supervisor said.

"How kind of you."

"Would you like tea?"

She was surprised at the question. "No, but thank you."

"I'll close the door for your privacy."

The report had been written by a Dr. Lawrence Edward, who had stated that a projectile of an unknown nature had made the wound. He noted that the weapon had created a puncture in the front of the body and pierced the deceased's left lung. The measurements of the wound corresponded to the dimensions of the bolt at the museum. Although she had been ninety-nine and nine-tenths sure, the report removed any uncertainty about her previous conclusion.

The exit wound at the back of Kent's body was lower than the entrance at the front. She was also right, then, that the killer had stood taller than Kent. The doctor reported that the projectile had also nicked a rib, denoting that it had traveled through the body with force. The cause of death was massive bleeding.

Kent's belongings at the time of death were listed on a separate sheet. One hundred and fifty pounds sterling. A silver watch. Gold ring. A paper notification about a photographic session with the royal family as part of Queen Victoria's Golden Jubilee celebration.

Felicity put down the report. From the description of the wound, William Kent had been facing his killer. He did not die instantly, but lay on the floor of the museum as his blood and life drained away.

She returned to the front of the office and handed the report back to the supervisor with her thanks. "By the way, did an Inspector Davies reread this report?"

"About an hour ago," the supervisor said. "Did *you* find what you were looking for, Miss?" He sniffled with smarminess.

"I'm not sure. That's the worst part," Felicity replied with all sincerity.

On the carriage ride home, Felicity closed her eyes and imagined the body of her friend on a metal table in this very building. *Who did you see holding the crossbow, William? What were you trying to say with your own blood?*

"Medra," Felicity whispered.

Opening her eyes, she looked through the back window of the carriage. Behind was a smaller, dark-brown carriage, the driver all in black, hat pulled low. It was as if death had followed her from the morgue.

She faced forward but heard the sound of the smaller carriage's wheels in back of them even as they made several turns toward her home.

"Matthew, speed up," she asked her driver, and he did.

The other carriage did the same.

"Pull over, please, Matthew."

When her driver did so, the small carriage drove past. From inside appeared the flash of an outline. A man with a large nose. He looked straight ahead.

"Everything all right, Miss?" Matthew asked.

"For the time being. Please, drive on."

CHAPTER 8

For the entire morning, Felicity didn't leave her room at the London house. She was teaching herself how to lift fingerprints. After trying different materials, she was ready to practice on a long piece of wood she had found outside near the kitchen door. She asked Helen to come to her room to help her.

"Hellie, please grab the wood at one end and pretend you are going to strike me on the head," Felicity asked. "Make believe the wood is a murder weapon."

"Really, Miss," Helen replied with an intonation combining worry and exasperation.

Helen had often used the same tone during her young mistress's scientific research—for example, when a twelve-year-old Felicity wanted to repeat the electricity test she had read about. Namely, American Benjamin Franklin's flying a kite during a lightning storm in 1752.

"Please, Hellie, the wood," Felicity said.

"Oh, all right." Helen picked up the wood at one end.

"Grab it good and tight, like you're going to pound me."

Helen tensed up on the wood and took on a menacing face.

"Very fine. Now please grab the wood at the other end in case I mess up and need another go."

Helen did so.

"You can set the wood down on the desk," Felicity said.

Helen wiped her hands. "Anything else you want me to touch?"

"No, thank you."

Helen laughed and curtsied. "I'll continue with me chores, none of which include smashing people on the head with a stick of wood."

"I hope not," Felicity said.

With an artist brush she had purchased, Felicity first swept fine charcoal dust over Helen's prints on the wood. Then she pressed a piece of paper over to record them. Felicity wore gloves so she wouldn't record her own prints. She had settled on using charcoal dust because it would show up clearly on the white paper. The process took a steady hand, and she had smeared prints more than once during the day. With practice, she had succeeded in removing fingerprints off a glass, a knife handle, and a gun she had borrowed from her father's set of antique dueling pistols. She grinned when prints on paper were revealed with iodine fumes, thanks to a method developed in 1863 by chemistry professor Paul-Jean Coulier.

The wood was problematic, given its rough surface.

Before starting her experiments, Felicity had read an article in the scientific journal *Nature* that had been written by Dr. Faulds. He described using printer's ink to capture fingerprints. She had tried his process—pressing her fingertips on an ink-soaked sponge and then pressing them down on paper. Several handwashings had been necessary to remove the ink, and she had created several black marks on her white blouse and on the wall near her desk, but the trial run had been a success.

She already knew that fingerprints were created from sweat glands in the elevated friction ridges on the outer layer of skin on fingers, toes, palms, and soles of the feet. She ran her hand along the coarse wood she had fingerprinted. One purpose of the ridges on the skin was to transmit texture information to sensory nerves—basically, how things felt, from rough to smooth and in between. They did not exist entirely to catch criminals. Yet, the swirls, arches, and loops of the ridges were distinctive for every person. Though not religious, she found something spiritual about how each man and woman had their own pattern, as if their soul had been published on their hands and fingers. First to recognize the uniqueness had been German anatomist Johann Christoph Andreas Mayer in 1788.

For years, fingerprint identification had been accepted scientifically. The Metropolitan Police or English courts, however, did not acknowledge the method useful for crime solving, as Inspector Davies had so vividly demonstrated. As with all things inventive, she was certain, fingerprinting would be a tool for future investigations of Scotland Yard. Taking a sip of tea with blackened fingers, she hoped the advancement would take place in her lifetime.

"At last!" After another attempt, she obtained a clear print off the wood. But her good mood didn't last.

Thanks to the interference of Davies, she had not been able to collect any fingerprints on the crossbow or bolt used to kill William Kent.

After clearing a spot on the desk, Felicity set down her typewriter and put in a piece of paper to organize her thoughts. She loved tapping on the new device. The machine ran not on steam, but on will and thought.

She set down the facts she had discovered.

1. *This was no ordinary theft. The killer knew precisely what he wanted—not only the priceless historical document, but to kill William. The culprit could have waited until William left and then stolen the manuscript. Instead, he sought out a weapon for murder.*

2. *This is a clever killer with a touch of irony. Using an historic crossbow and bolt and then concealing the murder weapon under the very eyes of the police.*

3. *Medra. The word William wrote in blood. The name of the killer? If so, the victim knew the identity of the man who shot him.*

Sitting back in the chair, she rubbed her temples and typed another fact.

4. *I need much more information.*

★   ★   ★

Felicity was absolutely comfortable in the offices of the soliciting firm of Morton & Morton on Oxford Street. That's because it was the unfriendliest place she had ever had the misfortune to visit. From what she observed, everyone was treated with the same frigid professionalism bordering on rudeness. She had not been singled out for her gender or wealth, which delighted her.

The reason for her visit was much less pleasant.

Throughout the four years she attended the University of London, she and William Kent had spoken often, either in class or at their regular meetings over tea. Their conversations had included a spectrum of topics ranging from history to the arts and present-day affairs. She had looked forward to the stimulating discussions, which made her part of a community of intellectuals. Despite all the chat, she really knew little about his private life, other than the death of his wife many years before and his distaste for attending functions of British society. She required more information about his background, because within it might be a clue as to why he had been murdered and his manuscript taken. She was not convinced by the police theory that a burglar had slain Kent while stealing *Le Morte d'Arthur* at the museum. To that end, she had made an appointment to talk with solicitor Joshua Morton. His solicitor firm had been mentioned regularly in *Illustrated Police News* articles. They had been hired by various clients to investigate the circumstances behind crimes, as well as to probe the lives of victim and perpetrator alike in many cases.

A white-haired clerk approached her. "Follow me," he ordered in an antagonist manner.

Waddling in squeaky shoes, the clerk showed her into the office of Joshua Morton. The solicitor held out his hand toward the black leather chair across from his long but tidy desk. He didn't stand or smile when she entered. She was content to see that the unfriendliness of the workers extended up to the owner of the firm.

Given the firm's association with criminal cases, Felicity had been prepared for a grim setting with death masks on the wall, like the office of Mr. Jaggers in Charles Dickens's *Great Expectations*. The place did not live up to *her* expectations. Shelves of legal books lined one wall in an office decorated in the fashion of the time. Stately wood. Forest-green wallpaper. Tasteful chandelier. Fireplace with a bust of the Queen on the mantle. Thick, lavish rugs. On the wall behind Morton was a painted portrait of the lawyer, perhaps ten years younger, with his hand on the shoulder of an older man who had the same close-set eyes. Obviously father and son. During her wait, she'd heard no one ask to see Morton Junior or Senior, so she figured the older partner must have died.

"How may I help you, Miss Carrol?" Joshua Morton asked with the rigidity of a ship's mast. His gray hair, plentiful both on his head and in his mustache, appeared just as stiff. But his eyes. She could have seen their acumen and fierceness at midnight from a league away.

"I would like your firm to investigate a man's life. Is that something you would undertake?"

He entwined his fingers on a portly middle. "As long as it is not illegal. Some of our clients' requests have bordered on the unlawful."

"This venture would be perfectly legal." Her certainty increased. "You may have read about the recent murder of Earl William Kent at the British Museum."

His nod was almost imperceptible.

"I would like for your firm to gather information on his life to help determine why he would have been targeted for murder," she said.

"I thought he was killed during a robbery." Morton's voice was made for oration, though as a solicitor, he didn't appear in court.

"Mr. Morton, that is precisely what I hope to learn. Which came first, the murder or the theft?" As she talked, Morton struck his finger against a pricy silver watch hanging from a chain attached to his pricy vest. He could have been tapping out in Morse code, *Time is money. Time is money.* She would not waste it. "I wish for information about his lordship's friends and enemies. Organizations to which he belonged. If possible, about his finances. Was he a gambler, for instance? Did he have any female companions? Any peculiarities?"

"In other words, the kind of man he was." He wrote down her list.

"I can see I have come to the right place, Mr. Morton. And in your investigation, you might look out for a person named 'Medra' or someone with a name beginning with those letters." She spelled it out.

"When would you like this information?"

"As soon as possible." She held up her purse. "I will pay a retainer, and you can inform me if you require more funds. I assume you will exercise maximum discretion in this undertaking."

For the first time since she had walked into his office, he smiled. A menacing one that might scare others. "Miss Carrol, everyone believes Michael is my middle name. But really it's 'Discreet.'"

CHAPTER 9

Felicity sat on her bed, a cup of tea in one hand and in the other Song Ci's book *Collected Cases of Injustice Rectified*, published in 1247. Song Ci wrote about forensic science and the many crime scenes he had examined while a judge in China. About damaged bodies and how they had been injured, about postmortem exams and causes of death. The book mentioned the particular case of a magistrate who had probed the murder of a peasant by a hand sickle. The magistrate asked people to put their sickles in the sun and watched as blow flies were attracted to the blade with remnants of blood. The owner of the sickle confessed.

"A blow fly, imagine," she said out loud.

The book had established Song Ci as a founder of forensic science. The book was also called *The Washing Away of Wrongs*. Felicity loved that title, which put into words what she was attempting to do. Wash away the wrong done to her friend and mentor William Kent.

She recognized Helen's knock and bid her enter. Helen carried a tray with plates of toast, eggs, and sausage. The ironed newspaper was under her arm. "You have to eat, Miss."

"I am hungry." Felicity knew the book about the physical

effects of murder on humans should have made her lose her appetite, but the passion to learn only made her hungrier.

Helen handed the newspaper to her mistress. "You won't believe this, but there's been another killing."

"When?"

"The day before yesterday."

Felicity sat up and turned to the article on the front page.

VISCOUNT RICHARD BANBURY'S BODY FOUND IN HOME

Viscount Richard Banbury was found murdered in the den of his gracious home Sunday night. The Metropolitan Police reported that his Lordship had suffered a ghastly wound to his head at the hands of an unidentified robber.

Melinda O'Keefe, who is a servant in the house, came across the body at five in the morning. She said she stopped in to clean the fireplace and made the terrible discovery. The servant saw her master slumped in a chair and screamed when she saw blood sprayed about the room. No one had been seen entering or leaving the previous night or earlier that morning, police reported.

Scotland Yard inspector Jackson Griggs Davies said the murder weapon was not found at the scene of the dread incident. Mr. Davies also stated that a costly twelfth-century tapestry was missing from the room where the late Viscount was slain. No other property was reported as stolen, but the inspector surmised the deceased caught the robber in the act and was slain.

The late Lord Banbury was fifty-one at the time of his death. His wife, Lady Charlotte, and their young daughter died in a rail accident nine years before.

One week ago, Earl William Kent was killed in the British

*Museum, another victim of robbery of a priceless antiquity. The
assailant in that case has not been apprehended.*

Davies could not say whether the crimes were related.

Felicity blew out her breath at the last paragraph. When she
raised her head, Helen had slipped out of the room.

Felicity's whole being swirled and eddied, as if she had jumped
into the turbulent ocean waters at Dover. She was positive the tapestry taken from the viscount's home had something to do with
King Arthur.

After ringing for Helen, Felicity took a bite of the toast and
hurried into her dressing closet.

Helen knocked and entered, as if she had been standing by the
door. "I thought you might get stirred up by that piece of information, so I waited."

Though it was awful manners, Felicity spoke with her mouth
full. "Hellie, you are wonderful. Can you help me, please? There
are many things to do."

Helen took the longest of looks at Felicity. One side of the
older woman's mouth raised up.

Felicity swallowed the piece of toast she had eaten while putting one leg into her cream silk combination knickers and cami-
sole. "What, Hellie?"

"I was thinking, Miss, about other women your age and rank.
They're probably busying themselves with the pianoforte, learning
languages, doing needlepoint, and trying to find a husband."

"Yes?"

"But your interests are as far from those as England to the New
World."

"Hellie, I don't want to learn the pianoforte. The idea of sitting behind a piano gives me a headache. I already speak German,

Italian, and French. And as for needlepoint, I would rather stick the needles up my fingernails."

Helen only grinned, making Felicity do the same.

"So why are you smiling, my old friend?" Felicity said.

"I do have a much more stimulating job than other serving ladies I could name. Sometimes, I am frightened for you, Miss Felicity, but there is not a day I would trade. So how do you go about finding a murderer?"

★ ★ ★

Helen was waiting for her at the carriage. She insisted on accompanying Felicity. "Where exactly are we going?" she said.

"To the home of the late Lord Banbury." Felicity had to know more about the stolen artwork and whether there was a connection with Kent's death.

"After reading about that murder, I just thought we might be heading there, Miss."

"Are you positive you want to come, Hellie? This might take time. That is, if I don't get kicked out five minutes after I enter."

"This way, no one will accuse you of impropriety, even though you are after a killer." Helen held up a large bag. "And take all the time you need. I brought along knitting and a book." Her eyes moved in the direction of the driver's seat. "Matthew and I can also play cards as we wait."

"As long as your time is occupied." Then Felicity leaned into Helen and whispered, "But if you play Matthew for money, take care. I've heard the servants say he cheats at cards."

"Where do you supposed he learned that?" Helen winked.

Before leaving the house, Felicity wrote a note to be delivered to solicitor Joshua Morton, asking his firm to also investigate the life of the deceased Viscount Richard Banbury.

Banbury's estate lay just inside the boundaries of London. The home was grand and suitable for a viscount. Fortunately, the Metropolitan Police, especially Inspector Davies, were not anywhere around. At this point, she wanted to be the one asking questions and not answering his.

She asked Matthew to pull the carriage to the front of the house. If nothing else, she would tell the truth and hope that gained her access and the details she needed.

An aged man answered the door. From his dress, he was a servant. White hair was scattered over his head as if painted there one strand at a time. Deep wrinkles and bereavement creased his face. His back was curved as a cane handle.

"May I help you, Miss?"

"First, my condolences for the death of Lord Banbury."

His nod was slow.

"I do apologize for appearing without an appointment, but I wanted to talk to someone about the tapestry that was stolen."

"May I ask why?"

"I too have lost someone dear. He was killed because he owned a prized and ancient manuscript. I want answers about my friend's death. Perhaps this will also lead to the man who killed Lord Banbury."

His blue eyes produced a minor spark. "Come in, Miss."

Once inside, she introduced herself. The servant called himself Macmillan.

"I have worked for the Banbury family for forty years, and the last few days have been among the saddest of my life," he said as they walked through the house.

She swore his bones crackled with each step. Without asking, he took her to the room where Banbury had been killed. She figured the old man just wanted someone else to share his heartache.

In front of the fireplace was a majestic chair. Lovely royal-blue velvet. Marvelously carved wood on the arms and legs. But its beauty had been spoilt. The right side of the chair was red with blood that pooled underneath. On the right wall were more sprays.

The significance: a right-handed killer.

"The police asked that we not clean up for a few days." The servant walked over to the chair and laid a craggy hand on the side without the bloodstains. "Lord Banbury died in this chair. It was his favorite in the whole house. The chair once belonged to Arthur Wellesley, the first Duke of Wellington. Lord Banbury was quite proud of that."

"It is magnificent."

Felicity's attention went from the chair to the door. Rugs lay between. That meant the culprit had probably gone unheard when he entered the room.

"Where was the tapestry?" she asked.

He pointed to a spot above the splendid fireplace.

"Can you tell me anything about the piece, Mr. Macmillan?"

"Certainly. It dated back to 1325 and depicted King Arthur sitting on a throne shaped like a lion. That's the symbol of England, you know."

"I do."

His wrinkles tilted up in a smile. "The late Lady Charlotte had given the tapestry to her husband for their anniversary. I heard her say quite often that she thought Lord Banbury resembled Arthur—when his lordship was younger, that is."

"Did anyone ever offer to buy the tapestry?"

"No, Miss. But it was quite expensive."

"Did the viscount have many visitors?"

Another shake of the head. "After her ladyship and their daughter died, he mostly stayed in the house. He did a lot of reading."

She made a slow turn. Even without the blood and signs of violence, the room exuded sadness. Dark even in the daytime.

"Has anyone ever attempted a burglary at the house?"

"Oh no, Miss. We don't even lock the front door."

Now Felicity shook her head. How easy they had made it for the killer to come in and leave death behind.

Macmillan walked her to the front door, and she gave him twenty pounds. "Please forget I talked with you in case the police ask."

"They have already asked me similar questions, so I don't feel the need to add anything more." Even his smile creaked.

At the door, she turned to the old man. "Mr. Macmillan, I would think that Lord Banbury was proud to have you."

He bowed.

Felicity headed back to the carriage where Helen waited, but realized she had to make another stop.

"Home, Miss?" Matthew asked Felicity as he held the door open for her.

"We're going to the coroner's office," Felicity said as she stepped inside. She needed to examine the body.

"Did you say *coroner*?" Helen said.

"I'm afraid so."

"I will most definitely wait in the carriage." Helen exhaled with worry, but then smiled. "Matthew will be happy we're moving. He's already lost a guinea to me in cards."

By the time they arrived at the coroner's building, Felicity thought of what she might do to gain entry into the mortuary. First, lie. Second, use bribery.

She thought it best to wait until ten minutes before the office was set to close. At that time, there would probably be fewer visitors. From the carriage, she watched the coroner's office supervisor leave and, right behind him, another well-dressed man carrying a physician's bag. Inspector Jackson Davies brought up the rear. With deliberate steps, the inspector walked with his head down and hands shoved in pants pockets. His Shakespearean actor's face carried worry. She sat back in the carriage so they wouldn't see her. After they were well out of the view of the building, she headed inside.

The same clerk Felicity had met on her first visit shook his head when she entered. He was not overjoyed. The sign on his desk stated MR. HOBSON.

She greeted him by that name.

"Miss, I never thought I would see you again," he said.

"Neither did I, but I must ask a favor."

"My supervisor went home, and every minute held up here, my supper gets cold."

When she had previously visited, she had noticed Mr. Hobson's shirt sleeves were frayed at the cuffs. His shoes were tatty, and one button was missing at the bottom of his coat. On his desk was a nice silver frame—probably pricier than he could afford—of an older woman with a similar chin and nose, but her face was compacted as the bricks making up the coroner's building. A blur of white cat hair marked his pant legs, and he wore no wedding ring. So here was a poor man with a cat who lived at home with his mother. He was wearing the same outfit that day.

"What do you want this time, Miss?"

She inclined forward. "The only information I can give you is that I am affiliated with a solicitor firm." She shaded her voice with secrecy. "The firm has been charged by a client to delve into the recent murders of Earl William Kent and Viscount Richard Banbury." She was also the firm's client but didn't mention that part. "Therefore, I would like to examine the body of Lord Banbury for a few minutes."

"I cannot allow that, Miss."

"Why not?"

He had no response. His brow creased. Obviously, he was trying to come up with one.

"As I thought, Mr. Hobson. You have no reason so say no."

His eyebrows burrowed into the middle of his forehead. "Well, no one has ever asked to see actual bodies except the police and those nosy reporters from newspapers and the penny magazines."

"I am no reporter. But I am wealthy." Felicity seldom heeded her father's teachings about the world because they were rife with pessimism and acrimony. Such as "Every man without money is a man to be feared. He will want to relieve you of yours." Or "The world is made for those who have means. All others must do what they can." She did recall one of her father's lessons she would use. "Most men have a price."

She would appeal to the pocketbook of the coroner clerk, thin as it appeared to be. Opening her purse, she took out a fifty-pound note and placed it in his dry hand. "Mr. Hobson, this is for your valuable time and inconvenience, such as a less-than-warm supper."

First, he brought the money closer to make sure it was real. Second, he gave her a review from head to slippers. "You don't look like someone who will do harm."

"I certainly won't. A look at the body is all I want. You can stay in the room if you like."

"Aye, that I will." He inspected the office although they were alone. "Follow me." He stopped abruptly, and she bumped into him. "You won't get ill or faint will you, Miss? I don't want to clean up your mess."

"I am used to dealing with corpses from medical studies in London." She did give up the truth in this instance, which felt good after some of the falsehoods.

"All right then, follow me."

The reek of death turned stronger with each step into the basement. The temperature dropped as they headed into dankness.

"I expect they will hold the inquest tomorrow, Miss," Hobson said.

"Then I have no time to lose."

From a room filled with ice blocks, Hobson brought out the body on a metal table. Its shaky wheels imitated the cries of tortured mice. A white sheet enveloped the deceased. Hobson placed the table under a large electric light hanging from the ceiling. The bare bulb layered the room with sickly illumination.

Removing her black leather gloves, Felicity donned white ones for ease of handling her investigative tools. From her purse, she withdrew the magnifying glass.

"I am ready, Mr. Hobson."

He pulled the sheet off of the top part of the body only. "His lordship doesn't have any clothes on, Miss."

Felicity coughed slightly. "That's fine. I am interested only in the head wound."

"From what I noticed, that was the only place where the body was damaged."

"Thank you for the observation, Mr. Hobson." She took shallow breaths, as if unconsciously keeping the death-filled air out of her lungs. She fixed her attention on the wound, which had been cleaned.

Terrible it was.

The right side of his head had taken the brunt of the damage. With her magnifying glass, she noticed several round perforations in the skin. She got out a piece of paper, folded it, and placed the paper in one of the holes to measure their depth.

"May I bother you for a ruler, Mr. Hobson?"

He obtained one for her. The holes were two inches deep, one inch in diameter, and evenly spaced from each other.

She stood up. "It can't be. It just can't."

"What can't be?"

She swiveled at a voice she had heard before. Inspector Jackson Davies had one hand on his hip and exasperation on his face. "What in the bloody hell are you doing here, Miss Carrol?"

"Isn't it obvious? Examining the body. What are *you* doing here?"

"I wanted another look at the victim." He took swift steps toward her. "You do work for a newspaper."

"Not at all."

The inspector turned a hostile gaze at clerk Hobson. Despite the cool bite of downstairs, Hobson began to sweat and shot a desperate look at Felicity.

"Inspector Davies, Mr. Hobson is not at fault here. I asked if there was any law against examining the body, and he couldn't think of any. I bullied my way into the mortuary." She glanced at Hobson.

"That true?" Davies asked the clerk.

"Absolutely. I could not eject a young woman out the door," Hobson said.

"He will also tell you I did nothing but look at the body of the deceased," Felicity added.

"That is true also, Inspector," said Hobson, who smiled at Felicity when the inspector wasn't watching.

Davies faced Felicity, his face forbidding in the dimness of the basement. At that moment, he could have been playing the ominous Richard the Third on stage.

"Why would an obviously well-brought up young woman like yourself want to look at a naked and mutilated body?" Davies asked, his voice matching his scary expression.

Felicity stepped under one of the lights in the basement. "Because I believe the murders of William Kent and Viscount Banbury were committed by the same person. I wasn't sure until a minute ago."

He blinked his eyes in curiosity only for a moment. "Miss Carrol, if you don't leave, I shall pick you up and carry you out."

She smiled. "No one has ever threatened to throw me out of anyplace. It's quite thrilling and frightening at the same time."

"You don't make anything easy do you, Miss Carrol?"

"One of my curses in life, Inspector. But please let me show you what I have found."

"Go on."

"The viscount was killed by a flail."

"A what?"

"A weapon of the Middle Ages. A metal ball covered with spikes attached to a chain or strap and wielded by a shaft."

"Something like a mace?"

"Except the ball is on a chain. Let me show you how I came to this conclusion."

"I wish you would." He took off his hat.

She pointed out the small holes in the head of the deceased. "Notice how the holes are uniformly spaced. No other weapon in the world leaves marks like those. Here, use my magnifying glass for a better view."

Davies scrutinized the wound and mumbled something. She didn't understand what he said and perhaps didn't want to.

"If not a flail, what did you believe made those unusual marks?" she asked.

"I couldn't say at this point." He half mumbled again. "We thought some kind of hammer or tool."

"Listen, why don't we have tea and chat some more?" She blew on her hands. "I may not be able to feel my fingers for a while."

"I would love to hear more of your whimsies, Miss Carrol."

Once outside the building, Felicity introduced the inspector to Helen and asked Matthew to drive Helen home.

"Will you be all right, Miss?" Helen threw an evil eye at Inspector Davies, who stood behind her young mistress.

"Hellie, if I'm not safe with a Scotland Yard inspector, I won't be safe anywhere on this isle. Isn't that right, Inspector?"

"As rain, ma'am, as rain." He opened his coat and touched the black Bulldog Metropolitan Police revolver in a shoulder holster.

"That's all right then," Helen said. "But mind you, Inspector, to take care with my lady, or you'll have me to answer to."

"You have my word, Miss Wilkins," Davies said.

Helen asked Matthew to drive on.

"That woman does love you," the inspector said.

His statement surprised Felicity because of its earnestness and also because of its source.

"And I her."

"Where shall we go for tea?" he said.

Felicity checked her watch. "Well, we might make that dinner, since it is well past six."

"There's a place nearby." He started walking and didn't wait for her to follow. She hurried to catch up. "You're interfering with a police investigation, Miss Carrol. I'm not sure why I'm even listening to you."

"Because I may be helping."

CHAPTER 10

W hen Felicity was younger, she and her father had dined at the kinds of restaurants where the napkins were crisp as his ironed money. Smartly outfitted waiters appeared at patrons' elbows like specters in white aprons. Glasses never wanted for water. Chandeliers brightened the room with shine and advantage. The diners appeared exhausted and bored from counting all their pound notes.

The place where Felicity now sat had no chandeliers or white aprons. In their stead were grubby gaslights and gravy-smudged shirts on waiters. Located a few blocks from the coroner's building, the café was about the size of the foyer at Carrol Manor. Dusky wood enclosed the eatery. The stink of grease and smoke was embedded in the walls. Cloths worn from washing covered round wooden tables. Pans clanged in the kitchen. Diners at their tables chatted so loudly Felicity could have probably carried on a conversation with them as well as with the inspector. The place was alive.

"I like this cafe," she told Davies, who sat across from her at a table.

"Me too."

She took off her hat and gloves. "You must come here often after examining murder victims in the mortuary. You probably don't want to go home to an empty house because you live alone. You want the company of the living." She held out her hands as if to enfold the café. "The food is probably good as well as inexpensive. I am not sure what wage an inspector earns, but I guess not much. But you're ambitious and smart."

He smiled. "You a mind reader or something?"

"They are from my observations of you." She sipped her coffee, which was flavorful and strong. "The barman waved at you when we walked in, so you must be a regular customer. You have no wedding ring, and when we met at the museum I noticed an iron burn on the front of your shirt. No wife or mother would have let you out of the house with such a mark. Therefore, you probably ironed the shirt yourself."

He looked down at his shirt.

"No mark today," she said. "But your hair needs a trim. Your top coat is fairly decent but your shoes less so. You smoke a pipe and take lots of notes in your black notebook. Given your accent, you hail from the East End. Coming from that poorer part of London, you must have fortitude and intelligence to have earned the rank of Scotland Yard inspector at your age. Ah, twenty-four."

"Twenty-three."

"Did I miss anything?" she asked.

"I'll be." Davies rested back in his chair.

"All from observation."

"I'm in that line myself. So it's my turn to list what I've found out about you."

"Oh, my. I have never been investigated before. By all means, tell me about myself."

From his jacket, he pulled out the notebook. "Felicity Margaret Carrol, the unmarried and only daughter of Samuel Reuter Carrol. Your father is the owner of Carrol Shipping London, Carrol Mills in Cheshire, and about five thousand acres of land near Surrey."

"Close to eleven, really. Sorry."

"My mistake. You took courses in medicine, history, chemistry, and mathematics and all sorts of other subjects at the University of London. Impressive. And that's where you met the late William Kent."

"What can I say? I love to learn."

"Any university degrees? I couldn't find out that information."

"Only in medicine and history."

He wrote it down in the notebook.

A short waiter arrived to take their food order, but Davies waved him back. "You have been described as brilliant and tenacious, but you have never been in trouble with the law and have lived a quiet life. That is, until we met." The inspector closed his notebook.

"I am flattered you spent so much time looking into my life. You could have just asked me."

He straightened his shirt. "Want my opinion about why you're meddling in my cases?"

"I don't believe I can escape it." She smiled.

"I believe you are a rich, bored know-it-all putting her nose where it doesn't belong for a lark." His tone was light but solemn.

She put down her coffee cup. "You are absolutely wrong, Inspector Davies."

"Am I?" His smile was edged with sarcasm.

"I shall tell you why I am, as you call it, sticking my nose in your case."

"This had better be good." He sipped his ale and wiped his mouth with the back of his hand.

"William Kent was no mere acquaintance. He was a dear friend to me while I attended the university. He encouraged me to continue my education while other men suggested I hide under petticoats and behind fans." Suddenly, the noisy café quieted—all in her mind, probably—as she hoped to make this man understand. "William Kent gave me so much, and I want to give something back."

"Like what?"

"By helping find the man who killed him so brutally."

Inspector Davies said nothing for a bit. "I should have added *frankness* to my list of your characteristics."

She laughed. "I never thought of myself as having characteristics. That makes me sound quite nefarious, like Lucrezia Borgia or at the very least the Red Queen in *Alice in Wonderland*."

"I'll add *sense of humor* to the list as well. So about the fail thing you called the murder weapon."

"Flail, Inspector." A thought occurred. "There is a wonderful example of one at the British Museum."

He checked a clock on the wall. "It's past seven and we haven't had dinner."

"Surely the guard will let in a Scotland Yard inspector."

He asked for the check. They took a cab to the museum. Felicity stayed quiet to give the inspector time to mull over her deduction.

"Why do you think the murders are connected?" he asked after a while.

"Because William was killed by a crossbow, a weapon from the Middle Ages, and Viscount Richard Banbury killed by a flail. Obviously, the murderer is obsessed with that period." She took a breath. "Both items taken were related to the legend of King Arthur. The manuscript is considered a literary foundation of the Arthur legend. And the tapestry portrayed the king. Nothing else was stolen except those items."

He crossed his arms again. "So what does that tell you?"

"The same man must have killed William Kent and Banbury. The killer could have waited for the viscount to go to bed and stolen the tapestry, but no. He slams him with a flail. Sound familiar? He followed his own twisted protocol. He kills and then steals. Not the other way around."

"He probably doesn't want any witnesses."

"Then why not wait for Lord Banbury to retire or William Kent to merely go home?"

Davies placed his hand on his mouth as if to stop himself from saying something. He sat back in the seat of the carriage. Felicity let him meditate on the information.

"I have one other item of interest." From her handbag she produced the list of the forty-two people who had been invited to the King Arthur reception at the museum held the night of Kent's murder. She had memorized all the names.

"Where'd you get this?"

"I asked for it."

"Naturally."

"I thought it might be a good place to commence my investigation."

"*Your* investigation?"

"The list was only a beginning, Inspector. Besides, Lord Banbury's name wasn't there."

"So?"

"I thought the killer might be stalking people interested in King Arthur relics, based on his thefts from William and Lord Banbury."

"Then that would have to mean the murderer was there, too." He glanced over the names. "This looks like a bunch of peers and rich people. Not thieves and murderers."

Her shoulders fell a bit with disappointment. "I'm afraid you might be correct." Still, she had sent a copy to Morton & Morton asking the firm to prepare short biographies on the attendees.

"Did you really think the killer attended the reception, Miss Carrol?"

"More like I hoped."

He folded the paper and placed it in his pocket. *A sign he is taking me seriously*, she thought.

At the museum, Inspector Davies knocked on the front door until a guard answered. He identified himself and said he was coming in with such gravity that the guard did not make any objections.

"I noticed the flail when I came looking for the crossbows," Felicity said when they were inside.

The guard led them by lantern to the medieval weapons exhibition and turned on the gaslights. A flail was displayed in a glass case. The weapon was as Felicity had described. An iron ball with spikes attached to a heavy wooden handle by a chain.

"This isn't *the* murder weapon, is it?" The question slipped from Davies.

Felicity didn't have to draw out the magnifying glass from her purse. "Not at all, Inspector. The spikes on this one appear to be approximately one inch long. Based on the wounds on the viscount's body, the spikes were twice that size and there weren't as many of them."

Inspector Davies rubbed both hands over his face. "My God. You're right. The inquest into Lord Banbury's death will be held tomorrow. I'm going to have to present this evidence and say how I came to the conclusion."

"Please don't mention my name, Inspector Davies. I beg of you."

"Why not?"

"I would rather my family not know about my activities in this matter." Particularly her father. Otherwise, he might cut off or restrict the money she needed to continue the investigation. She would tell her father when the case had been resolved and the murderer in prison.

"The flail was your discovery, Miss Carrol."

"Say it came to you in a dream or that you noticed the weapon the last time you visited the museum. Even better, say the information came from a confidential informant." She had read about those in the newspapers. "I'll bet Mr. Foxborough the curator will even let you borrow this flail as an example."

Davies smiled. "I'll bet he will."

"Please, keep my name out of it?"

"I promise. It's the most I can do."

They stepped out of the museum. Davies pointed to a food vendor a little ways down the street. "Look, you've had no supper and I'm hungry as well."

"Then by all means, let's eat."

From the vendor, Davies purchased two ham sandwiches, two boiled eggs, and two cups of coffee. They stood next to the cart while they ate.

"This is quite good," she said. "My first food vendor."

"Only the best for you, Miss Carrol." He finished his sandwich and wiped his hands.

"Inspector, why did you become a police officer?"

Surprise looked good on him. "No one's ever asked me that before. Not even my mum and dad."

"Then it was high time someone did."

"You were right, I did grow up in the East End. Lots of bad things happen there, and I saw plenty. But my dad and mum kept the bad out of our house. They taught me and my brothers always to appreciate the good in life. And that good is worth protecting."

"And so it is. I have another question."

"Oh no."

"Were you always this grim, Inspector?"

For the first time, he gave a smile that lasted more than a few seconds. "I'll tell you about my first day on the job as a constable. I was so proud of my new uniform."

"I bet you cut quite the figure."

"I thought I did. My mum thought so, too. Anyway, I'm patrolling in the East End. Taking myself *very* seriously, probably more than the people there. Then, a skinny man runs past me. Behind me, another man yells, 'Stop him, Constable! He stole my money. Stop that thief.' So I chased the bloke through the streets."

"Did you catch him?"

"I spun around a corner, slipped on the street, and fell right on my backside into a pile of horse manure."

She laughed. He joined her, and they both had to wipe the tears from their eyes with the napkins.

"I bet nothing like that ever happened to you," he said.

"Inspector Davies, did I ever mention how I blew up part of my house?" she replied.

"No, but I would like to hear it."

She told the story about her laboratory accident, the fire, and her homemade bomb to save the rest of the manor from that fire.

"I always knew you were a born criminal," Davies said.

She laughed. "I suppose that's a kind of compliment."

"I have another. You *have* been a help today, Miss Carrol. Thank you." The last two words sounded as if they had lodged in the inspector's throat like a piece of his sandwich.

"You are very welcome."

"Now do I have your promise that you will stay out of this case?" Davies said.

"I cannot make such a promise. I'm sorry. I really am."

He stopped short. "Then you best not hide any evidence you stumble across or get in my way."

"I don't stumble." She would not mention her visit to the Banbury crime scene. She and the inspector were having such a pleasant time. She didn't want to ruin it by having him get mad again.

Davies insisted on riding home in the cab with her though Felicity said she was capable of riding alone.

"Am I really a know-it-all?" she asked him.

He gave a curt nod. "It's quite maddening, because you do seem to know an awful lot."

"By the way, Inspector. Judging by the location of the wound on Lord Banbury's head, the killer is right-handed. But you probably already knew that."

He made no reply, but the grinding of his teeth sounded like boots on concrete.

Chapter 11

For the second time, Melinda O'Keefe fainted in the witness box.

The surgeon rushed to the fallen girl with a capsule of smelling salts. He placed one hand under her neck and with the other he broke open the capsule, releasing alcohol and ammonia into a piece of cotton fabric. He waved the cloth under the nose of the waifish serving girl.

The coroner's inquest into the death of Viscount Richard Banbury halted while the serving girl revived one more time. With the salts, her eyes fluttered to normalcy. Standing, she brushed aside pieces of her red hair that had drifted down from her small hat when she swooned.

"Are you well enough to proceed?" asked the coroner of the City of London.

She nodded.

The coroner rotated his gray eyes under the bushiest of brows. This was the liveliest Felicity had seen him during the proceedings, where she and Helen sat in the gallery with ten other people. For most of the morning, he had come off as half dead one moment and half asleep the other. His skin was paler than a typical London resident, with hair slicked down as if pomaded for a journey into the grave. His voice sounded like it struggled out of ten feet under dirt. He tapped a pen against his desk.

"Tell us what you saw, Miss O'Keefe," the coroner asked the serving girl.

Melinda gripped the sides of the witness box where she sat and took the deepest of breaths. "Well, sir, I went down to Master's den at five in the morning to clean out the fireplace, as is my duty. I didn't knock because I believed the Master was in bed. Then I entered."

"And what did you find?"

The serving girl's teeth clicked like senseless crickets. Felicity thought the girl might pass out for a third time, but Melinda sucked in more air.

"The first thing I noticed was blood on the right side of the wall. Splatters of it."

Felicity sat forward.

"I took a few more steps into the room, and I saw Lord Banbury slumped over in his chair. His head was awash in blood." Her tiny face recoiled with tears. "Blood soaked his favorite chair and spread out all over the floor. I will never get that sight out of my mind." She covered her wet face with her hands and wept anew.

Sitting at a separate table, three male newspaper reporters scribbled down the quote. People in the gallery muttered in disgust. The coroner tapped his pen again to quiet them down.

"Was Lord Banbury dead when you entered?" the coroner asked.

"Can't say, sir. I screamed bloody hell and ran out of the room."

Someone snickered. The coroner widened his eyes to search for the culprit but apparently didn't spot him. He returned his attention to Melinda O'Keefe. "Did you witness any person entering or leaving the house before your discovery of the body?"

"No, sir."

The coroner told the serving girl he had no more questions.

Shaky on her feet, she hurried out of the hall. "Let us continue with the surgeon who conducted the postmortem."

Coroners had the power to call for an inquest with a jury to investigate suspicious deaths and then determine the circumstance and the cause of the death, or so Felicity had read in stories in *The Illustrated Police News*. The inquest into the viscount's murder was taking place in the Coroners Court building on Golden Lane. The jury of men had been selected from voting lists, and they earned a few shillings for the job. Earlier in the proceedings, the jury and coroner had walked down the street to inspect the body in the coroner's mortuary.

Taking the stand was the surgeon who had a few moments ago helped the serving girl after her bout of fainting. The witness portrayed the word *eminence* with his refined clothes and manner, as if he realized his superiority over all the living in the room.

"The cause of death was massive blood loss from a severe head wound to the right side of his head." The surgeon did sound a bit bored. "Extremely severe."

"In your opinion, what was the time of death?" the coroner asked.

"Lord Banbury died an estimated seven hours before the serving girl found the body."

"No other injuries to the body?"

"Apparently one blow was enough."

Six servants then took turns testifying that they had neither seen nor heard any person enter or leave the manor the night of the murder or the next morning before the body was found. Only Melinda the serving girl and a cook said they had been awake when the killing occurred, but both resided in the servants' wing in the back part of the large manor.

Mr. Macmillan the butler, who appeared to have aged even more since Felicity had spoken with him, repeated the information she already knew. Priceless tapestry. No prior burglaries. House unlocked.

Sitting up in the gallery, Felicity asked and answered her own question. How had the killer even known about the valuable tapestry? He must have previously scouted the viscount's home. He knew the location of the tapestry as well as the fact that the doors were never locked at night.

Wearing a new gray suit, Inspector Jackson Davies took the witness chair. His face was rigid as he answered the coroner's queries. "No murder weapon has been located in the den or anywhere on the grounds at the residence. A complete search of the premises inside and out was conducted by several Metropolitan Police officers."

"And as for the likely weapon, do you have any speculation?" the coroner asked.

Davies licked his lips with uncertainty before he answered. "We suspect the killing tool used was a flail."

The panel and coroner were as baffled as Davies had been when Felicity told the inspector about the medieval weapon.

"I have an example right here." From a brown cloth bag, Davies proceeded to pull out the flail the museum had let him borrow. "I believe a weapon like this killed Viscount Richard Banbury." His voice lowered.

A collective gasp came from people in the audience.

"How did you come up with this outstanding assumption?" the coroner asked.

"Based on the wounds of the deceased. They are similar to those a flail would make, sir. I would not be wrong to say this weapon makes a distinctive mark on a body."

"What are you doing to attempt to find the weapon, Inspector Davies?"

"We're planning to speak with dealers who handle antiquities such as these," Davies replied.

Felicity bit her lip. The idea had not occurred to her.

"Anything stolen from the premises?" the coroner asked.

"Only a tapestry dated 1325 and worth several thousand pounds, sir."

"Any suspects, Inspector Davies?"

"Not at this time."

The coroner wiped his pale nose with a handkerchief. "So, Inspector Davies, please tell the panel your conclusions about this death."

The inspector contemplated the flail he held in his hands. His eyes went to the panel of men sitting on wooden seats on one side of the wall and then flashed up at Felicity sitting in the gallery.

The coroner rapped the end of his pen on the desk. "Inspector?"

"I conclude that Viscount Richard Banbury was murdered during the commission of a robbery. A burglar was stealing the tapestry when the Viscount discovered him. The thief then killed his lordship."

"Any other relevant information on this case, Inspector?" asked the coroner.

"No, sir."

Felicity stood up from her seat.

"We leaving, Miss?" Helen whispered into her ear so as to not disrupt the proceedings. "The panel hasn't made their ruling."

"I'm sure it will echo the inspector's conclusion. I've heard quite enough, and it amounts to a small pile of animal droppings."

*　★　*

Inspector Jackson Davies called her name several times, but Felicity paid no heed. She quickened her step, as much as her skirts allowed, to hurry down the street to the carriage. Helen puffed to keep up. Felicity slowed her step for her friend.

"Miss Carrol, wait," Davies called from behind.

Across the street was the smaller brown carriage she swore had followed her days before. As she walked nearer her carriage, the smaller one sped off. The same man sat in back. The one with the large nose. What was going on? Maybe she was becoming obsessed and seeing danger where there was none. No, it was not that. She was being followed and had been since she started her investigation.

Felicity reached her carriage. "Forgive me for making you rush, Hellie."

"Good for these old legs," Helen managed to say.

Davies was also out of breath when he reached the carriage. He still held the bag containing the flail he had borrowed from the museum.

"Please, Hellie. Get in first." Felicity held out her hand to help Helen into the carriage.

"Thanks, Miss." Before taking Felicity's arm, Helen tossed the inspector a fuming look before she stepped inside.

"Why didn't you stop when I called?" Davies asked Felicity.

Felicity refused to reveal her high level of aggravation. A few years back, she had developed a trick she used whenever her father punished her for no good reason. That is, back when he even bothered to do so. She raised a shield of calmness and let his ire bounce back at him. Her father would get even angrier and halt the reprimand.

But in addition to being angry at the inspector, she was hurt. Turning toward the young man, she wielded similar armor against him. "What can I do for you, Inspector Davies?" she answered in a composed manner.

"You heard what I said. Why didn't you stop and talk with me?" His cheeks flamed.

"Except for the use of the flail as the murder weapon, you didn't believe anything else I said. You dismissed my theory about a single murderer and how Kent and the Viscount were murdered first and robbed second. In other words, you dismissed me."

"I know you weren't expecting to hear that," he said, finally catching his breath.

"You discounted my deductions. So, my dear Inspector Jackson Griggs Davies, I am discounting you." She spun back toward the carriage.

He gently touched her elbow. "Please."

Felicity did not move.

"Despite all your obvious academics, Miss Carrol, you don't understand police work. I need evidence. Not the intuitions of a rich young girl. I'm not saying I don't believe you. You are indeed brilliant . . . in a strange way."

She faced him and half smiled, although the compliment did contain an insult.

He took off his hat. His brow shone with perspiration from running to catch up to her. "Until I get solid, hard-as-hell proof the two murders are linked, I must go on the assumption it was robbery first, murder second." Searching his pockets, he could not find a handkerchief. He used his sleeve to dry his brow.

Felicity fished out her handkerchief from her bag and handed it to him. He accepted it and dotted the perspiration. "I understand what you're saying, Inspector. I don't agree with you, but I understand."

Davies grinned. "You did lead me to the murder weapon."

"I did, yes."

"So how can I make it up to you?"

"Let me accompany you when you interview the dealer of antiquities. I am learned in history and can help."

She could have sworn the breath left his body. He didn't answer quickly.

"Inspector?" she said after a while.

He shut his eyes as if in pain. "Very well," he said, as if surrendering a lost war to a victorious general.

She stepped into the carriage.

The inspector put his hand on the door. "I'll pick you up tomorrow morning at eight."

"I will be waiting." She rapped on the roof. "Drive on, Matthew."

Inside the carriage, Helen gave her head a shake. "You had no doubt about him, did you, Miss?"

"I believe our Inspector Davies wants justice as much as I do, which means he will take any route to obtain it, even employing someone like me."

"He did call you brilliant."

Felicity smiled with a satisfaction she couldn't help but enjoy. "He did, didn't he?"

CHAPTER 12

At Landon and Son, Felicity tripped over history. Her foot slipped on a javelin on the floor. Standing next to her, Davies grabbed her waist so she wouldn't hit the ground. When he helped her to her feet, their faces were close. In the afternoon light, his eyes showed speckles of forest green in the brown, similar to the colors of the woods near the lake back home. *Concentrate, Felicity.* She gave him a nod of thanks.

"I am so sorry, my dear," Mr. Landon Senior said.

Stout as a good chop, he walked sluggishly with age. But his clothing was flawless. He picked up the javelin and placed it in the hollow hand of a suit of armor near the door. "It does tend to fall off and roll."

"No harm done, Mr. Landon." Felicity righted her hat, which had tilted when she slipped.

The antiquities dealer on Charing Cross was the seventh shop she and Davies had visited. The first six of them did not deal with any medieval weapons, although they each exhibited a suit of armor in their establishments. The last dealer had referred them to Landon and Son, a shop specializing in such items of war.

When he had picked her up that morning from the London house in a cab, the inspector wore a new suit smelling vaguely of bay rum. His hair and nails were trimmed. Felicity didn't want to say anything about the improvements to mortify him, though he had obviously taken special care with his looks. While she did like to tease him, she wanted to be prudent about it and engage when appropriate, such as when he took himself too seriously.

Davies had insisted he do all the questioning when dealing with the antiquities dealers. "That way I can justify my pay from Scotland Yard," he had told her on the cab ride there.

"I can't tell if you're joking again," Felicity said, and she truly couldn't.

"A poor joke, I admit it," Davies replied.

But the inspector had never gotten past the question of whether the dealers sold flails. Not until Landon and Son.

"Why, yes, we have a good assortment of flails and maces," Landon said with marked pride.

"May we see them?" Felicity asked.

Landon waved a chubby hand toward the back of the shop, which was stuffed with history but in an orderly fashion. He sold not only suits of armor but also antique swords, javelins, lances, knives, daggers, bows, arrows, crossbows, and bolts. All arranged by type of weapon and well maintained.

"Your collection rivals that of the British Museum." Felicity surveyed his offerings with admiration.

The older man blustered from the praise. "I have tried to make it so."

Inspector Davies held up a sword from the fourteenth century and ran his finger along the dull blade. "Sell a lot of these old weapons, sir?"

"Enough to keep me in business for forty years."

"Why an interest in such items, Mr. Landon?" Felicity asked as they made their way among the historic weapons.

"I truly believe I was a knight in a former life. As a lad, I would play with sticks and pretend they were swords and lances. That I was Sir Lancelot or Sir Gawain. Sometimes I'd dream about finding the Holy Grail and bringing it to King Arthur himself."

"I did the same," Felicity said, and both men stared at her. "Well, such imaginings were more fun than playing a pathetic damsel in distress."

Landon's laugh was heartier than a good stew. "My son does not share my interest or love of medieval weaponry. He opened up a haberdashery down the street. Ah, here we are," the shopkeeper said.

On the back wall, five flails and maces were on display. The wooden shafts measured up to three feet in length, while a chain or rope holding the striking head to the shaft varied in span. Most of the heads had spikes. A few had smooth surfaces.

"Those weapons with the short shaft can be wielded with one hand. Longer ones require two," Landon said.

"Awful-looking things." The inspector leaned closer to one and touched the tip of a spike.

"And we've seen evidence of what they can do," Felicity added.

Landon pointed to one of the flails on display. "This is my oldest. From the sixteenth-century German Peasants' War."

"Have you sold a flail with spikes measuring two inches long?" Davies asked.

The antiquities dealer gave an enthusiastic nod. "I have sold three of them."

Felicity and the inspector raised eyebrows at each other.

"To who?" Davies said.

The merchant blustered again. "I would have to look at my records."

Davies held out his hand. "Please look."

Landon's record keeping was comprehensive. He set glasses on his nose to read. "I have records for each item based on the type of weapon," he told them. He licked a finger and turned to one sheet on his desk. "This is my flail page. The first flail I sold five years ago to a Mr. George Baker of Connecticut in the United States of America." His finger went down another column. "The second was four years ago to a museum in Germany."

Davies wrote down the information as Landon pronounced it. Felicity memorized it.

"Three years prior, I sold one to Sir Percival Trent." Landon consulted his paperwork again. "It was a two-headed flail. Very rare."

"That was not the murder weapon, according to the wounds," Felicity said.

"Why not?" Davies said.

"Inspector, if there were two spiked balls wielded, the damage to Lord Banbury's body would have been even more severe. Namely, there would be twice the number of wounds."

"Sounds logical."

Landon narrowed his eyes as if concentrating on a memory. He opened them wide. "I do recall Sir Trent already owned a single-headed flail with the spike measurements that you mentioned. A fine specimen, from what I saw."

Davies wrote in his book. "Where can we find this Sir Trent?"

"He passed on last year, and his family sold all his collection of medieval weapons at an auction," Landon said. "I heard Lady Trent never did take a liking to them."

Davies put a line through Trent's name. Felicity thought that a mistake. Someone had purchased one of those flails.

"Are you aware of anyone else, perhaps not a shop owner, who collects such medieval weapons?" Felicity asked.

"I thought I was supposed to be asking the questions, Miss Carrol?"

"It is a good question," Landon said.

"Well, do you?" Davies added.

"My customers usually buy a piece here or there to decorate their castle or ancestral home. I wouldn't have termed them significant collectors by any means, except for the late Sir Trent," Landon said. "But London is a big city, and other people besides myself also sell such antiquities."

"Like criminals?" Felicity said.

Landon gave a slow nod.

"We have visited other reputable dealers of antiquities, but are there others who, shall we say, are not?"

Davies tossed Felicity a terrible look as she asked the question.

Landon shifted about but didn't answer.

Felicity smiled. "Mr. Landon, you do know of one."

"Yes."

"Well, what is it?" Davies said.

"Rawlins House. It's located near the Aldgate Pump."

"Why would you consider them disreputable?" Felicity drew closer to the shop owner.

"Rumor is they sell items not usually obtained in a lawful manner." Landon's eyes darted about as if to make sure no one else heard him.

"Stolen goods?" Now Davies wrote the name in his book.

"That is just the gossip." Nice man that he was, Landon added, "I have heard that they do have some very lovely and unique items."

"Such as flails?" Felicity asked.

"I can't say. I've never been in their shop."

Inspector Davies thanked Landon for the information and his cooperation.

Landon gave a little bow and checked his watch. "My pleasure." The bell rang over his door, and he grinned. "That's my next appointment. A gentleman has expressed interest in the sixteenth-century ballista in my warehouse."

"Ballista?" Davies said.

"A sort of giant crossbow," Felicity answered.

Landon smiled at her and entwined his fingers. "You don't need a job, do you, Miss Carrol? I could use your expertise in my store."

Her face brightened with the offer. "Mr. Landon, I am flattered." She tossed a glance at Davies. "But I have another duty at the moment."

"Pity," Landon said, and hurried to meet his customer.

CHAPTER 13

The Aldgate Pump stood at the junction of Leadenhall and Fenchurch streets. Water poured from the spouts on the stone pump that stood almost twice as tall as an average man. A metal lamp sat on top.

"The well has supposedly been around since the late fifteen hundreds," Felicity said. "It also marks the start of the East End." This she knew from reading a history of London.

"You don't have to tell me. I come from here, remember. And see that wolf head plaque? This is where the last wolf in London was shot." He grinned, gathered a handful of water, and drank. "Me mates and I used to splash around the water as kids on hot days. The coppers would come and tell us to take off, but we'd be back soon as they left." His East End accent took over as he talked.

She could imagine Davies and his friends dashing about in the small pools where the gushing water collected. Laughing and making as much noise and mess as possible. He was doubtless the leader. "That sounds like fun."

"It was. Suppose you had a pool or something to play about in."

"Actually, I have a lake."

"Figures." Davies brushed at the water again. "It wasn't always fun. A young friend of mine died from drinking at the pump. One of hundreds who did."

She had read about that also. The Aldgate Pump Epidemic. On its way to the well, water had flowed through cemeteries and been contaminated by the bodies. The city had had to hook up the pump to the main lines.

"I'm sorry, Inspector."

"That's life in the East End." He shrugged. "Enough of that. Let's get to the business at hand."

Rawlins House sat a little ways down on Leadenhall Street. The windows were drab, and anyone passing might consider it abandoned.

Patting the place where he kept his gun, Davies took a step and then stopped. "Maybe you should wait here, Miss Carrol. It could be dangerous if they are thieves."

"Maybe *you* should wait."

"What?"

"If the operators do sell stolen property, how cooperative do you think they'll be if a Scotland Yard inspector walks through their doors?"

He thought about it. "You have a point. But I can't let you go in there alone."

She had been afraid he would suggest that. "Then let's pretend we are a couple shopping for antiquities. We can be Benjamin and Sarah Smyth."

"Sadly, that is an excellent idea. And I must say, you've got somewhat of a devious nature."

"What a wonderful compliment. Now don't dawdle, Mr. Smyth." She put out her arm for him to take.

"You're going to let me do the talking, correct, Mrs. Smyth?"

"Probably not."

He gave an annoyed sigh.

The bell over the door didn't ring. Rather, it sort of clanked when they walked in. No one was about. Unlike Mr. Landon's business, which was full of relics but neat, this shop was packed and not organized. The windows were smudged and dirty. Felicity's heart jumped at the closeness, as if the walls were ready to implode at any second. The building was long as a tunnel with no end. It stank of tobacco and dirt. She ran one of her gloved hands over a suit of rusted armor that was missing an arm. Her glove came back gray with dust. Then again, everything in the place appeared smothered in it.

Davies sneezed and drew a handkerchief out of his pocket to wipe his nose.

"Bless you."

Felicity and Davies turned. A lanky man stood at a short counter against the right wall.

"May I help you?"

His suit and shoes were as natty as her father's. His scent was of peppermint and cigarettes and his blue eyes resembled the color of melting ice. He had a high forehead and slicked-back ginger hair over a lean and taut face. He did not so much sneer at them as appear uninterested, which was unusual for a shop owner. While a mustache that curled up at the ends gave him the appearance of smiling, he was so stiff it didn't appear as if he had ever done so. Felicity guessed him to be in his thirties. He was attractive, in a menacing way. The kind of man to kiss you one moment and dispatch you the next.

"Oh hello. My grandfather is a collector of medieval armaments, and we wanted to find him a gift for his eightieth," Felicity said, adding a touch of simplicity to her voice. "Maybe a sword or suit of armor. Something like that."

"Yes, old Granddad loves this stuff," Davies added, burying his East End accent. "Doesn't he, love?" He kissed Felicity on the cheek.

"That's right, sweetums," Felicity said, and then turned back to the man. "You do carry such items?"

"Just what you see." The man raised his left arm to the walls. "Look around."

"I like to know who I'm doing business with," Davies said.

"Thornton Rawlins."

"Very good."

"Shall we browse, sweetums?" she told Davies.

"Of course, my darling."

They split up. The inspector browsed with leisure, probably looking for stolen items, she guessed. The man divided his attention between them.

On the walls and shelves were swords, lances, knives, daggers, bows, and arrows. Similar items to those Mr. Landon sold. The antiquities at Rawlins House, however, were scratched, tarnished, or damaged. A push-lever crossbow was displayed, but half of the handle had been broken off. She didn't spot one item related to the King Arthur legend.

A black curtain hung in a doorway at the back of the shop. Before she could reach the curtain, the man moved quickly and headed her off.

"Nothing back there, Missus."

"No hidden treasures?"

"Unless you count a broom and boxes as such."

Time to move along this surveillance.

"Do you have one of those ball-and-chain things?" She smiled sweet as an apricot tart. "What do you call those, darling?" she asked Davies.

"A flail, my love, a flail."

"Do you have one of those, sir?" she asked the man. "Granddaddy would be so happy if you did."

"No."

Davies patted his chest as if tapping a large wallet. "Mr. Rawlins, we don't especially care where and how the item is obtained. We just want one."

The inspector is clever, Felicity thought. She would help him along. "Yes, money is no object at all, right, sweetums?"

"Correct, my darling."

"We always get what we want."

Rawlins's face didn't move. "You're talking nothing but air." He drummed long fingers. He wanted her and Davies to leave.

"Well, if that's the case, I don't see anything that would interest Granddaddy. Shall we, dearest?" She held out her arm to Davies and he took it. They headed back toward Aldgate Pump to catch a cab.

"That man is hiding something. I'd love to see what's in that back room," she said.

"You're right about that, Miss Carrol. Thornton Rawlins is a tough one. Underneath his clean nails is dirt, I suspect. I've been around criminals long enough to smell them."

"And what does that smell like?"

"Smoke and greed. Rawlins House does need a second look, but without you."

"Why?"

"Because they're criminals."

They didn't speak for a while in the cab. The horses' hooves clomped on the stone street and the wheels churned. She suspected that Davies was thinking about what he had learned. Felicity was also thinking—thinking about what was behind the black curtain at Rawlins House and how to find out what it was.

"You got to watch a real detective at work," Davies said after a time. "How did you enjoy it, Miss Carrol?"

"You mean you?" she said with all earnestness.

"Yes, I mean me."

She smiled with mischief. "That's right. You are the only inspector around."

"How nice of you to say." He held on to the sarcasm.

Even so, her cheeks warmed like a stone under the sun and her pulse thumped. She was almost giddy. She *was* part of an actual, honest-to-goodness police murder investigation. "I did find it exhilarating."

Davies brushed specks from his hat. "I'm so delighted to have entertained you, Miss Carrol. Now you can return the favor and tell me something."

"It depends on the question."

"When we first met at the museum, you spouted out all those names and dates about medieval weapons and fingerprinting and history. How do you do it, remember such facts?"

"I recall everything I read."

"This some sort of parlor trick?"

She shook her head. "Merely the way my mind works. I can evoke the information I have read anytime I need it."

"You're not at all how you appear," he said thoughtfully.

"I hope to be something better."

He didn't answer. But the silence between them was not awkward. Without his usual annoyance, he became even better looking, but she would never tell him that and was unnerved she had even considered it.

"Well, here is a fact I read about Sir Thomas Malory," she said after a bit to break up the quiet, nice as it was.

"Who is Sir Thomas Malory?"

"The author of the manuscript stolen from the museum."

"Ah." His cheeks pinked up from embarrassment.

"Don't be ashamed. Few people probably recognize the name."

"Good. Don't want you to think me a dunce."

"Never. As I was saying, Sir Malory was a member of Parliament and a soldier but also a criminal. Malory faced accusations of theft, extortion, attempted murder of another nobleman, two rape charges, and even stealing from an abbey."

"Sounds like someone I would love to arrest." He grinned.

"Oh, he was. Malory was imprisoned but escaped twice. He went to prison again for trying to overthrow Edward the Fourth."

He placed his hands on his lap. "You making this up?"

"Truth is much better than fiction. And it was while he was imprisoned that Sir Malory wrote the beloved *Le Morte d'Arthur.*"

"Ha!" His laugh blew back her hair. "Sorry," he said with a bountiful grin.

"No, I like your laugh. The gentlemen I have met at social events look like they have never laughed in their lives. If they did, it would break their spine."

"I forgot. You go to balls and hunts and all those things."

"Unfortunately."

"Well-off gents?"

"With all their wealth, they can't afford any personality."

Davies's smile faded.

"What is it, Inspector?"

"I wonder what your Sir Malory would have thought about someone committing murder over his manuscript."

"An excellent question. I do want to thank you, Inspector."

"For what?"

"Agreeing with me about Rawlins House."

He smiled. "Better appreciate it. It may not happen again."

"I do, sweetums."

He laughed.

CHAPTER 14

The messenger from Morton & Morton arrived at the door at midmorning. A lad held a note for Felicity.

Elaine Charles found dead in her bedroom at her home in Hampstead. Expensive medieval painting lifted. Police believe she died of a heart condition after being frightened by the robber. Thought you might be interested.

—Joshua Morton

"Mr. Morton, I do believe I owe you a bonus," Felicity said out loud.

Felicity knew Elaine Charles, though only enough to nod at her with recognition. They had met at several London events for the rich and ripe to be married—the ones Felicity's father had coerced her into attending. Elaine Charles was a slight creature with the pallid skin of someone who had recently recovered from illness, but her hair was of the richest and thickest brown. No matter her wan appearance, Elaine always showed the most robust of smiles, especially when she talked about her engagement to a good-looking officer in the Corps of Royal Engineers. Since birth, Elaine's heart had not been the strongest, and she took care not to exert herself too much, as she had explained to Felicity and a group of other women at one social event. With the possibility of death nearer than she liked, every day became as precious as diamonds, Elaine had said. She thought of her life as a necklace made up of those flawless gems.

Poor Elaine. Now the necklace had been broken.

Felicity had to visit the crime scene to find out whether the stolen painting had a King Arthur theme. If so, then Elaine's death might be related to the murders of William Kent and Lord Banbury. One thing she did know: Elaine Charles not had attended the reception for the King Arthur exhibit at the museum, according to the list she had gotten from the curator. That signified that the murderer had to have another source of information about who owned what Arthur relic.

Felicity did ask Helen to stay home this time, and Helen bade her to take care.

Two Metropolitan Police constables stood in front of the fine home of the newly departed Elaine Charles. In their tunics and helmets, the men were upright as the grand pillars outside the white stone mansion in north London. Parked in front were several carriages.

"Matthew, please drive around the back," Felicity asked.

If this house was anything like Carrol Manor and other grand homes she had visited, there would be a servants' entrance by the kitchen where food supplies were delivered. That would also be her entrance. Felicity spotted the door. It was not guarded by any police officer. Fortune was on her side.

She asked Matthew to stop a little ways down. Once inside, how could she roam about the house unnoticed? She looked down at her simple blue dress. With more luck, she might be mistaken as a servant. First, Felicity removed her hat and pearl earrings, leaving them in the carriage. Because she had no pockets, she placed her small bag of detection supplies down the front of her dress. She kept on her white gloves so she could examine evidence without leaving her fingerprints or obliterating those of the guilty. She conceded that Scotland Yard did not care about such prints, but they did exist and might point to the killer.

Surveying the area to make sure no one was watching, she entered the house. The sizable kitchen stood empty, and she dared to smile upon getting that far. Where *were* all the servants, anyway? A house this size would have more than twenty, not including those manning the stable. Wherever they were, she was glad they were someplace else.

She completed her masquerade as a maid with a white apron and cap she found hanging from a hook in the kitchen. In the reflection of a shiny platter was the image of a serving girl. She could now move around the house undetected.

Where to find the bedroom? *You didn't reason that part out, did you, Felicity Carrol?* she reproached herself. Bedrooms normally lay on the first floors. She couldn't go up the main staircase because the police might be roaming around. However, many of the older homes of the rich had similar layouts for servants. Specifically, back stairs leading up from the ground floor to the bedrooms for staff to better aid their employers. She would have to find those servants' stairs. She began opening doors, including one leading into the larder. Carcasses of chickens and geese, pieces of ham, and sausages hung from the ceiling. She peeked into nearby hallways and took a few wrong turns, ending up near the front hall.

Loud voices came from two men walking down the elegant front staircase. She backed up and pressed herself against the stairway to listen. Inspector Jackson Davies was talking with another man.

"When was the last time anyone saw Miss Charles alive?" the inspector asked the older man.

"Miss Charles retired at ten thirty at night. One of the maids found her body at six this morning. God rest her soul."

"Any other items taken?" Davies wrote down the information in his notebook.

"No, Inspector."

Felicity moved to where she could see the men but not be seen. She hoped so, anyway. The older man was clothed exactly like Horace Wilkins. Black coat cut shorter in the front, white tie, shoes shinier than glass. Tidiness personified. The look of prim. The head butler, to be sure.

"And what was the value of the stolen painting?" Davies said.

"Miss Charles' mother paid thirty thousand pounds for it, Inspector."

"What was the painting of?" the inspector asked.

"Of the fabled Queen Guinevere holding a red rose in a garden. A famous rendition, really, and quite striking. It was painted in the sixteen hundreds."

Davies stopped suddenly and shook his head with vexation. "Bloody hell."

"Sir?"

"Nothing."

Another item associated with the Arthur legend, Felicity thought. *So this incident must be connected to the other murders.*

"All the servants ready to be interviewed?" Davies said to the butler.

"I set up an area in the west dining room. They are lined up waiting there as you asked."

At that moment, a young military officer rushed through the front door. A handsome man with buffed golden hair and a mustache. The constables who were out front ran right behind him. The soldier's face paled with so much grief that even Felicity began to tear up.

"Sorry, Inspector, but he didn't give us a chance to get his name," one of the constables told Davies.

"This is Lieutenant Henderson," the older servant told the inspector. "He's Miss Elaine's intended."

"Where is she?" the lieutenant said. "Where is my beloved?"

Davies introduced himself to the soldier. "We're investigating the death of Miss Charles."

"Where is she!" the lieutenant repeated.

"Her body has been moved to the coroner's mortuary."

"Where are her parents?"

"Just yesterday they went to their estate in Buckinghamshire, Lieutenant. But we've sent word for them," the servant said.

"My God, what happened?" the soldier asked.

"We believe a robber was stealing the painting from her room when she woke. Her heart couldn't handle the fright of the moment, and she passed. I talked with her ladyship's physician this morning. He said she had an acute heart ailment," Davies said.

"Where is the damn bastard?" the lieutenant shouted. "I want my hands on his neck!"

"Lieutenant, we haven't caught the suspect yet," Davies said.

"We were going to be married in four months." The lieutenant's voice faltered, and he collapsed on the steps. "Even the Queen was supposed to attend. She's a good friend of Elaine's grandmother."

"I'm truly sorry, Lieutenant Henderson." Davies placed his hand on the soldier's back.

"For years, my love always had trouble sleeping. Elaine said she had been blessed all of her life. She worried those blessings would be taken away if she closed her eyes. That a thief would steal inside and pinch everything when she wasn't looking. And that's exactly what happened." He smiled but cried as well. "I had assured her she would sleep soundly once we were married. Now she will never wake."

"She is finally at rest." Davies's voice carried compassion for the bereaved lieutenant.

Felicity leaned in. Davies had treated her mostly with cynicism and even rudeness, yet here he had displayed kindheartedness to the victim's fiancé. Perhaps she had underestimated the inspector.

"Has this house ever been robbed?" Davies asked the butler.

The older servant shook his head. "Never, sir."

"Did Miss Charles have any enemies?" the inspector continued.

"Everyone loved her. She was sweet and kind, an angel really," the lieutenant added with conviction.

"That is an enormous tribute for any person," Davies replied.

The lieutenant stood and wiped at his eyes. He stared up at the staircase. "I almost expect to see Elaine coming down. Wherever she went, she brought the sun and happiness with her. Inspector, please find the killer."

The young man made his way back outside. The two constables followed.

"Let's go talk with the servants," Davies told the butler, and they headed off in the direction away from the kitchen.

Felicity doubled back in search of the servants' staircase she had somehow missed. As she walked about, she felt the disagreeable serenity of the place. She might as well have been wandering around a fancy crypt. More disturbing was how she had remained so unruffled sneaking into the house of a recently murdered woman. No perspiration or rapid breathing due to fear. No impulse to get out of there at once and go home. As if breaking and entering, breaking the law, really, traversed her blood. She wondered if she had inherited the trait from one of her ancestors. One who had used less-than-legitimate means to help the family secure its fortune. She promised herself to ask her father the question, though she was positive he would never answer that one.

Returning to the kitchen, Felicity opened another door leading to a set of worn wooden stairs. The narrow space smelled of body odor and cabbage. At the top of the stairs, she pushed open the door slightly and slowly. Ahead was the main gallery, stunning with fine carpeting and paintings that would make even her fastidious father jealous. At the end of the hall were a set of double doors and a constable out front. Hands at his sides, he was looking at one of the paintings on the wall. That had to be Elaine Charles's bedroom.

Felicity straightened the apron and cap she wore and walked with her eyes on the carpet as she had seen the servants do at her house. *Breathe, Felicity, and act like you belong here.*

She walked to the door, hand reaching out to the knob.

"You can't go in there, Miss." The officer turned around as she walked past.

Felicity gave a deep curtsy and kept her head low. "But the inspector downstairs wanted me to look for the mistress's appointment book and other items." She imitated the accent of their Irish cook, Colleen, who had been with their family for ten years. The imitation was so good, Felicity imagined she could have doubled as Colleen's daughter. "Please, sir. Won't be but a minute." Another curtsy.

"All right. But touch as little as you can." He opened the door for her.

"My thanks, constable sir."

Heavy curtains had been moved aside, and the windows were open. The room was lovely. Lilac in color but not too ostentatious. A large bed of oak dominated the room. The faint scent of lemons and lavender came from the rumpled bedclothes. Indentations on the pillow on the left side of the bed revealed where the deceased had slept. There was no pillow on the right side of the bed. The sheet was missing, but she guessed the authorities had probably used it to cover the body.

On a thick rug at the left side of the bed stood a night table with an empty teacup on top. Felicity picked up the cup and took a sniff. Chamomile tea. Nothing odd there. She set the cup back in the exact spot where she had picked it up.

Felicity bent down. From depressions in the rug, she could see that the night table had been moved from where it normally stood. At the foot of the table was a small vial. With care, she removed the stopper and placed it to her nose.

A slightly sweet odor with a touch of saffron, musk, and nutmeg. Laudanum.

She peered under the bed. An empty glass lay on its side. Picking it up, she sniffed the inside. More laudanum. She took the glass to the window to see if fingerprints had been left behind. In the light, she saw a print from a small hand, but the prints were smudged. She replaced the glass where she had found it underneath the bed.

Felicity walked around the bed. A white coverlet lay rumpled on the floor. She lifted it up. A pillow lay under that. Picking up the pillow, she turned it around. Smears of blood marked the middle.

"Scared to death, my eye," she whispered.

Felicity closed her eyes and saw the room the way it must have been the night before. The house had settled for the night. Elaine Charles lay in bed. The man entered without a sound. He saw the sleeping woman, picked up the pillow, and shoved it down on her face. Already half drugged, she struggled but ultimately was forced into a sleep from which she would not awake. Opening her eyes, Felicity exhaled at the life extinguished so cruelly.

Felicity walked to the doorway and asked the constable to summon Inspector Davies, calling it urgent. She lost the fake Irish accent at that point.

Davies's face tensed when he saw her. "Did you lose all your money? Have you taken up domestic work?"

"Perhaps."

He shut the door. "I could have you arrested for disturbing the scene of a criminal investigation."

"I did not disturb anything, Inspector. I was observing."

"Is that what you call it?"

"Elaine Charles did not die of fright. That is ludicrous."

"She was frail."

"She was suffocated."

"That is the grandest of assumptions."

"No assumptions, but deductions based on what I observed in this room. May I demonstrate?"

His nod was so sharp, she thought his neck bones might snap.

"Elaine Charles took laudanum to help her sleep last night. Under the bed is a glass and vial reeking from the opiate. I heard her fiancé say she had chronic trouble with insomnia."

"When did you hear that?"

"Downstairs."

"How?"

"I was listening."

His teeth clamped down hard,

"May I continue?"

"I'm afraid I won't be able to stop you."

"When the house was asleep, the murderer sneaked into her room and suffocated her with a pillow. I'm sure the coroner will concur when he conducts the postmortem."

Felicity showed him the red marks on the pillow. "This came from the bleeding in her lungs due to lack of oxygen. And when you examine her body, I'm certain you'll find broken blood vessels in her eyes from hemorrhaging. Those are sure signs of suffocation." Her hand pointed to the bed. "Although drugged, Elaine Charles did have fight in her."

"Why do you say that?"

"The night table."

"We never moved it."

"Yes, but as the murderer suffocated her, she knocked the table over. The thick rug muffled the sound of it falling. When the killer had finished his terrible deed, he replaced the table, but not in the correct position, based on the marks in the rug. He did replace the teacup, but apparently didn't have time or couldn't see enough in the dark to pick up her drinking glass and a vial of laudanum from underneath the bed."

She pointed out where they were located.

Davies took the pillow from her. "How did we bloody miss this?"

"Because the killer set the stage. And he took another piece of artwork with a King Arthur theme. That makes three."

"I can count."

She paced. "As with the other murders, the killer could have waited until she was asleep and then stolen the painting. But again, his aim was murder as well as the theft. The suspect must have been familiar with her medical condition and that her parents were gone." She stopped pacing. "Heavens in a basket! He knew her! May I see the body?"

"Get out of this room and this house!"

"There may be more clues."

His hands grasped the sides of the pillow. "Miss Carrol, my patience is thinner than rice paper."

"But . . ."

"Out!"

Felicity nodded with compliance. Logically, retreat was the best action at that point. "Thank you for not arresting me, Inspector."

"I won't be so generous next time."

CHAPTER 15

Lady Trent basked in the sun as if the light were meant exclusively for her. Her chaise sat in the middle of a glass-enclosed garden off the house. She was surrounded by roses and greenery. An attractive woman in her forties, her skin was a pastel cake and contrasted her upswept black hair and black dress. Her conceit fluttered about the room like her luxurious scent. The lady appeared as if she would break into a thousand pieces if she moved from the chaise. Felicity was tempted to push her, but not without getting information she required.

The home was the poshest of places, but Felicity was used to such surroundings, having been raised in them herself.

The woman's green eyes barely moved over Felicity's card.

"Your father is Samuel Carrol?"

Felicity acknowledged it with a dip of her head.

"An amiable fellow, witty and enchanting." Her smile was delicate.

Lady Trent must have been talking about some other Samuel Carrol.

"I understand your late husband had a wonderful collection of medieval armaments. And I would like to buy one for my father." Felicity congratulated herself on a marvelous acting job.

Mr. Landon had told her and Inspector Davies that the collection had already been sold, but Felicity wanted to gauge Lady Trent's reaction. Like Hamlet watching his uncle's response to the play dramatizing the murder of his father.

The woman had no reaction at all. Not exactly a surprise. Felicity couldn't see Lady Trent killing anyone for fear of mussing her beautiful hair.

Lady Trent sighed. "Young woman, you made this visit for nothing. I disposed of all that soon after my husband died. I detested those medieval things. Brutal they were. And horribly ugly."

"How large was his collection?"

"Too large for words."

This woman gave the term *vague* a whole new meaning.

"Perhaps you can give me the name of the person who handled the auction of the weapons."

"I do not recall. But our butler will." She moved as if with great difficulty to pick up a silver bell on a nearby table. Within seconds, the tall man who had shown Felicity into Lady Trent's presence appeared and bowed.

"Simonds, do you recall the auction house that disposed of those terrible medieval weapons?"

"Rawlins House."

Felicity suppressed an "Aha."

"There you have it," Lady Trent told Felicity. "My regards to your father."

"I shall relay them." Of course, Felicity wouldn't. She did, however, give Lady Trent her thanks.

Felicity would try her questions on the butler as he walked her to the front door. "Mr. Simonds, were you well acquainted with Sir Trent's collection of antiquities?"

"I did help him inventory the lot and supervised their cleaning. He used to tell me about each item. He very much admired them."

"Did Sir Trent ever obtain any antiquities from Rawlins House?"

"I believe so, but couldn't tell you which weapons. One of their representatives did deliver packages to the house on occasion."

"A slender ginger-haired man?"

"I believe so."

"Among Sir Trent's collection, was there a flail? Specifically, a weapon with one spiked ball attached by a chain to a wooden or metal handle?"

His eyes stared straight ahead. "Sir Trent did have one of those, but it was stolen a few days after his death. Come to think of it, several of his artifacts were stolen."

Felicity stopped. "Did you contact the police?"

The butler kept walking. "Lady Trent did not wish to. She said it just made fewer items to get rid of." He opened the front door for Felicity. "Goodbye."

The butler had apparently had enough of her questions.

★ ★ ★

"Hungry, Miss?" Helen asked when Felicity entered the London house.

"What?"

"Dinner?"

"Famished."

"Put your things away and I'll have Cook prepare you a plate. By the way, a package came for you." She pointed to one of the tables in the hallway.

It was from Morton & Morton.

"Hellie, I'll eat in my room. And please send up lots of hot coffee. I'd like it served in the mug you use in the kitchen and not one of those dainty things we normally drink from."

Helen gave her a warning head shake. "You'll be up all night, Miss."

"That, my lovely Hellie, is exactly what I intend."

Upstairs in the dressing closet of her room, Felicity took off her shoes and worked at getting out of the outfit she had worn to Lady Trent's home. She cursed the number of articles required for women. Dress, corset, bustle. Mounds of fabric weighing as much as two helpings of iron. She donned her favorite piece of clothing, a powder-blue chenille robe given to her by Helen on her eighteenth birthday. Because the robe had come from Helen, it was even more cozy.

Sitting on the floor of her bedroom, Felicity spread out the papers from the soliciting firm.

Helen knocked and entered with the tray, which she placed on a small table near Felicity. "We have perch, potatoes, and green beans."

"Coffee first, please, Hellie." Felicity held out her hand.

Helen handed her the large steaming mug.

"I have much to read."

"I will leave you to it, but please eat. You need to feed your brilliant brain," Helen said with a smile, and departed.

Felicity sipped the coffee. "All right, Mr. Joshua Morton, let's see if you are worth what I have paid," she said out loud.

The first account focused on William Kent. The report had been typewritten, which impressed Felicity. The solicitor firm noted Kent's birthplace as Warwickshire. That was within sight of Kenilworth Castle, once a medieval fortress and later a palace of Queen Elizabeth. Felicity stopped reading. Growing up in a place like that, no wonder her friend William had become fascinated with the knights of old.

Educated at Cambridge, Kent was a member of the House of Lords and a philanthropist. He aided several charity organizations helping poor children to attend school. In addition to his generosity to the British Museum, he gave to the London Hospital to help pay for the care of John Merrick, who suffered frightful deformities and was called the Elephant Man.

Kent had many friends and no pronounced enemies. The lord was admired by those who met him, according to what the firm had uncovered. He suffered no financial troubles and indeed showed as great a talent for increasing his money as he did for teaching history.

William Kent was recognized as one of the leading collectors of King Arthur artifacts in England.

"I am quite familiar with that fact, Mr. Morton," Felicity said to herself.

The report on Viscount Richard Banbury listed similar facts but fewer of them. Born in London, he had served in the military. The Viscount didn't collect anything except an abundant amount of income from his investments, land holdings, and businesses. The King Arthur tapestry had been purchased by his wife, as Macmillan the servant had reported. Not a member of the House of Lords and not much of a philanthropist, Banbury had loved to hunt until the death of his wife and young daughter. After that, he had withdrawn from society and didn't leave his house for weeks at a time. In recent years, Banbury had not ventured out in society at all.

Neither of the men was a gambler, womanizer, or frequenter of prostitutes. Nor did they have illegitimate children, added the report, as if such vices were to be expected of males. Neither man had received his noble title for a service to the crown. They were first cousins to the Queen. In other words, the blood spilled by the killer was royal.

Felicity set down those reports and placed her hand on top. William Kent and Richard Banbury had shared rank and wealth and had both owned an item related to the King Arthur legend.

And they had both been killed by medieval weapons. No matter what Inspector Davies thought, the cases were linked.

She picked up a separate report on the guests who had attended the reception at the museum the night Kent died. None were collectors of antiquities related to King Arthur. The guests, as Davies had guessed, were indeed wealthy donors to the museum, noblemen and noblewomen, and acquaintances of William Kent. Probably not a thief among them because they could afford to buy the art that had been stolen.

The inspector would call the list a dead end, she supposed.

Joshua Morton had added a note to the reports.

Miss Carrol,

None of our investigators found the word 'Medra' associated with either of the deceased.

JM

Felicity sat up. The piece of bread she chewed began to taste like uncooked dough. She swallowed hard. How to proceed with her investigation? First, she required more information about Elaine Charles and would ask the investigators to create a similar dossier on the deceased young woman.

Felicity typed on her machine.

1. *William, Banbury, and Elaine Charles all owned expensive or priceless Arthurian artwork.*
2. *All were killed but needn't have been.*
3. *Did the killer murder them for a purpose or out of a love to kill?*
4. *And who is following me in that brown carriage?*

She poked at one key.

YYYYYYYYYYYYY?

Inspector Davies had mentioned the existence of thieves who specialized in antiquities. Since they hadn't found a clue in the legitimate shops selling weapons, she might have to look in the darker corners of London. After all, Sir Trent's flail had been stolen.

"That cuts it."

Felicity walked into her dressing closet. She slid her hand over the silks, satins, crepes, and velvets in her wardrobe. On another wall were caches of shoes, hats, bows, and shawls. Dresses and accessories for all occasions. Dresses she had worn when she was younger and attended the society events she detested just to please her father. Dresses for teas, balls, opera galas, and calls on other families of fashion and money, especially if they had sons, because her father had wanted her to marry one of them. While at Carrol Manor, she had worn only simple skirts and blouses or plain dresses. She could move and breathe in them.

Putting her hands on her hips, she surveyed the abundant amount of clothing. She had to choose the right outfit for a different kind of event now.

"So what does one wear when meeting a thief?"

CHAPTER 16

From her frequent reading of *The Illustrated Police News*, Felicity understood very well she was not visiting Wonderland. She was not even venturing down the street from her house in London or going to luncheon.

She was heading to the East End.

Helen's face turned red as fall beets when Felicity mentioned her plan.

"You're welcome to accompany me, Hellie, but my solicitor will be there—for my protection," Felicity added in an attempt to relax her friend.

"Then one more person won't make a difference. I'm coming, too. I grew up in Spitalfields, and we can handle those East Enders," Helen replied, and put her solid hands on her solid hips.

"I believe you can, my dear."

When they boarded the carriage, Felicity glanced across the street. She spotted the same small brown carriage that had been following her.

"Helen, see that carriage over there?"

"Aye."

"Have you seen it before?"

Helen looked. "No, Miss."

"I think it may be tailing me."

Helen laughed. "You always had a good imagination."

"We shall see if this is a fancy or not." Felicity got out of the carriage and walked toward the smaller one. In the back was the same man with the large nose. When she got halfway across the street, the carriage took off with haste.

"Now that wasn't my imagination," she told Helen when she got back in her carriage.

"Who is it then? It's not the killer, is it?"

"I hope not. Good thing I have no King Arthur treasurers."

"Then I'll keep my eyes open and summon the police if I see it again."

"You can go now, please, Matthew," Felicity told her driver.

Solicitor Joshua Morton had arranged the meeting—for a fee. Felicity would talk with a man who dealt exclusively with stolen antiquities. In other words—a thief, but one with good taste.

The meeting would take place at nine in the evening at a public house named the King Cock in Whitechapel in the heart of the East End of London. The solicitor would accompany her, also for a fee, because the man with whom they had the appointment was suspicious and cautious. Who wouldn't be if he was a criminal?

At eight that evening, her carriage picked up Joshua Morton from his office and they all headed to the East End. Felicity had decided not to tell Inspector Jackson Davies where they were going, whom they were meeting, or invite him along. No thief was going to talk freely with a Scotland Yard inspector in the room. If she were a thief, she certainly wouldn't. Keeping Davies away from the meeting was essential to her own query, but her conscience pinched her for not telling him. She comforted herself with the fact that, if anything came out of this meeting, she *would* tell Davies—eventually.

On their way there, Helen nudged Felicity. Joshua Morton had his eyes closed and snored. "Soliciting must be hard work," Helen whispered so as not to wake him.

"Let him sleep," Felicity said.

When the carriage drove into the East End, there was a palpable change in the air, like the crackle of an electrical storm about to strike. The East End had no tidy boundaries with the exception of the River Thames to the north and to the east, where the old City of London's stone walls had once stood. The area bore the reputation of being one of the poorest sections of London. The title was nothing new. The East End had held the station since medieval times, when tenants had labored for lords who held the unfortunates in their pocket like so many gold coins.

The carriage drove on. People ambling down the streets wore clothing only a few degrees above rags. Felicity had read in the newspaper how impoverished families packed single rooms lacking sanitation and fresh air because of meager ventilation. Workers made meager wages, and crime sprang up out of desperation fueled by poverty. Under the dim street lights, the faces of the inhabitants appeared destitute of hope, as their bodies lacked the resources to barely survive.

Women with low-cut dresses, tattered feathers in their hair, and shabby shawls passed under the streetlights like silhouettes. They wore counterfeit smiles of red lips and solicitation. Felicity could not condemn these women, who, without education or income, probably had no other route to make their way in the world.

Sluggish brown liquid flowed along the gutter as if the streets bled sewage. Shabby people slept in doorways of houses and buildings so clustered together Felicity wondered how anyone could take a breath there. A scrawny dog loped along with his nose on the ground and proceeded to fight another dog for a dead rat. At one doorway, a woman pushed out a boy, tugged in a man, and slammed the door. Dingy wash hung on lines like ghosts rising up from a grave. Poverty turned the crammed stone streets claustrophobic. People shouting at each other, music from pubs, and clomping horses on the cobblestones created a din of violence.

The place stank of dead animal smoke from the nearby tanning factories and slaughterhouses where many of the residents worked. Inserted into the mix were garbage and manure from the passing horses. The result: a vile tier of inescapable air deposited on the people who lived there. Dominant winds from the rest of London rolled right into the East End and dumped their own stench onto the area.

"This is what poor looks like." Helen peeked out the window and then sat back to look straight ahead. "I saw the same thing in Spitalfields."

"Hellie, I'm sorry," Felicity said.

"Just makes you stronger."

The carriage drove by a group of people who smiled and wore cleaner clothing. Felicity had read about them. They were "slumming." This new trend had upper classes clad as the common residents of the East End. Or what they interpreted as such. In their costumes, they toured the squalor for a warped kind of stimulation, as if gazing at a zoo of creatures. They desired the same "guilty pleasures" enjoyed by the people of area, who were thought of as sinful. Felicity had heard such ignorance at the social parties she used to attend. Specifically, the poor were poor because they were wicked. They did not deserve to prosper. When Felicity declared their views "rubbish," the society toffs had turned up their noses and walked away. She hadn't minded seeing them go.

Not all of the well-off wanted to exploit poverty and sin. Some people came to aid those in the slums with their charity projects, offering better housing and food.

Felicity sat back in the rocking carriage. Her body seized with shame because of her wealth in the face of what she was witnessing on the streets of the East End. She vowed to donate money to the people working to improve conditions here. Ever stoic, she also understood that without such riches, she would never have been educated or had the resources to do what she was doing. That is, seeking out a murderer.

Matthew stopped the carriage in front of the King Cock. The scarred wooden sign out front showed a proud bird wearing a crown.

"Mr. Morton, we're here." Felicity touched his hand.

The man woke with a snort and eyed the sign. "So we are."

Matthew came down from his driver's seat to help Felicity and Helen out of the carriage. A husky fellow in his thirties, Matthew was built to take care of not only himself but any other trouble coming along. His physique contrasted with the kindness on his upright face. He scanned the area. "If you and Helen need my help, yell and I'll be there."

"Thank you, Matthew," Felicity said.

In a dark-blue skirt and jacket with no jewelry, Felicity had donned attire that would not draw any attention to her. Her hat had a thin veil pulled over part of her face. Despite her effort, people gawked as she entered the public house. Her cheeks flushed red.

"You're too beautiful for your own good, Miss," Helen said in a quiet voice.

"Not the impression I wanted to make," Felicity replied.

The inside of the pub appeared to have been carved out of ebony. Above the thick bar, shelves held bottles of liquor. Instead of a place of enjoyment, it carried the mood of a wake where no one had liked the person who died. Patrons grasped cups of whiskey and ale like lifelines. A few had half-closed eyes, as if they were on their way to drinking themselves into oblivion to forget they were already buried. A stone wall with a fireplace broke up the decor, if anyone would have called it that. Layered over the smell of stale ale and cigar smoke was the perspiration of the working people frequenting the pub, judging from their heavy boots, soot-smeared faces, and patched clothing.

Dishes and mugs clacked in the kitchen. People shouted, and Felicity couldn't tell if they were laughing or arguing. There was not one tablecloth in sight. Marred wooden tables were bedecked with rings from the plentiful mugs of ale and glasses of whiskey that had sat on them.

Joshua Morton gave the briefest of nods to the bartender, who could have been formed from soil and grit. The bartender jerked his head toward a door at the rear of the public house. Felicity and Helen followed the solicitor.

Only a few tables were in the back room, which was a little quieter than the pub out front. At a table near a back door sat one man. Felicity had to stop her mouth from flopping open. He resembled Thornton Rawlins from Rawlins House. Same taut face and same ginger hair. Same gemstone-blue eyes. But the man at the King Cock had no mustache and appeared younger than Thornton Rawlins. If they weren't brothers or cousins, she would eat her hat and that of Inspector Davies.

From his stare, the man was evaluating Felicity as well.

She stepped forward. Morton motioned for Helen to stay back. In response, Helen put on her iron face and prepared to follow. Felicity gave her a small smile, and Helen returned to stand next to the solicitor. In all their years together, Helen had come to read Felicity's expressions, and that one meant, "Yes, I will be all right." Whenever her father had missed one of her birthdays, spent Christmas elsewhere, or not visited Carrol Manor for months at a time, Felicity had slipped on the same mask to conceal the hurt.

Yes, she would be all right.

Felicity was not afraid. Like Joshua Morton, she had paid the criminal for his time. One hundred pounds was the price. This was her conference. Her time. To emphasize that, she took leisurely steps toward the table. He didn't rise to his feet but instead sipped at a mug of dark ale.

Felicity didn't give the customary curtsy women were supposed to when introduced. But then, they hadn't been properly presented to each other. She held out her hand in the American tradition. He took it but did not get to his feet. His grip was noncommittal. She sat across from him. She didn't want to let him know that she knew about his brother or cousin at Rawlins House.

"What shall I call you?" he said, and yawned, not bothering to cover his mouth.

"We agreed to exchange information but no names." She put on a winning smile.

"You got nerve, I'll give you that." Her eyes lifted. His accent was as refined as that of any gentleman she had ever encountered. This was probably necessary when selling stolen antiquities to wealthy people who didn't mind dealing with thieves as long as they didn't sound dishonest.

"How nice of you to say." Felicity nodded.

"Not every young girl wants to sit down with someone in my line of work. That is, unless they would like to purchase one of my items." A glint of greed invaded his blue eyes. "Do you, Miss?"

"Perhaps another time, but I do appreciate you meeting me."

"Your payment was appreciated. What do you want? Don't got all night."

"In the last two weeks, three people have been murdered and priceless items stolen from them."

"Let's see. Malory's *Le Morte d'Arthur* manuscript, an ancient tapestry depicting young King Arthur, and a painting of Guinevere."

She buried her excitement and a little fear about his knowledge of the stolen items. Was he the killer? "You *are* well informed."

"It's my business, plus I read *The Times* same as you, Miss."

The name of the manuscript and the subjects of the tapestry and painting hadn't been mentioned in the newspaper. "Just what is your business?" she asked.

"I don't deal in gold plate or silver tray. Nor comely jewels like others gents with nimble fingers. My interest is in the items having history in them. Buyers here and on the continent will pay good coin for those and not bother to ask how you got them."

"These men with the nimble fingers, do they commonly kill the owners while in the process of absconding with property?"

"They aren't murderers, young lady." He pressed his manicured fingers on the table. "Those gents like to get in, remove their treasure, and get out. Without notice or confrontation. 'Course, I have heard tell of some accidents here and again. Like an owner coming home and catching a man at his work." He straightened his shirt. "Thieves steal. Murderers kill." He spoke with principle, although the principle dealt with criminal acts.

"That is enlightening." Felicity had suspected this all along, given the cases she had read about in *The Illustrated Police News*.

"Murder is bad for business."

"Do you know who took these particular items?"

"You mean who killed those people?"

"Yes."

"I'm no informant."

"Then you know?"

"No." The man finished his ale.

"How about a hint?"

He laughed.

She did not. "Sir, I am determined to learn the identity of the culprit with or without your aid."

"You?" A chuckle rumbled in his chest. "Looks like you couldn't survive one day without a lavish holiday or a new frock."

"I suppose my aspiration can be construed as humorous." She

placed her hands flat on the table with her own challenge. "But what would you do if someone murdered your friend, a man you thought of as a father?"

"That's simple. I'd find 'em and kill 'em."

"I will find him and let the Crown do the rest. So I repeat, have you heard of anyone who might have murdered those people and taken their property?"

He leaned back in his chair.

Felicity smiled. "Have you ever considered that if *I'm* asking these questions, the police soon will be?"

"The coppers have already been asking around. No one's telling 'em nothing."

"Have they talked with you?"

"And they won't."

She recognized an opportunity. "Scotland Yard can be very resourceful. If I could find you, so could they. As a dealer in pinched antiquities, you would be measured a qualified suspect in those murders." She smiled. "Isn't that the accurate term, 'pinched'?"

He drank more beer, then crossed his arms.

"In addition, the police could detain you with lots of questions," she said. "And what buyer would want to do business with a suspected murderer? However, if the real culprit was apprehended, the focus would be off of you and yours."

He uncrossed his arms. "I have no idea who killed those people."

"No gossip or guesses?"

"None. Satisfied?" The man drew out his watch. A gold antique. "We 'bout done here? I have an appointment with a man interested in a chair once owned by Louis the Fourteenth."

"That must be a wonderful piece."

"Want to make an offer, love?"

"If you do hear any pertinent information, please contact Mr. Morton. I will pay well," Felicity said.

"Ain't no snitch, little Miss Nosy." The man's genteel accent gave way to pure East End.

"Think of it as acting as a dealer in precious intelligence. One more question."

"One is all you get."

"Have any of your buyers shown a particular interest in purchasing items related to King Arthur?"

"No," he snapped.

Why so testy? she wondered. Was he protecting someone?

"Never did believe in King Arthur and Camelot and all the other knightly nonsense this country admires. Life is life and it's not pretty." Menace dictated his expression. "Given that someone is slaughtering the owners to get those pieces, I might have to give the ole boy another look. King Arthur might make me a rich man."

With that, he slipped out the back door.

CHAPTER 17

Through her copper field binoculars, Felicity counted rats. She had spotted five so far. She was watching the alley behind Rawlins House, which was grim as a passage to hell. Sweaty brick walls on both sides. The stench of sewage drew the rats she counted.

She wore a black dress and her riding boots just in case she had to run. Her primary accomplishment had been getting away from Helen, who fortunately had gone to bed early. Concealing herself in shadows, Felicity had been observing the double doors at the back of Rawlins House for three hours. This was her second night doing so.

Given what she knew about the antiquities dealer and the art thief, she suspected the stolen painting once belonging to Elaine Charles might show up for another buyer who probably didn't care where it came from. And if they had killed Elaine for her art, then they might also have killed Lord Banbury and William Kent for theirs. The Rawlins brothers or cousins, however they were related, knew and sold medieval weapons, so they could easily have wielded them to kill. For Elaine Charles, they hadn't needed a knife or lance, only their hands.

Felicity hoped they hadn't already disposed of the stolen manuscript, tapestry, and painting. How wonderful it would be to catch them, as the police would say, red-handed.

Another rat scurried by.

Was she nervous? Well, yes, even though Matthew and the carriage were around a corner on Fenchurch Street. The driver had offered to accompany her, but she had said she would yell if she required aid or needed police summoned to apprehend the Rawlins brothers or cousins.

"Hurry on now, Mr. Rawlins," she whispered.

Her body stiffened. Behind her came the sound of footsteps on stone. She clutched the leather strap of the copper binoculars. If she swung them hard enough, she could discourage whoever was sneaking up on her. Immediately she thought of the big-nosed man in the carriage. With caution, she turned.

Inspector Jackson Griggs stood there, pistol in hand. Behind him was a bobby twice her size. Davies emitted an iciness, sure as if he had just returned from the North Pole. He took her arm and led her in the opposite direction of Rawlins House.

"Now tell me what in blazes you're doing here," he whispered.

In returning whispers, Felicity told him about her visit to Trent's widow. How the late Sir Trent had done business with Rawlins House, which had also handled the auction of his armament collection. There was also the matter of the stolen flail and other items from that same collection.

"You should have told me, Miss Carrol."

"I just did. Besides, the details didn't seem important until now. Inspector, that shop was in a dreadful condition, so why would the late Sir Trent choose to deal with such people?" She didn't wait for him to reply. "The answer probably lies in what is not displayed. Didn't you notice how the clerk got addled when I neared the back room?"

"I noticed. I could arrest you."

"On what charge? Annoying you is not an offense."

"Why are you here?"

She told him about meeting the thief at the East End pub.

"My lord," he said. "You're going to get yourself killed."

"Not if I can help it. Now, may I continue?"

"Nothing will stop you, I suppose."

"So what we have is two men who are most likely brothers, based on their physiognomy. One is a thief and the other sells the stolen goods behind closed curtains. Because Thornton Rawlins handled the Trent estate auction, he knew the items to be sold. He and his brother probably chose to steal the items they wanted, such as the flail. Perhaps we might even find the one that killed Lord Banbury. And that means they also killed William. Both men are right-handed and the right height."

"I was going to make a return visit to Rawlins House as a Scotland Yard inspector," Davies said.

"I realize that. You're not stupid," she replied. "Wait, that didn't come out correctly."

He breathed out.

"In fact, I believe you are quite intelligent, Inspector Davies."

"Your praise is overwhelming."

"'Cuse me, Inspector. A wagon is coming up the other end of the alley," said the bobby.

A wagon with a lone driver stopped in back of Rawlins House.

"May I borrow your binoculars?" Davies said.

She handed them over. A man got off the wagon. Doors opened in the back, spilling light into the alley. The ginger-haired man she had met at the King Cock was the driver.

"That's the art thief, Inspector."

Thornton Rawlins exited the building's door and joined the other man at the back of the wagon. With all gentleness, they picked up what appeared to be a painting wrapped in a cloth.

"Well, go get them," Felicity said to Davies.

"The thought had occurred to me." He pointed at her. "You stay back." To the constable, he said, "Gather the men."

The bobby ran around a corner. In a few seconds, he returned with four more officers.

"Nichols and Branch, watch the front. The rest of you, come with me," Davies said to the policemen.

He handed her back the binoculars.

"Now here's how Scotland Yard works." He dashed off.

He and the officers sneaked up as best they could, but not perfectly.

"Coppers!" said Thornton Rawlins, who dropped the painting back into the wagon and headed back inside the building.

Weapons drawn, Davies and the officers ran up to the man near the wagon. "Nothing hasty, or else this will go bad for you," the inspector said.

The other Rawlins put his hands up.

Felicity drew nearer but stayed out of sight.

"Let's see what you have in the wagon." Davies took the canvas off the painting and frowned.

Two of the other bobbies brought Thornton Rawlins through the doors.

"He was trying to beat a path to freedom," one of the officers told the inspector.

"I thought there was something fishy about you and that girl," Rawlins said. "Where'd you recruit your lady spy? From the streets?"

Felicity had never been so insulted. How exciting.

Davies grabbed Rawlins's lapels and drew him near. "Another disparaging remark about her and I'll roll you into the Thames with chains wrapped around your feet."

And how exciting to see Davies defend her, even though she irritated him plenty.

"No need to get bothered," the man said.

"You two brothers?" Davies asked them.

"We ain't got nothing to say," Thornton Rawlins replied.

"Yeah, nothing," said the other man.

"You'll have plenty to say before a magistrate, because this painting is stolen," Davies said. "And we're going to see what other treasures you have inside."

"We didn't steal the painting," the other Rawlins said, using his gentleman's accent. "We bought it from some bloke at a good price. He was the one who nicked it, not us. Told us he bought it at an auction."

Davies smiled. "I do love a good bedtime story. Puts me right to sleep."

"It's the truth, blast it."

"Give me his name and I'll arrest him too."

"We ain't no snitch," the art thief Rawlins said.

"Given your interest in art and medieval weapons, you're also under suspicion for the murders of William Kent, Lord Banbury, and Elaine Charles."

"You can't put those on us," Thornton Rawlins said.

"We were both in France when that Kent man died. We can prove it, too," the art thief said.

"My brother's right. You got the wrong gents," Thornton Rawlins said.

"Since you're brothers, maybe they'll put you in the same cell." Davies looked to the officers. "Clap irons on them and take them to the yard."

"Our pleasure, sir," replied one of the constables.

Once the police carriage had rolled away, Davies waved Felicity over. She picked up her skirts and ran. The back of Rawlins House could hold the answers and evidence, and her friend and the others would finally get justice.

"May I see the painting?" she said.

"It's not what you expected."

The painting showed a woman, but not Guinevere. A group of women and men from mythology celebrated spring amid a lovely forest.

"That's Sandro Botticelli's *Primavera*, circa the fourteen hundreds," she said.

"The painting was stolen while being transported by train to a museum in Prague for display. No one was hurt during the robbery."

"I read that article also, but didn't give it much thought because the painting had nothing to do with King Arthur. This painting *does* prove the Rawlins brothers are thieves and may be killers, too."

"We need evidence."

"Then let's look." She went up the stairs to the back of Rawlins House. The space was tidier than the shop. Two dozen wooden crates were stacked around the room. For an hour, she, Davies, and another officer searched for a flail and the items stolen from William Kent, Banbury, and Elaine Charles. In the crates were medieval weapons of all sorts, all in better condition than the ones in the Rawlins House shop. In other crates were more paintings and sculptures. But none of the items were related to the King Arthur legend.

"There's got to be something here that links them to the murders." Frustrated, she kicked one of the crates.

"The Rawlins brothers might have already sold them. Look, Miss Carrol, without evidence linking them to the murders, we can only arrest them on thievery and dealing with stolen property. If they can prove they were in Paris when William Kent died, then they are innocent of that crime."

"Oh dear."

"Don't worry. We'll keep looking for something to connect them to the other two murders. Want to kick the crate again?"

She didn't but smiled. "No, thanks."

CHAPTER 18

Felicity's religion was knowledge and the London Library her church. The building of gray Portland stone on St. James's Square in Westminster became her cathedral whenever she visited London. The floors of book stacks and collections amounted to stairs leading to the celestial of wisdom. Not to mention the tall windows letting in the most ethereal of light. So lovely for reading.

Carrol Manor boasted a sizable library first started by her grandfather and added on to by her father. Their books of choice dealt with history, biographies, economics, and business. Helen said her mother had built up the family library by acquiring the many novels and books of poetry and philosophy, not to mention all of William Shakespeare's works. Her parents had used to sit and read in the evenings, but after her mother's death, her father had rarely spent time there. That left Felicity to sit in front of the fireplace and read alone in the big room, which is why she preferred the London Library.

This visit was not for enjoyment, though. In the spacious reading room, she spread out on a table several books and writings. She wanted to know why someone would be driven to kill over King Arthur. She read a copy of *The Annals of Wales*, or *Annales*

Cambiae in the Latin translation. Written in Welsh and dating back to the tenth century, the chronicles were thought to be one of the primary sources of the Arthur legend and included descriptions of his battles—one in the year 516 where Arthur bore the cross of Jesus for three days and nights, earning the Britons a triumph in the Battle of Badon. Felicity thought that a commanding image. The warrior king in armor humble enough to carry the wooden cross.

To some scholars, Arthur's mention in the Welsh chronicles, which documented mostly real historical events, meant he was a real person.

In the *Historia Regum Britanniae,* or *History of the Kings of Britain,* Geoffrey of Monmouth did portray Arthur as a genuine British king who beat the Saxons and organized an empire in the fifth century. Geoffrey was the first to write about Arthur's father, Uther Pendragon, as well as the magical Merlin and unfaithful Guinevere. In Geoffrey's version, Arthur's mortal wound came at the hands of his traitorous nephew, Mordred. In other versions of the tale, Mordred was described as Arthur's son with his half sister. Utterly shocking for the England of Victoria, even if it was fiction.

Geoffrey described how the fatally wounded Arthur was carried to the mythical island of Avalon by the Lady of the Lake Nimue and her sisters.

Avalon. Where the mighty sword Excalibur had been forged.

Avalon. Even the word seemed to carry an enchantment to it.

From that same century, poet Chrétien de Troyes enhanced the Arthur tale by introducing Lancelot and stories about the quest for the Holy Grail, as well as many romances between knights and ladies of the court. Using these older tales and more, Sir Thomas Malory wrote his *Le Morte d'Arthur* manuscript, which had been stolen the night William Kent died.

Her chin resting on a pile of books, Felicity gazed out the beautiful windows of the library. In her childhood, she had loved all those tales of Arthur and his knights. Like other characters in the novels she had read, they had become her fictional family.

One summer when she was ten, Felicity had asked Helen to take her to Guildford Castle, which was located north of Carrol Manor. Her nanny packed a lunch, and they headed to the castle in the carriage, driven by Matthew. While Helen sewed and Matthew slept under a tree, Felicity explored the former Norman fortress.

Sitting among the ancient stones, Felicity reread the tale of King Arthur and his Knights of the Round Table. She felt excitement when Arthur married Guinevere, and sadness when Arthur's wife betrayed him with Lancelot. Sorrow when Arthur died, and finally, amazement when a knight returned Excalibur to the magical Lady of the Lake.

"Think King Arthur might have stopped at Guildford Castle?" Helen asked Felicity when they ate their picnic lunch.

"I am positive he did." Although Felicity realized Arthur was a fairy story, she did not want to spoil the tale for her friend.

From the wildflowers around the castle, they fashioned hair wreaths and pretended to be ladies-in-waiting in Arthur's court. Felicity soon grew tired of the wreaths and challenged Matthew to become a knight with her and fight a dragon to protect Helen. Reeds stood in for their swords.

Returning to Carrol Manor, Felicity snuggled against Helen. *This is what it is like to have a family*, Felicity had thought, and closed her eyes.

When she grew older and studied at the university, those stories of Arthur fell away from her. Along with her childhood, they were literally left behind in the nursery. Fantasy had no place in all the science and mathematics she was learning from tutors and at the university. Even in the literature courses, she had to view the

Arthurian stories as a serious academic and put aside the magic and fulfilment they had brought into her early life. The characters became leftovers from her imagination—until her discussions with William Kent. Oddly enough, during this murder investigation, she had again found her love of those amazing tales. Sadly, the renewal of affection arose from the death of her friend.

Emotion aside, she needed to find out why a man would murder out of an obsession with King Arthur antiquities. Her mind craved a pattern to the events of the last three weeks and sped through the observations and deductions she had made. Her catalog of facts was not as long as she would have liked. On her way home from the library, Felicity sighed.

How many other people had to die before she figured it out?

★ ★ ★

Felicity strolled the familiar grounds of the University of London. She could have been fifteen again, when she had first applied and gained entry. She had lied and told the university administration at 6 Burlington Gardens she was eighteen. They had never asked for proof of her age, probably assuming a young woman had no reason to tell such a fiction in the name of gaining an education. For four years without a break, she had been blissful in her studies there. She had sought truth.

She had returned seeking a different kind.

Professor Clarence Mitchell sat in his office in roughly the exact place where she had last seen him. Thin of face and hands, he bent over his desk writing as if his glasses weighed him down. The chamber was gloriously packed with papers and books as if they protected him from the world beyond. In addition to being an instructor, he was working on a book about the differences and similarities between King Arthur's Camelot and the present monarchy. Word around the campus was that the book was rife with scandal, which was remarkable for a man whose very pores appeared filled with decorum and a staid academic life.

Despite the apparent frailness of his body, Mitchell's voice was formidable when discussing Shakespeare, Milton, Marlowe, and other literary titans in the classroom. Felicity could have sworn she heard his mind revolve like a steam engine during the lectures. He had treated her no differently than the other predominantly male students in his courses. She admired him for that.

Felicity knocked on the open door to his office.

"Miss Carrol." He didn't raise his head from his writing.

"How could you tell it was me, Professor?"

He faced her. His smile was a crack among his wrinkles. "How could I forget that expensive perfume in my English literature courses?"

She smiled. "May I have a word, Professor?"

"For you, several. Please sit."

"I am working on a special project, and I hope you might help, given your expertise in the Arthur legend."

"Did you take that class, Miss Carrol?" He blinked.

"No, but I wish I had."

"Before we start any discussion, let's have tea." He rang a bell and asked a reedy youth for a pot and two cups. The lad brought the service quickly. The professor added two teaspoons of sugar, sipped the tea, and grinned. He straightened his neck. "You may proceed at any time."

She took a breath and described the murders of Earl William Kent, Viscount Richard Banbury, and Elaine Charles, as well as the thefts of their artwork and documents.

"I knew William and grieved at his passing. His collection of Arthurian art and documents was superlative. He had a great mind and was a great man, too," the professor said.

She dipped her head in agreement.

"I do find it disturbing and fascinating that medieval weapons were used and that the King Arthur artwork and antiquities were stolen," the professor said.

"I have read what I could, but I want to understand why a man would become so fanatically preoccupied with Arthur." She scooted up on her chair. "A preoccupation resulting in murder and robbery."

His expression became that of an uncle whose niece had asked him to explain the meaning of God in baby words. "Miss Carrol, I could teach a whole course on the subject."

"I realize that, Professor. Forgive me for asking you to encapsulate something so expansive, but this is important."

"I can tell you what it means to me, and I hope this will suffice."

"Anything would help."

He shifted about in his professorial robe. "When I was younger, I loved the charm of the Arthurian tales. The divine interventions, such as the passing of Excalibur to Arthur from the Lady of the Lake. The guidance of the wizard Merlin. The revered hunt for the Grail. Camelot ascending the plains like Valhalla on earth." He closed his craggy eyes. "I could see in my mind Arthur's mortality slipping away at the Battle of Camlann. Arthur bidding Sir Bedivere to throw Excalibur into the water. How the mystical hand of the Lady rose out of the waters to catch the mighty weapon. And finally, how she drew Excalibur back into the water and into legend."

"'There drew he forth the brand Excalibur / And o'er him, drawing it, the winter moon / Brightening the skirts of a long cloud, ran forth / And sparkled keen with frost against the hilt: / For all the haft twinkled with diamond sparks.'" From her extraordinary memory, Felicity recited Alfred, Lord Tennyson's passage about the sword from his poem about the death of Arthur.

The professor opened his eyes, which appeared ageless. "So beautiful."

"And now how do you feel about the legend?" Felicity asked.

"Ah, in my older age, I see King Arthur not as myth or a real historical figure but as an allegory for mankind." His voice turned to one of a parent, bestowing a life lesson on his child. "Arthur was a boy raised without a father or mother. He had to learn to be king and dreamed of a utopia he named Camelot. And for a while, the ideal flourished. But his dream shattered because of human weakness, that of a wife who was unfaithful with one of his knights. And then to die at the hand of his own nephew."

"Tragedy the like of a Shakespearian play."

His nod was slight. "Yes, betrayal and death at the hands of people you loved and trusted. And because of or in spite of that, Arthur shines through the ages because his is a story of hope, of what we can become. He presented us with a nobility to which we can aspire, despite our own foibles. The forging of a kingdom comes not through power, Miss Carrol, but through will and willingness to do good for others."

"Lord Kent expressed similar views."

"And because of such greatness, how can you not become gripped by Arthur?"

She smiled. "Even if he is a mere folktale?"

"Believe in Arthur or not, he has become a thread in the fabric of this country. Academics still debate his existence. Believers claim his tales did not spring out of a writer's vision. Instead, they were seeded by a genuine person who helped forge our nation. On the other hand, there are academicians who find that notion dribble of the highest order." He chuckled and rubbed his creased hands together. "The lines between reality and myth have become terribly distorted through the years because of the many versions and sources of the Arthurian stories. You see, Miss Carrol, we scholars do not always know everything."

"Well, you know an all-encompassing amount, sir."

"How kind of you." He scrunched his eyes as if capturing a memory. "At any rate, the belief in King Arthur has become more vocation than bedtime story for numerous people. There are those who have even spent their life and resources seeking the real Excalibur."

"But the Lady of the Lake took away the sword, according to the tales."

He gave a nod. "Yet, obscure writings do hint that the sword was found and is waiting for a new king. And don't forget, in another version of the tales, Arthur was healed at Avalon, ready to return to England in another form."

She smiled. "A lovely image, Professor. Aside from William Kent, do you know of anyone else who was a large collector of King Arthur–related art or documents?"

He scratched at his thin hair. "Only museums. William's accumulation of antiquities was far more extensive than most. I'm sure others have collected items here and there, but I can't tell you who they are."

She had hoped for a name. But what she had gotten was an understanding of a possible motive behind the murders. "As you said, the name King Arthur means greatness in this country. Perhaps the man who killed to obtain these Arthurian antiquities craves that greatness."

"And that is heartbreaking." The professor touched the pot on the small table between them. "Oh dear, the tea has gone ice." He rang again. "Tea, Michael."

The young man took away the teapot.

The hot tea arrived, and she poured him a cup. Then she stood and again thanked the professor. "How is your book coming along?"

"I shall soon be finished. Then off to the printer." He shook the page he was holding. "The book will be quite a story, and I only hope the Queen won't take too much offense."

"An amazing accomplishment, and I look forward to reading it."

He gave her a wrinkled smile. "This shall be my legacy. Maybe not what Arthur left behind, but it will do."

She headed back to the London Library. Although she retained what she had read, she again poured over the books about King Arthur. She thought about the comments of Professor Clarence Mitchell and was touched by them. She had concentrated so much on the stories of the mythical king, she had not considered the humanity of them. Of Arthur's own desire for goodness and love. How he must have suffered from the betrayal by his wife and Lancelot. And then to be fatally wounded by his own ambitious nephew who tried to take the kingdom Arthur had envisioned and achieved.

Mordred.

She slammed her hand on the book before her. "Stupid, stupid," she said out loud, and was immediately shushed by a reader next to her. Although she didn't need to, she opened the pages of the *Annals of Wales* that referenced Mordred.

Medraut was the Welsh name for the legendary traitor Mordred.

"Medra" was what William Kent had written in his own blood at the museum. An Arthurian expert, he was writing "Medraut." With his blood, he called his killer a traitor.

William Kent knew the man who shot the crossbow. But why was the killer also a traitor?

CHAPTER 19

With a shake, the carriage pulled up in front of the London house. Her mouth withered as the front door opened. Samuel Carrol stood in the doorway.

Never mind diamonds. His stare was the strongest substance on earth at that moment. He stood erect as a soldier who had declared war—on her.

Helen stood behind her father. Her face was leaden with worry. Her hands clamped down on her apron.

Felicity stepped into the house.

"Helen, see to your duties," her father announced. "I will speak to my daughter in the drawing room."

The older woman curtsied to him. Helen's eyes went to Felicity's and she gave her mistress a smile, as if that would protect her from whatever the older woman feared might come.

"Go, Helen," Samuel Carrol ordered.

Helen went off in the direction of the kitchen.

Felicity had never liked the ornate drawing room in their London house. Brocade busied the walls. Light-blue valances hung from the arched doorway like opulent shrouds. The furniture was unyielding in its conformity. Ceramics, sculptures, and paintings with no soul or passion decorated the walls. Plush rugs deadened the sound of footsteps and anything else that might carry a pulse.

Her father motioned for Felicity to sit in one of the chairs.

"I prefer to stand, Father."

He held his hands behind his back. "Have you become engaged to Lindsay Wheaton Junior?"

"Pardon?"

"Are you engaged to be married to him or anyone else?"

"Not that I know of."

"I thought so. I have registered you at Miss Whittle's Institute for Young Women in Switzerland."

Felicity wondered how her father got out the words. His lips were pressed so tight together they almost disappeared into his face.

"At the Whittle Institute, you will be taught all the qualities required of a lady in society. You will learn how to behave."

"When would you like me to start?" Felicity said.

From his coat pocket, he pulled out a thin case and from that a cigarette, which he lit. "Immediately would not be too soon. I can't stand to look at you much longer than that."

Removing her hat, she placed it on the chair and faced her father. They were duelists preparing for battle. If she faltered, she would lose everything she had struggled to acquire.

"No, Father. I believe I will not be attending Miss Whittle's Institute." She could not believe her composure.

"What did you say?"

"You have exceptional hearing, Father. I said no. I am not doing anything of the sort."

"How dare you talk to me in such a manner." He threw his cigarette into the fireplace. "I have heard reports how you have scandalized this family's name throughout London. How you are making a fool of yourself playing some kind of detective, traipsing about in the company of Scotland Yard inspectors, and unescorted."

"Helen was with me most times."

"My God, you even attended a public inquest into a murder. That a young woman would concern herself with such obscenities is shameless."

"The process was illuminating." How had he found out about all of her activities? She thought immediately of Horace Wilkins spying on her, but he had accompanied her father to the continent. Someone else had tracked her whereabouts.

The man with the large nose in the small brown carriage.

"After we are through here, I intend to dismiss Helen Wilkins for allowing you to engage in such behavior."

Felicity became incensed he would even mention firing Helen. "Please, leave her be, Father."

"I can dismiss anyone in my household."

She lowered her head, hoping the gesture might help Helen.

"Then you deny your conduct?"

Felicity raised her head. "I do not deny any of those activities, but none of this was Helen's fault. She attempted to stop me, but I carried on. And I am neither a scandal nor shameless."

The color of his face faded despite his hands balling into fists. "If you do not go to Miss Whittle's Institute, I shall . . . I shall turn you out of this house and Carrol Manor. Tonight."

Felicity thought about the dismal streets she had seen on her visit to the East End. The roads leading to a void. She should have been terrified about the possibility of being disinherited. Trembling in her corset and petticoats. Fainting from fear.

She wasn't afraid. She wasn't trembling or about to faint.

"Father, you have already done your worst to me. You have turned me out of your life. Your warning of disinheritance does not scare me. I can make my way in the world." She stepped toward him and wondered where she found such strength. Maybe she was exhausted from the unspoken truths that had skittered around their lives like bugs over a pond.

"And tell me, what would you do with no friends or connections?"

"I can teach, become a governess, a nurse. Perhaps even a doctor. And I have friends." She thought of Helen. Her best friend.

He sputtered with antagonism, leaving Felicity to wonder how this man could be related to her. "Father, has it occurred to you what kind of scandal you *would* generate if you did throw me out of the house?"

His eyes were on her. "No one in polite society would blame me after what you have done."

"Go on, then, if you must, turn me out. Wherever I land, I will lead a good and useful life. One of learning and perseverance. The first thing I will do is discover who murdered my friend, William Kent. He was more of a father to me than you have ever been." As soon as she uttered those words, she questioned whether she had gone too far. But now was the time for the truth, as much as it might hurt both of them.

"I should never have paid for those tutors and schools you wanted. You have become too educated for your station in life." He flinched as if in pain and rubbed his left arm. "If my son had lived, he would have been a gentleman, not a savage. He would have made me proud."

She smiled at the openness. At last. "And that sums up our relationship, doesn't it?"

"What on earth are you talking about?"

"You can't forgive me for living. First, Mother died of the consumption, weakened by my birth. Then my older brother died of pneumonia. But I survived."

"Do not speak of them." He closed his eyes.

"They were my family, too. I grieve and mourn them as you do."

He slowly opened his eyes, which were red and teary.

"Father, how I have wanted you to love me as you loved them. Every day I made that wish." She did not mean for her voice to falter on the last phrase. "It's not too late." She held out her arms for an embrace and took a step toward him. "Please."

His body stiffened and his face turned gray. He took a step back. She was still a phantom in his eyes. She lowered her arms.

"No family of mine is fancying themselves as a detective. How unbelievably vulgar," he said.

Never had she seen him so angry. She thought he might splinter in two. A shudder seized her body as if she had passed from one world to another. One existence to another. She had to go forward. The only way to go. "Father, I am not *playing* detective. I am quite excellent at it. At observing what people don't. Take you, for example."

"Me?"

"I can usually do this with strangers, but we two are very much strangers." She took a step toward him. Her voice grew bolder and assured. "Let's see. You are a fussy man with exclusive, handmade clothing so anyone can see from a mile away you have money. Lots of money, with your polished fingernails and polished shoes. Your immaculate suits are made to give you the appearance of a man years younger, which speaks of vanity and denying your age. You spend lavishly on art and comforts but haven't given the servants an increase in wages in twelve years. You look no one in the eye whom you consider inferior."

"How dare you."

"Each time you leave the house, you remove your wedding ring. And when you come home, you smell of cigar smoke and brandy." She sniffed. "You also wear a costly scent to mask an odor of—what? Oh yes, another scent. A female scent. One down-right cheap and worn by a woman who came with a price for her companionship."

"Enough!"

"When you return from town, there are several long blonde hairs on the back and shoulders of your clothing. Sometimes, red curly ones."

"Stop this."

"For the past few months, your color has blanched and your breath has become labored, even from minor exercise, such as climbing stairs. Your posture has eroded. On occasion you take a white pill, which I suspect is nitroglycerin for angina pectoris."

"How did you . . ."

"Why did you really go abroad, Father? The trip was not due to your irritation at me or only for business. You traveled to Switzerland, but not to register me in that woman's school. You went to see a specialist so your business competitors would not find out about your ailment. I have also read in *The Times* how the Malmstrom Clinic in Stockholm excels in the treatment of heart conditions." She let go of her temper. "You should have told me, Father. I would have cared for you."

He said nothing. Swiveling toward the door, he fell to his knees and went down on his right side with a dreadful thud.

Felicity rushed to him. "Father!"

His eyes fluttered and he mouthed silent words. She took his hand. "Wilkins, come quickly," she shouted.

Horace Wilkins dashed into the room without knocking, not his custom at all. His face contracted with worry. "Sir, how can I help you?"

"Quick, summon a physician. See if Dr. Theodore is at home," Felicity said. The doctor resided two houses down from them. "I'll stay with him." She struggled to steady her voice. "Go!"

The older man left, and quicker than she had ever seen him move.

"Father, stay with me." She put her head on his chest, which barely moved. Her tears wet his fine shirt. She placed her fingertips on the carotid vein in his neck. His blood felt like it was ebbing at low tide. "Where are your pills?"

He mumbled. She patted his pockets and found a small tin of white pills in his jacket. She placed one under his tongue. His condition didn't improve. "We don't have to leave our relationship like this. We can heal. We can be family. I want that so much." She squeezed his dry, cool hand. "Father," she whispered.

With a quivering movement, her father slid his hand away. Even in the throes of death, as in life, he had nothing for her.

CHAPTER 20

Every time Felicity moved, the black dress crackled. The black veil hiding her face cast the world in a dreary tint. Sitting on the window seat in her room at Carrol Manor, she didn't remove the veil. She wanted the darkness. Downstairs the servants prepared the food for the funeral reception later that afternoon. Plates and silverware probably clattered in their hands. She would have welcomed the noise. In her room, all was stillness and remorse.

The evening before, Samuel Carrol's costly coffin of oak wood and brass had been set up in a separate room off the library. A servant stood near, guarding the body through the night. Another tradition from the old days when corpses were snatched and sold to medical schools for practice autopsies. Horace Wilkins had personally hung black crepe over the mirrors on the ground floor of the manor, and she didn't stop him from carrying on with the stupid custom.

Earlier that morning, she had ventured into the room with her father's body. Several flower arrangements surrounded the coffin, imbuing the room with honeyed perfume to hide the odor of death. The light from the windows had transformed her father's face into a translucent and stark mask. She had not cried when he died days before. She did not cry at his coffin. He had caused her enough tears when he lived. But she was aching nonetheless.

Her father would be buried beside her mother and brother in the family crypt in the cemetery east of the house. By orders of her father, the crypt had been well maintained through the years by the groundskeepers. There he had left flowers on the birthdays of her mother and brother. He had always gone by himself and never asked Felicity to accompany him. He would not even share his grief, leaving her to mourn on her own.

Rising, she studied herself in the mirror of her room. Under the veil, her face was as washed out as laundry left too long in the sun. She stood very small in that large house.

Helen knocked and poked her head inside. "It's time, Miss."

Soon, she would follow the coffin to the crypt, where it would be set beside her mother's and brother's. Following custom, Felicity had sent expensive invitations to her late father's colleagues and friends to attend the burial. Responsibility for the list of attendees she had left up to Horace Wilkins, who had known her father much better than she ever had.

Felicity straightened her veil and mourning clothes. She had a daughter's duty to fulfill. She would give him that.

★ ★ ★

The funeral reception was well attended, which would have pleased her father. Felicity curtsied to each person who entered the house and accepted their condolences with as much grace as she could rally. Several men were acquainted with her father from his London club, while others were managers at the family mill and shipping line. Banks and other businesses with which he had dealt also sent representatives. Standing near the door, she thanked each person for paying their respects. They in turn talked of her father's business acumen and characterized him as a man of good qualities. A true gentleman. A true man of England. Samuel Carrol had showed them another face and not the one she had been raised with.

Horace Wilkins stood at her side near the door, taking hats and directing other servants. In the days after her father had died, she had caught Wilkins staring at her with condemning eyes, only to turn his head away when he noticed her gaze. He wore accusation like his well-fitted butler's suit. From the way his eyes moved from here to there, he appeared to know everything that took place at the manor and in the London house. As head butler, it was his business. To that end, he must have heard their argument in the drawing room before her father collapsed. And from his polite glowering, he clearly blamed her for his death. Just as her father had blamed her for the deaths of her mother and brother. Felicity was relieved when Wilkins left his spot at the door to attend to other matters.

As Horace Wilkins treated her with increased indifference, Helen made up for it with abundant understanding. She stood by Felicity the night her father was pronounced dead and helped her plan the funeral and reception.

"My deep condolences, Miss Carrol. You must be strong at times like these." The man who spoke was Martin Jameson.

Jameson was not only her late father's trusted solicitor, but also his friend. They were members of Brooks's gentlemen's club in London and shared a passion for whist, cigars, and arrogance. She suspected Jameson, like her father, viewed her as the worst of the worst in England—an educated woman. A wealthy girl who squandered time and money on schools and books in lieu of forging a good match and taking her place in British society. The solicitor had a daughter her age who had been married for three years and had already produced two children.

And when measuring austerity, Martin Jameson made Horace Wilkins appear like a dancing girl on the Strand.

"Your father was a great, great man. His presence shall be missed not only in commerce, but by society. He was a colossus of industry." Jameson always snuffled, as if dispelling a bad odor or something else he disapproved of. He snuffled a lot when he was around Felicity.

"You are kind, Mr. Jameson."

"When you are ready, we must talk about your late father's will and other business concerns. But those matters can wait for another time."

"I understand. Until then." She curtsied.

"What will you do now that your father is gone, Miss Carrol?"

"I shall live, sir."

He gave a sharp inhale and went off to talk with other people gathered in the house.

After a time, she left her post at the door and wandered around the ballroom, where the mourners had gathered to chat and have tea and refreshments. No one spoke to her as she walked around the room, and she was glad of it. They apparently wouldn't miss her, so she entered the library to be alone. A portrait of her mother and brother hung over the fireplace. They had been posed sitting in this very room in front of the window with a view of the garden behind them. Her mother's arm was draped around her brother, and both had smiles in their bright-blue eyes. Would they blame her, too, for what had happened?

"Miss Carrol."

She turned.

Inspector Jackson Davies stood in the middle of the room, pulling at his collar with obvious discomfort at the surroundings. He wore a fine black suit. From its gleam, his hair had been freshly trimmed. His shoes were new.

"Inspector Davies."

"I'm so sorry, Miss Carrol."

She rushed over and hugged him.

★   ★   ★

After the carriages had left with the last of the mourners, she and Inspector Jackson Davies made their way to the lake. She had suggested the walk to get away from the house and the scent of flowers and fatality.

His footsteps munched down the pasture grass, while her hem brushed over it. They took the path through the thick woods, which dimmed the afternoon light. The police inspector said nothing on their way there, as if reading her mood. From his glancing about and the way he held his hands behind his back, she could tell he wanted to ask something.

"Does all this belong to you now?" Davies asked, as if he couldn't wait any longer.

The question made her laugh. "I'm afraid so."

"I knew you were, well, rich, but not this rich."

"I can take no credit at all. My father and grandfather are the ones who built this place and the enterprises supporting it. They were very exceptional businessmen." She should have complimented her father for his talent. She should have. Guilt weakened her legs.

"You could fit my entire flat inside your library with room to spare."

"Wealth is not all in life, Inspector. Your position is as valuable to society, if not more so. Upholder of the law. Bringer of justice."

He yanked at his collar. "When I can."

They came to the lake. Davies whistled. "Never knew someone who owned a lake," he said.

"Every spring, my grandfather paid to have it stocked with trout so he wouldn't have to venture far to catch fish," she told Davies.

"That was nice of him."

"He probably didn't want to recreate with the rabble."

"Like me?"

"Most definitely." She smiled.

She and Davies boarded the small boat tied up at the shore and rowed to the island. He insisted on rowing.

"The lake is my favorite spot on the estate." She let her hand slide in the water. "I used to row out to the island and read."

"I can see why. There's a magical quality to the place, and I'm not one to say *magical* very often."

She smiled. "I believe that."

Upon reaching the island, he tied the boat to a cement post put there for that purpose. They took a seat on the stone bench. Sensing she was an infinite distance from Carrol Manor and the rest of English society, she placed a hand on his. "Please, call me Felicity. We have examined a body together. I believe this entitles us to be less formal. And what shall I call you?"

He laughed. "I'm Jackson to my friends."

"Then, Jackson, let us be friends."

He placed his hand on hers. It was rough and wonderful. His warmth sapped her breath.

A young woman should not have been so bold, but the gesture was appropriate because she wanted to show her gratitude. "Thank you for coming today. Besides Helen's, yours was the only friendly face to me. I assumed you didn't like me because of my interjection in your cases."

"I can't help but like you." He squeezed her hand.

"Even though I annoy you to no end?"

"You keep me on my toes with all your questions and theories. You're also funny and smart."

She didn't fight his compliments. She turned and placed her other hand on his.

"Besides, I understand how you feel." His voice quieted.

"When did your father pass?"

"Eight months ago."

"Tell me about him."

His smile was heartfelt as a child's. "He worked in a cotton mill. We didn't have much money, but we were wealthy in his love. He was a good man who taught us how to work hard and respect the law. I was glad he lived long enough to see me become an inspector."

"He must have been proud."

"He was."

Even in the shade of the arbor, his eyes held tenderness. She slid her hands away. "I envy you more than I can say."

His big thumb pointed at this chest. "Me? Why, for heaven's sake?"

"You were so loved by your father."

"And you weren't?"

"No." She gave a feeble smile. "I must come off as incredibly wretched."

"You're just being direct. And here's my confession. I envy you, too."

"For my money? I would gladly trade you this very moment."

"No." He stood up and stretched out his arms. "Not for all your money and properties. Or your fine house and this lake. For what you did with it. You used money for a good purpose, for an education and to better yourself. Most young girls in your station would have gone for the money and a richer husband. You should be proud."

"I always wanted my father to feel like that, but he saw my education as more of a detriment. So I replaced his love with learning. Now I *do* sound wretched."

Davies didn't say anything, but he wore a slight smile. "Forgive me for speaking ill of the dead, but your father must have been a fool. He should have been honored to have you as a daughter."

She clasped the bench.

"What's wrong, Felicity?"

Her eyes teared. "Jackson, I believe I drove my father to his death."

"What?"

Standing up, Felicity told him about their final argument in the drawing room. "He collapsed and died soon after we quarreled. I might as well have taken up a crossbow and shot a bolt through my father's back."

"By telling him the truth?"

"I should have kept my tongue. The truth can be as sharp as any weapon."

He slanted his head. "Did you make that up?"

"Yes, but it's true as the moon passing through the heavens. My father and I didn't have a relationship, but we excelled at burying the truth."

He stood up and went to her side. "You weren't to blame, Felicity."

"Is that your professional opinion?" She lowered her head, unable to face the inspector, as if he would arrest her for the crime of ingratitude and being a bad daughter. "I suspected he had heart problems, but I didn't let up on my verbal attack."

He placed his hand under her chin and raised it. "His illness killed him. Not you."

"Ever since that night, I keep telling myself I should have tried to be what he wanted. I should have become a lady of society, a wife, a mother."

"I can't see you as one of those pasty-faced women in silks and satins. I can't see you flirting behind a fan. A woman with no voice or thought."

Suddenly, she was exhausted at another truth. He was right.

He gently took her arms. "Felicity, a person can't live his or her life for someone else. If they do, they become hollow inside."

She started to cry. Davies took a handkerchief from his pocket and patted her face.

"Can't you let me feel terrible?" she said.

"Do you want to?"

"Since we are being honest, I have one more confession, Inspector Jackson Davies. I started my investigation into the murder of William Kent only to prove to my father and to myself that I had goal in life. I had forgotten why the work is so important."

"For justice."

"An amazing word." Felicity started to cry again. She wiped at her face. "I never cry, and for some reason I can't stop."

He put his arms around her. "There, there. Wipe your tears away. My mum used to say a cry is good once in a while. Gets rid of the excess salt in the body."

"Medically, I don't believe that is correct."

"Neither do I, but my mum is a kind woman and a darned good cook."

"She sounds wonderful, too." She continued to cry, and he dotted at more of her tears.

"Felicity, I have been irritated with you since we met. And I may be drummed out of the Yard for saying this, but I'm glad you are investigating."

"Why?"

"You may have a point about this case."

She pulled out of his arms and wiped the last of her tears with his handkerchief. "Are you saying this to comfort me?"

"No." Placing his hands in his pockets, he gazed out at the lake. The water was golden in the sunset. "There *is* something odd about these killings." He rotated to face her. "In my experience, the motivations for murder are straightforward. Too much drink. Fights over women or money or even business disagreements. But with these . . ."

"The reason feels more complicated. A reason other than robbery and gain from selling those antiquities." She blew her nose in his handkerchief. "So sorry. I will buy you a dozen new ones."

He waved his hand.

She blew her noise again. "Then let me tell you what I have discovered."

He crossed his arms. "Is this the right time?"

"Always, for insight." Taking a breath, Felicity launched into her meeting with literature professor Clarence Mitchell at the university. "I wanted to find out whether someone's obsession with King Arthur could transform into murder and robbery."

"And did you?"

She shrugged. "Professor Mitchell's observations are more of a literary and philosophical bent, but the answer is yes. The next question is why the killer's obsession has resulted in the murder of three people. And this is my most significant find, Jackson. In his own blood, William Kent was starting to write the word *Medraut* on the floor of the museum."

"Who is he?"

"The Welsh name for the legendary traitor Mordred."

"I'm sure he wasn't the killer. He's not even real."

She didn't smile at his joke. "The point is, William knew the identity of his killer. He was calling him a traitor."

"Why didn't he write the man's name instead of using some King Arthur code?"

"I have no idea. William was dying. In great pain, especially because he knew the man who fatally shot him."

"Assumption, Felicity."

"Logic, Jackson. The killer had the opportunity to rob but not kill. But kill he did."

Davies covered his middle with his arms. "All this is making my gut ache."

"Me, too, because we haven't discovered the real cause behind the murders. The why. It must be more than robbery." Felicity drew back her shoulders. "We learn the motive, we find the murderer."

"We?" Davies blew out a long breath.

"My God. I've done it again. I've annoyed you," she said.

He laughed this time.

They both sat down again on the bench as the evening claimed the woods around them. The light of the sunset and his smile amplified his attractiveness. His actor's face might now have been playing Romeo or another onstage lover. She could see why women relinquished themselves to such desires and emotions. She had no time for them.

"Jackson Davies, I conclude you are a decent, noble man."

"You're just trying to get on my good side." He held out his hand. She placed hers in his. "Can I tell you what friendship means to me, Felicity? Sharing information and not lying to each other."

She smiled. "I shall try. But friendship also means believing in each other. Can you try?"

"Maybe."

Felicity glimpsed her watch. "Time for dinner, and all you had to eat were the biscuits and cucumber sandwiches at the reception. You are going to come and eat dinner with me. Matthew can take you back to London tonight." She stood and held out her hand. She realized she hadn't given him a chance to respond. "I mean, if you would like to have dinner."

"I would love to stay and eat with you as long as we don't discuss murder."

"We can talk robbery if you like." She winked and took his hand. They walked toward the boat. "Thank you for listening to me."

He gave a clumsy gentleman's bow. "And about your father, Felicity. No man is perfect. Regardless of what he might have done, he was your family."

"The old blood-is-thicker-than-water scenario, Inspector?"

"Aye, there is that."

She took his arm. "But history books are rife with stories of family killing family as easily as killing anyone else. Sometimes, even easier."

CHAPTER 21

The office of Martin Jameson was as sober as the man whose name was etched on the brass plaque beside the door. Reddish chestnut wood coated the place with an atmosphere of no-nonsense. Clerks walked around as if metal rods had been pounded down their backs with a mallet. Papers lay in neat piles. An odor of ink and coffee permeated the wood. Felicity preferred the untidiness and rude clerks at Morton & Morton. Their unfriendliness was sincere. The clerks at Jameson's place of business were disingenuous in their behavior.

"He don't seem to be bothered by being prompt on his appointments," Helen whispered to Felicity as they waited on a stiff wooden seat in the hallway.

They had been there for fifteen minutes.

"I don't mind. Besides, I don't really want to hear what he has to say to me," Felicity said.

The office was busy with employees and clients. All men. Clerks shuffled papers from one room to another, while others scribbled at desks.

A man entered the front door. He didn't appear to be a solicitor. Rather, he looked like a man who did jobs that a solicitor didn't want to do. The man hung up his coat and greeted a passing clerk. The man glanced at Felicity and rapidly turned his head away. She knew that profile. He was the man in the carriage who had followed her around town.

"You!" She stood. Everyone in the room stopped and stared. "Why were you trailing me? Do you work here?"

"Don't know what you're talking about, Miss." His voice was lower than a pit.

"Yes, you do."

"Excuse me." The man spun and hurried out the door.

"Wait. I want answers!"

At that point, Martin Jameson emerged from his office and waved a large hand in Felicity's direction. "Miss Carrol."

Helen kept her seat as Felicity rose and marched into Jameson's chambers.

Felicity breathed in rich tobacco and old book pages. Jameson took his place behind a huge but oddly clean desk, which reminded her of her father's desk at Carrol Manor.

"Sit, please."

She didn't sit. "Did you have that man follow me?" Her mouth dried with anger. She pointed toward the door.

Jameson tugged at his tie.

"Please answer me, Mr. Jameson."

"Before your father left on his trip, he contacted me and wanted a report on your activities while he was gone. This was spurred by your unusual interest in murder."

"My friend was killed. That should interest anyone."

Jameson shook his head with admonishment. "Your father was worried you might create a scandal for the family. So we sent an operative to observe you, where you went, who you met, et cetera."

Her jaws closed tight. She could barely speak. "In other words, to spy on me."

"Before he left, your father had discussed the possibility of creating a trust in the event of his death, with myself as trustee. That way we could guide your life. Miss Carrol, your father wanted more than anything for you to become an esteemed woman of society."

"I take it the trust wasn't set up."

"We had no time to draw up the papers."

"I want to see a copy of the surveillance report you gave my father."

"That was for his eyes."

"His eyes are closed."

From a drawer, he took out the report and slid it over to her. She folded the papers and placed them in her purse.

"Are there other copies, Mr. Jameson?"

"No."

"Now let's talk about why I'm really here," She sat in a leather chair rasping with newness.

Felicity disliked talk of money. She was pragmatic enough to realize her dislike stemmed from the fact that she had always had plenty of pounds and then some. She appreciated the privileges afforded to her with the money, specifically education. Yet the plentiful income had also been an encumbrance that came with a bill. Namely, continued pressure on her to follow the stream of society. The sharpest of double-edged swords.

"Your father left a will." He handed her another piece of paper.

She scanned the text. "This says everything should go to my brother with the exception of a marriage dowry for me." The piece of paper was a reminder of her place in her father's soul and heart, even beyond the grave. "Obviously, my father did not change his will after my brother died."

Jameson blew his noise and cleared his throat. He was about to make an important announcement, Felicity concluded.

"Because your father did not change the document after the

passing of your brother, this renders the document invalid, legally, that is. That means, in practicality, he died without a will."

"And . . ."

"You inherit all the property in your father's estate." He read from another paper on the side of the desk. "This inheritance consists of an income of an estimated twelve thousand pounds per annum from the family's business investments and enterprises, such as the mills and shipping line. That does not count all the property you own, including Carrol Manor and the London home. Your father also had an apartment in France."

She didn't know anything about that one.

"This makes you a very wealthy young woman."

Her ankle shook under her petticoat. Not the title she valued most. One thing was certain, she did not want to spend her life in business.

"Tell me, Mr. Jameson, did my father personally supervise all of our business enterprises?"

Jameson let go a hiss not unlike a boiling kettle. "He left the daily operations of the mills and shipping line to the managers already in place. He did visit once a year, maybe twice. He also read the annual financial statements." The solicitor ran his hands over his lapels. "Our office was the clearinghouse for such information."

She smiled. "Then, sir, I shall do the same."

He fussed with his collar as if he abhorred talking business with women. "Clearly your father wanted you to marry so you could concentrate on family."

"Without a trust and as sole heir, it appears I may do what I want with the money and without your advice or guidance."

The blood left Jameson's face, probably settling in his pricey Italian shoes, Felicity hoped.

"It is *your* money, Miss Carrol."

She pushed down her resentment against the solicitor. "My

grandfather and father built a remarkable business empire, and I will put every effort to ensure it remains so. I also plan to study ways to modernize those operations. With progressive methods, we should be able to increase capacity and profits, as well as lessen the workload on our many employees."

"Modernize? Progressive?"

"Please send me the past year's financials on our family's businesses and any other information related to the generous legacy left by my father. I wish to study all there is about the fortune I have inherited."

"I can provide an assistant to help you understand such documents. They are complicated."

Her hands knotted together. "That won't be necessary, Mr. Jameson. I did take economics courses at the university." Maybe she could not read the financial statements, but she could learn.

His eyes beaded.

"One additional issue we must discuss, Mr. Jameson."

"Yes?"

"I realize how difficult it might be for you to be employed by a woman, especially one interested in murder."

"Miss Carrol . . ."

She held up one of her gloved hands. She should not have enjoyed tormenting this man, but she did. "No, no, no. I can understand your position. I believe I can find other solicitors who will not have such a problem with my gender or interests." She thought of Morton & Morton.

"Miss Carrol, I promised your father to look after you, and I shall."

"I will not hold you to that promise, Mr. Jameson. After reviewing the financials, I will decide whether your office will or should continue as my solicitor in those matters." She stood but was ashamed of her treatment of a man solely doing his job. Her breathing steadied. "Thank you for being my father's friend."

"Our firm has served your father and grandfather, and we hope to continue our services to you."

"But change is always a good thing, don't you agree? By the way, if I ever see your man following me again or hear that you shared the information he gathered with anyone else, I will use all of my twelve thousand pounds per annum to ruin *your* reputation."

"Miss Carrol, I would never do such a thing."

"Good." She curtsied and left the office.

"Everything all right, Miss?" Helen asked on their way out of the building.

"I have been loaded down by inheritance."

Helen appeared confused.

"I don't mean to sound ungrateful for the advantages I have received, Hellie. I hope I can do good things with the resources."

"You will, Miss. Of that I have no doubt."

They walked out of the stern office and onto the street. Groups of people gathered along the Strand where Jameson's office was located. Matthew and the carriage had vanished.

"What is this?" Felicity glanced at the growing crowd around them.

"A parade for the Golden Jubilee. I heard two of the clerks in Mr. Jameson's office talking about it," Helen said. "She'll be in the parade herself. Imagine that. I've never seen the Queen."

Matthew appeared out of the crowd. "Sorry, Miss Felicity, but a copper, an officer that is, asked me to move the carriage off the street. For a few shillings, a nice gent let me tie up the horses in front of his store three streets away. But it might be some time before we can leave with the parade and all."

Matthew's and Helen's eyes gadded about, and they grinned with anticipation.

"You two want to watch the parade," Felicity told them.

"If it's not too much trouble," Helen said. Matthew nodded vigorously.

Felicity was not interested in watching the royal pomp roll down a street. She had already seen the Queen. Before she went to the university, her father had suggested they go to an opera and reception, another one of his repeated attempts to get Felicity noticed by eligible men. With a flourish and cheers, the Queen had taken her seat in a box across the venue. Felicity hadn't cared for the entertainment and had instead spent the evening studying the most powerful woman in the country and the world. Victoria had petite hands, but her eyes combined strength and sorrow. Her Majesty still mourned the loss of Prince Albert many years before, or so Helen had said. Although a short and tiny woman, the Queen exuded significance.

She was England.

From down the Strand came lively band music. Helen and Matthew got up on their toes to look. As they enjoyed the scene, Felicity spotted a vendor and bought Helen and Matthew each a small Union Jack flag to wave.

"You enjoy yourselves. I'll take a walk. I would like to think," Felicity said.

"I'll go with you, Miss." Helen said.

"I won't hear of it. How often can you see the Queen? The National Gallery is a little ways down on Trafalgar Square. You can meet me in, say, two hours."

"We'll be there, Miss Felicity." But Matthew was paying more attention to the activities up the street.

"Have a good time. Wave to Victoria Regina for me," Felicity said, and started off.

As Felicity walked down the street, she noticed how many storefront and business windows displayed reproductions of famous paintings and photographs of the Queen at various ages. A young Victoria. Victoria on her wedding day. Victoria and Prince Albert. Victoria with family. Victoria in her old age.

Victoria had become queen in June 1837 when her uncle William the Fourth died. Many of the photographs and paintings Felicity saw depicted Victoria's coronation, which had been held one year later in Westminster Abbey. Draped in royal finery and holding a regal scepter, Victoria always appeared to be looking up to heaven for guidance. Her lips together in the solemnity of the event. Felicity imagined the then nineteen-year-old inwardly asking the question, "What do I do now?" as the crown was placed on her head.

Walking along and dodging people hurrying to the parade, Felicity realized she and the Queen had both had responsibility thrust upon them. She from the death of her father, Victoria from the passing of her uncle. While Felicity's inheritance was a pittance compared to Victoria's on coronation day, it would prove weighty nonetheless.

Felicity did look upward and whispered, "What do I do now?"

She had not been joking with Helen when she had said she wanted to make good use of the funds left to her. She would do her best to make sure that happened, such as good compensation for the workers at the family companies and ensuring their safety. Last year after reading a newspaper article about the hazardous conditions mill workers faced, she had asked her father if this was the case at the enormous Carrol Mills operation. He had replied that it was none of her concern. Now she would make the workers' safety her concern.

She slowed her pace. The irony of her situation did not escape her.

As a young girl, she would beg Helen for stories about her

deceased mother before going to bed. What her laugh sounded like. How she wore her hair. What kind of books she read. Felicity took in every account as if they were fairy tales and she was a character in them. A little girl waiting for her princess mother to return from the ball.

Helen's eyelashes had flicked with enthusiasm as she talked to Felicity, who lay in her bed with covers up to her chin. "A grand lady she was, Miss Felicity. A beauty like you. A kind and gentle mistress who held everyone in high regard."

"Was she intelligent?" Felicity would always ask.

"I should say so. She could hold the brightest conversations with your father. I can still see her doing needlepoint by the fire in the library while your father smoked cigars and read the *Times* when I brought in his brandy. He loved your mother so much he wore it on his sleeve. She was his sun and moon."

What a different man her father must have been then.

Felicity did have a few memories of her brother Christopher, who was two years older. She recalled a liberal smile and his sharing toys in the nursery. Christopher would punch their father in the leg and then fall back on the floor and giggle. Her brother loved to chase butterflies and frogs at the lake on their estate. He was rowdy and fun. Felicity would chase after him and loved his daring. Then one day, a quiet summery day, Christopher collapsed out on the lawn. Their father picked him up and carried him to his room. She never saw him alive again. She had not been allowed near her brother in his illness. Her father had been so grieved by her mother's death, he had disappeared into his study for hours. After Christopher died, her father retreated back into the study after putting a lock on her dead brother's bedroom door.

William Kent had lectured in class on how the past changed the future. If the past had been altered, how would that have affected her? If her mother and brother had lived, what would her existence have been? Would she have grown into a young woman who loved house parties in the country and insipid balls? The kind of daughter her father desired with no goal but marriage and children of her own? Would her father have shown her the kind of love she had always wished for? Would she have wanted an education outside the walls of Carrol Manor?

She liked to think she would have been the same person but wasn't certain.

In truth, the passing of her mother and brother had brought her to this very point. She could not change the past. She could determine her future. And she could not ascertain what that was until she had solved the mystery of who had killed William Kent, Richard Banbury, and Elaine Charles.

Still, Felicity would have traded everything to have her family back.

CHAPTER 22

Columns topped by a dome highlighted the classical marble facade of the National Gallery. Behind the face spread out the different exhibition rooms. When Felicity entered, the building was more subdued than usual, probably because of the full glory of the parade ready to proceed down the Strand.

She had long admired the place for its humble beginnings. The British government had purchased thirty-eight paintings from the heirs of art collector and banker John Julius Angerstein for fifty-seven thousand pounds in 1824. Angerstein's former townhouse at 100 Pall Mall was the new gallery's first home. Years later, a building was constructed on the site of what had been the King's Mews, which were the stables and carriage house for English monarchs. So masterpieces were displayed on the spot on which royalty had once kept their horses. Such was the history of art.

She regarded the structure as another work of art, although the architecture had been criticized as hodgepodge. The light filtering though the dome cast the building in a hospitable glow. Patrons in fine clothing and others in humbler attire admired the art. The gallery's mission was to open the collections to everyone, privileged and not. All were welcome, and Felicity loved that attitude.

Drifting about, Felicity only half paid attention to the wondrous collection of paintings. In honor of Victoria's fifty years on the throne, the gallery spotlighted several paintings of the Queen and her royal family throughout. Felicity climbed a set of stairs. At the top hung a painting twice her height. Depicted was an oak tree set in a typical English pastoral setting with small portraits painted on the branches.

"A pleasant way to record a lineage," said a young man with spectacles who appeared to be taking in Felicity as much as the painting. "Literally a family tree." He chuckled at his joke.

"What did you say?" she said.

He adjusted his spectacles. "In the Queen, our country does have solid roots to support the mighty oak that is the British Empire."

Felicity stepped closer to the painting. At the pinnacle of the tree was a portrait of Victoria. On the branches underneath were the names and portraits of her still surviving children and grandchildren. On the branch immediately down was the likeness and name of the late Earl William Kent. On the same branch was the name of the now deceased Viscount Richard Banbury.

"It can't be," Felicity said. Once she had touched an electrical current to see how much voltage the human body could accept without stopping the heart. After the initial *zzzt* throughout her body, her nerves had tingled for hours. She had the same sensation now.

"Sheer blindness."

"Beg your pardon?" The young man's voice climbed high as a woman's.

"Not you, me."

He threw her a quizzical look and walked away.

The killer's sole interest was not hunting down King Arthur artifacts. He might also be after the nobles who owned them. Two out of the three killed were royalty, and that percentage was good enough for a new lead in her investigation. Really, she had nothing more promising at this point.

She studied the name and portrait on the branch directly below Viscount Richard Banbury. The next victim could be the Marquis Thomas Wessex.

★   ★   ★

At the National Gallery, Inspector Jackson Davies's eyes went from Felicity to the legacy painting and back again to Felicity.

"The victims are all there, Jackson. We must warn Thomas Wessex straight away. My carriage is waiting. We must not tarry."

Davies didn't move.

"Jackson, another person is going to die if we don't hurry!"

A few gallery patrons gawked at her with irritation. She was shouting.

"Hold on." Davies held up one of his large hands. "I thought you were convinced the murderer was after King Arthur items because of the medieval weapons he used. Now you're saying the suspect is really killing off members of the royal family. Why?"

She didn't want to answer but had to. "I have no idea. But if we talk to Lord Wessex, we might obtain an answer to that very question."

"We?"

"Yes."

He folded his arms. She had come to realize the gesture signaled skepticism. "Don't you believe me, Jackson?"

"Let's go outside. We can have more privacy."

Davies led her through the doors of the gallery and across the busy street. They ducked the carriages and horse-drawn trolleys rambling past Trafalgar Square. The street noise reverberated even louder in her ears from her impatience to act. She couldn't tame her rapid breathing.

In the square, Davies walked to the 169-foot-tall monument of Lord Admiral Nelson. Images from Nelson's battles and his death at the Battle of Trafalgar were etched on the bronze panels of the column's pedestal. Topping the Corinthian-style column was the statue of Nelson in full-dress uniform, his face stoic and brave. He held on to a sword with one hand. The arm with the lost hand lay on top of his tunic. A mound of nautical rope behind him reminded all of his heroism at sea.

"Nelson is one of my heroes." Davies put his hand to his eyes to view the statue against the afternoon sky. "He led the country's greatest naval victory against a Franco-Spanish fleet at the Battle of Trafalgar. My God, what bravery. Only to die when a French sharpshooter laid him low." The inspector's attention went to Felicity. "I must have been a naval officer in another life. How can you not dream of a sea adventure?"

"I do appreciate you sharing your dream with me, but we are wasting time," Felicity said. Her arms shot out. She couldn't seem to control her limbs. She wanted to run. "We must find Lord Thomas Wessex straightaway."

Davies took off his hat and swiped a hand through his thick hair. "Felicity, I respect your intellect. But . . ."

She was beginning to hate that word. *But.*

"You can't expect me to go to a member of the royal family, a knight of the realm, and tell him he is in jeopardy based on the suspicions of a young woman who is playing detective."

Her excitement at the discovery in the gallery gave way to disappointment. Her mouth tasted chalk. "My late father used the same phrase. *Playing detective.*"

"There is only one detective on this case." Davies looked away as soon as he spoke.

"I thought we were friends, Jackson."

"We are. That evening by the lake, you trusted me enough to

talk about your father." His voice was kind. "I was so grateful you let me into your life."

She took his hands. "Because I did have faith in you not to betray my confidence, and that we could understand each other. Besides Helen, I counted you as someone I could talk with and share what was inside of me."

"Felicity . . ."

"And I have shared the facts I have gathered on this case."

"That is not enough." The kindness in his voice disappeared. He pulled his hands out of hers and took a step back. "I have listened to your theory. Although interesting . . . it is a theory and, I believe, a poor one."

The inflexible man she had first met in the British Museum had returned. Uncompromising as ever.

Fatigue sank into her very bones. "Friends believe in each other. I thought you would trust *me* at this point. Near the lake you admitted these killings were odd. Well, the killing of royalty is supremely odd. No, it is extraordinary."

"If I tell my superiors about this, I will come off as a madman and you will come off even worse."

"I don't care about what people think of me. Not when someone's life is threatened."

"You're brave as well as smart, Felicity." He placed his hat back on his head. "But you should care about such things. If the newspapers find out and report how you unnecessarily alarmed a member of the royal house, your companies could be in trouble. Your income."

"I don't give a hang about the money."

"You should. You should care about all the people who make a living at your mills and shipping line. All the people who work in your houses. What will happen to them? Have you thought about that?"

"No." She hadn't, and the answer parched her tone. She swallowed. "Then it is up to you to warn him. You are the Scotland Yard inspector, as you so vividly pointed out."

"I'm sorry, Felicity. I just can't." His voice lowered. "I don't believe what you believe." He began to walk away.

His words amounted to a blow to her stomach by a mallet swung by a giant. "Inspector Davies." Her tone was as chilled as the bottom of the Atlantic.

He stopped and turned to look at her.

She pointed up at the statue of Nelson atop the picturesque column. "Are you familiar with your hero's famous quote? 'England expects that every man will do his duty.' Isn't it your duty to warn Lord Wessex he is in jeopardy?"

Davies dug his hands in his pockets and walked away.

Felicity glanced up at the naval hero on the pedestal. *Lord Nelson, if he isn't going to do his duty, I will.*

★ ★ ★

The clerk eyed Felicity as if she was Mrs. Guy Fawkes ready to blow up Parliament with explosives packed in her small purse. "Lord Wessex has no time to see anyone, Miss Carrol."

"This is urgent, please," Felicity said.

"Can you state the nature of the urgency?"

Felicity blushed. How could she tell this clerk that the Marquis Thomas Wessex could be the next victim of a murderer? She had to talk with Wessex personally to explain. That way the man would understand and take caution. "I can wait until he has time."

"Not possible."

"Is he in a meeting with the House of Lords?"

"No, he is working in his chambers."

"May I go see him there?"

"He gave instructions not to be bothered." The clerk neatened his tie, which wasn't crooked in the first place. "Lord Wessex is one of *the* organizers of Her Majesty's Jubilee celebration." He bowed his head when he mentioned the Queen. "In fact, earlier today, Lord Wessex signed off on a commemorative bust of the Queen by sculptor Francis John Williamson. So you can see, Miss, he is a very busy man."

"If I can't meet with him, please give him this message."

The clerk picked up a fountain pen and shook it. Then he placed a piece of paper on the desk before him, smoothing the paper with his hand. The movements all slower than a Galapagos tortoise just waking from a nap. "Proceed, Miss."

"I must talk with Lord Wessex because it is a matter of life or death."

"Whose life? Whose death?" he almost giggled.

"Please write it down."

He wrote "life or death" on the paper and placed the words in quotes, but didn't stir a muscle as he did so. "I am sure the matter is important to you, Miss Carrol, but Lord Wessex is extremely occupied."

"Is he accepting visitors at his home? Where does he live?"

She might as well have slapped the clerk on his freckled face.

"Unless you are a personal friend, business associate, or on government business, I would not advise visiting Lord Wessex at his home." His words became terse syllables.

"Does he collect King Arthur artifacts?"

"I have no information about his hobbies."

Felicity breathed out, handed the clerk her card, and wrote down the address of her London home on the back. "Please have him get in touch with me as soon as possible. I cannot stress how important it is that I speak with him."

The clerk took her card as if it was dipped in Fawkesian gunpowder. He placed it on the far corner of his desk, where she was sure the card would be forgotten or likely dispatched into the refuse.

"I shall come tomorrow and wait," she said.

"Tomorrow is Saturday. The government offices are closed."

Felicity had forgotten. She might have to track the potential victim down another way. She curtsied to the man and he bowed, although she wanted to snap a finger on his ear.

Not sure whether Thomas Wessex was a member of the House of Lords, she took a gamble and headed to the Palace of Westminster to warn him. Westminster was the meeting place for the House of Lords and House of Commons, which made up the Parliament of Great Britain. Sure enough, Wessex was a member of the House of Lords, but she couldn't get past the maddening clerk there either.

Discouraged, Felicity stopped in the octagon-shaped Central Lobby where the corridors from the two houses and Westminster Hall met. Grand mosaics and windows decorated the vaulted ceiling of the lobby. On the wall were mosaic panels portraying patron saints. Statues of the past kings and queens of England also stared down at the visitors. What history had passed through these doors and over the floors! The first royal palace had been built on the site in the eleventh century. Coronations and courts took place in Westminster Hall. A fire had destroyed the palace in 1834, but its subsequent rebuilding had turned the structure into the grand center for England's government.

Felicity paced the beautifully tiled floor. She didn't have time to appreciate the splendor or the history right then. She was set on locating Thomas Wessex.

The House of Lords was located south of the Central Lobby, the House of Commons to the north. Waiting for the clerk to turn away, she hurried down the hall to the House of Lords chamber. Attempting to look like she belonged there, she strolled down the arched and splendid hallway searching for a door belonging to Wessex's chamber. She had seen his portrait at the National Gallery, so she knew whom to look for. A man with a noble, somewhat haughty face. Small eyes and mouth. Neat beard and mustache and dark hair behind a receding hairline. She didn't know his height.

The doors she did find were all locked, and she didn't come across anyone to give her directions to Wessex's chamber. Continuing on, she came to a door marked PUBLIC GALLERY. If the House of Lords was in session, she would wait and attempt to find him after the proceedings.

She opened the door and stepped onto the gallery above the chamber. On the floor below were raised red benches running along both sides of the gigantic, opulent room. The benches were unoccupied. At the end of the chamber, the sumptuous and gilded Queen's throne sat vacant. The tall stained-glass windows spread marvelous light on the emptiest of places.

"Sorry, the House of Lords isn't meeting today, young lady."

She spun. An older man carried a pile of papers. Wrinkles dominated his face, but his blue eyes belied his age.

"Can you tell me where I might find the chamber of Lord Thomas Wessex?"

"He just left Westminster for a meeting. He won't be coming back today that I know of."

"Can you give me his address in London?"

"'Fraid not, Miss. I'm only a clerk toting around the paperwork for them high-and-mighties."

She sat down.

"When the place is bare like it is this afternoon, I often come here for the peace." The older man sat down, also. "But when it's filled with them lords, there's too much talk and debate. Even shouting. I guess that's what we call a working government."

Felicity returned to her carriage.

The gigantic gothic building ascended behind her with its

spires aimed at the skies. The Victorian tower with the gigantic clock and the massive reflection of the Palace of Westminster wavered on the Thames. They made her feel even smaller for her unsuccessful mission.

She asked Matthew to drive her to the office of Morton & Morton, who might be able to find the home address of Lord Thomas Wessex. Once there, she discovered that the offices were closed for the weekend. She rattled the doors but chided herself for not making the request sooner.

At home, she pulled her knees into her chest and wrapped her arms around herself in defeat. The clock's ticking reverberated the setback. One minute, two minutes, three minutes. She could have been a prisoner in the Tower of London, fearing for the dawn and the executioner's ax in the square.

One hour, two hours gone. Now, three.

Time was coursing on for Lord Thomas Wessex, and she could not stop it.

CHAPTER 23

Delivered by a clerk of Morton & Morton, the message arrived at five thirty in the morning to the London house. Felicity had paid the solicitor firm a retaining fee to keep her informed of anything out of the ordinary involving people of wealth or nobility. Murder was definitely out of the ordinary.

If such a message should arrive, Felicity had asked the servants to wake her at any time of the night. And so, in her nightgown and robe and carrying a candle, Helen brought up the note from the solicitor firm to Felicity's bedroom.

Body of wealthy man found in Belgrave Square garden. Police arrived at the scene. Identity of victim unknown.

"Please ask Matthew to bring out the carriage, Hellie," Felicity said. "We're going out."

Her friend curtsied and left.

Felicity washed her face in the basin to wake but didn't need the water. Her senses pulsed. Her dread swelled. Morton & Morton had no information about the victim, but she was certain who it was before taking a step outside her house.

She closed her eyes and saw the body of Thomas Wessex lying

in the garden. If she was wrong, she would give up this investigation. But she knew she wasn't wrong.

As she dressed, her feet were ponderous as stone and her brow perspired with guilt, which was turning into an unwanted acquaintance. Felicity felt her chest go taut as a sail in a high wind. She couldn't save Thomas Wessex. She should have found his house and gone there. Beaten at the door until let in. Convinced him he had been targeted for death.

She should have. Tears formed in her eyes and she wiped them away roughly with her hand. *Use these feelings to become stronger and find the murderer,* she told herself. *Tears do no good.*

Felicity hurried down the steps where Helen waited.

"Where we going this time?" Helen asked.

"Belgrave Square," Felicity replied.

"At least your murderer is staying in the nice part of London."

★ ★ ★

The garden of Belgrave Square was a tranquil summer refuge with trees downy as green clouds and a lush mat of grass. One of the oldest squares in the city, the property had been arranged for the first Marquis of Westminster and named for one of the Duke of Westminster's other titles, Viscount Belgrave. Encompassing almost five acres of chestnut and lime trees, grass, hedges, shrubs, and gravel paths, the garden appeared to be a personal oasis for the wealthy who owned surrounding homes. The area was serene and untouched, really, except for the dark uniforms of the Metropolitan Police encircling a body at the north end. Helen grimaced at the sight.

"Why don't you wait in the carriage, Hellie." Felicity placed her hand on her friend's shoulder. "You probably won't like what you see."

"Probably not. Please be careful, Miss Felicity." Helen headed back to the carriage on the street.

"I'll be back soon, soon as the police throw me out, that is."

Helen started to smile, but then her face went somber as if remembering why they were there.

The pinkish light of morning tinted the sky. Milkmen delivered their wares to the elegant houses surrounding the garden. A horse tugging along a milk cart clomped on the stone street as the day began. Besides the vendor and the police, Felicity was the only visitor to the scene. She noticed Inspector Jackson Davies standing off to the side. He inspected the victim's body with a look of distress. He raised his head and saw her. His face crumpled with irritation.

Why did she have such an effect on men? Felicity asked herself. Was her interest in murder all that outrageous? No matter. She would rather he be annoyed at her than flattering and fawning. To Felicity's ultimate surprise, the inspector motioned for her to approach the circle of men.

As she came closer, several of the constables rolled their eyes and shook their heads at the sight of a woman in fashionable attire approaching a body. Felicity dipped her head to them to gain entry to a secret club of men.

"Miss Carrol." Davies moved his head in a less-than-inviting way.

Obviously, he didn't want the other police officers to know they were friends. Make that former friends. "Inspector. May I examine the body?"

"Let her pass." Davies told the officers. They moved aside like a gate.

In her studies, she had seen cadavers in her medical classes. But examining the recently dead was another matter. The body was a pitiful sight. Love. Ambitions. History. Memories. They had all departed like the breath from what was once a man. In this case, they had been robbed by a killer.

She leaned down to examine the face, white with mortality. "Lord Thomas Wessex," she said quietly.

"How'd you know?"

Felicity raised her eyebrows.

"Never mind," he said.

Davies wore his predictable black suit, though it was a bit rumpled. He had gotten ready in a hurry. One of the buttons on his shirt was askew. The stubble on his cheeks and chin was substantial.

She leaned in closer.

"How did you even find out about the body in Belgrave Square?" he said.

"Informants, Inspector Davies. The best money can buy."

"I wish I could afford them." His hands tightened on the notebook and pencil he held. "Go ahead, then. Have a look."

The body lay on its front. The head of an ax penetrated the middle of its back, almost square between the shoulder blades. A metal handle, which was as long as her arm, rode down the victim's body. In the dim light, the blood from the wound was dark as mortality.

She focused on the victim. The deceased's hair was immaculately cut and perfectly in place despite his position on the ground. From its appearance, his clothing had been tailored especially for him. The soles of his shoes were not worn. Even in death, his face held nobility. His left arm was at his side, but his right arm and hand were stretched out, as if reaching. She looked up in the direction where the dead man pointed. A terraced house with Corinthian pillars. A constable stood out front.

"His home is right over there," Davies said.

"Dying within sight of his home and family. This is a horror," she said.

"Since you're here, you might be able to help. You being a student of history and all," Davies said. "What can you tell me about the murder weapon? That is, if you aren't going to faint or anything."

"I never faint," she replied.

A few of the officers snickered.

Davies threw a lethal look at them. "Settle down, officers. This lady is an expert in weapons of the Medieval Ages. If you all can tell me about this old ax, I will send her home."

The officers quit snickering.

From her bag, Felicity took out the magnifying glass. "Oh well," she said with a shrug. With no other choice, she knelt down on the gravel path and bent over to examine the weapon. The single ax-head had been polished, judging by the shine. "The ax and haft are made of steel, Inspector."

"That's what I thought, too."

"Quite old, from the etchings on the blade. Probably late fourteenth century, when battle axes were constructed all of metal. This is the weapon of a knight."

"I thought they used only swords."

"Not at all. Richard the Lionheart wielded many an ax in his battles. As did King Stephen of England in the Battle of Lincoln and Robert the First of Scotland at the Battle of Bannockburn. I could go on."

"I wish you wouldn't."

"Whoever wielded this weapon was strong, gathering from the depth of wound." Half of the ax's blade was buried in the back of Lord Wessex. "The weapon is in admirable condition. Polished and sharpened. From the location of the wound, the weapon probably pierced the heart and lungs, which would have caused fatal internal bleeding within minutes." There was more to see. The victim's trouser pockets had been yanked out. Scratches marred the ring finger on his left hand. She studied the angle of the weapon in the victim's back and then clicked her tongue.

"What?" Davies asked.

"Inspector, don't you see that the weapon leans toward the right? The killer must have been right-handed and very strong."

Davies put out his hand to help her to her feet. She brushed dirt off her hands and skirt. While mad at him for not believing her theory, she was grateful he had allowed her to examine the body. "Why was he in the park at all, Inspector?"

"According to his wife, Lord Wessex went for a walk in the garden each evening before turning in. He did so last night, but also told her he was going to return to work on Jubilee business at Westminster after his stroll. As a result, Lady Wessex retired. A milk deliverer found the body."

Felicity surveyed the park. A killer could easily conceal himself in the darkness under the many trees and tall bushes. She wanted to examine as many as possible.

"Where are you going?" Davies followed her.

"To look for clues. The killer hid somewhere and then sprang. The most obvious places would be close to the path."

She checked the ground near several trees and bushes. Behind a large chestnut tree with branches almost touching the ground, she spotted a half-burned-down cigar and a match. With her gloved hands, she picked it up and inhaled. Strawberry and wood. She called Davies over to the spot.

"What did you find?" Davies said.

"A cigar. A pricy one." She held it up to show him.

"How'd you reach that conclusion?"

"Expensive cigars are not usually sweet as taffy. This one is more like the kind my father used to smoke."

"Not surprising at all. We're in a pricy neighborhood."

"Yes, but what kind of robber smokes such a costly cigar? This sort comes out of humidors and costs more than a shilling."

"That cigar probably didn't even belong to the killer."

Since her outfit was already soiled, she got down on her knees and examined the ground with the magnifying glass. "Jackson, look. Deep boot marks in the ground. The murderer stood there for a while, smoking his cigar and waiting for Wessex."

He bent down for a look. "Pure speculation."

Ignoring him, she retrieved a ruler from her bag and measured the length of the print. "Almost eleven inches long."

"An average size."

"More than average. The man was probably six foot."

"Why do you say that?"

"How many tall men have you seen with tiny feet?"

He didn't answer.

"This also indicates the killer waited for Lord Wessex. The murderer must have known where he resided and about his habit of going for a walk at night. Therefore, this was not a random attack," Felicity said.

"You can't support that notion." Still, he wrote the information down in his notebook.

A wagon arrived for the body.

"Well?" she asked.

"Interesting but inconclusive, like all of your theories." Davies walked back toward the body.

Placing the cigar in her bag, she followed him. The morning sun was up and warming the park. "Before you remove the body, I would like to check the ax for fingerprints."

"No."

This man infuriated her. "Why?"

"Fingerprints carry no weight in any court in England. So there's no need."

She couldn't argue because he was right about that point, only that point. "This is the fourth murder by the same killer."

"Miss Carrol, this homicide is different from the others. Lord Thomas Wessex *was* robbed. and not of some King Arthur knick-knack. He didn't even own anything like that, according to his wife. Your theory is wrong."

"What?"

Davies consulted his notebook. "His manservant said his

lordship always carried two hundred pounds with him whenever he went out. Kind of an idio . . . idio . . ."

"Idiosyncrasy."

"Yeah. One of those. Well, his wallet and the money are gone, along with his pocket watch and rings." He returned the notebook to his pocket.

"That accounts for the pulled-out pants pockets and scratches on Wessex's finger."

"The killer did not take anything related to your King Arthur."

"But a medieval weapon was used, just like the ones used on William Kent and Richard Banbury."

He held up a finger. "Except for Elaine Charles. She was smothered. And you were correct about the cause of death, according to the postmortem."

"Three of the victims were royals, for goodness' sake, Jackson. That demonstrates a connection, a pattern."

"So why did the killer leave the weapon this time, Miss Detective?"

"He probably ran out of time or heard someone coming. Try yanking out that ax, Mr. Detective."

Davies attempted with one hand and then two. It barely moved away from the victim's back. "All right. I can see why he left it behind."

He signaled, and two men began loading the body into a wagon.

He brushed off his hands. "Maybe this is the work of some kind of lunatic who thinks he's Sir Galahad reborn. Or an anarchist. In other words, your so-called connections are full of bloody holes. So many they could fill Buckingham Palace. These people were murdered because they had valuables someone else wanted. Time for you, Felicity Carrol of Carrol Manor, to retreat back into your money and books."

"Inspector, I might agree a lunatic is involved, but one who employs weapons of medieval knights? Who chooses members of the royal family as his victims? You saw the painting. Their names were all there. The same person is responsible for all four murders."

Davies held up his arms as if warding off her logic. She had to try another tack with him, although risk lay within. "Inspector, I told you the Marquis Thomas Wessex, a lord of England, was going to be the next victim, and you disregarded my warnings. So here we are, and he's lying dead with an ax in his back. Aren't you feeling a mite accountable for his death? Is that why you won't listen?"

He glared. Her words had hit their mark in his sense of justice. Her voice turned intimate. "Jackson, you and I could have prevented his murder."

His jaw tensed. "Constable Royce," Davies called to an officer, who came running. "Please escort Miss Carroll to her carriage."

"My pleasure, sir," said the constable, who was built like he could carry her *and* her carriage. The officer saluted Davies and pointed his big chin toward the street. "Miss, shall we?"

"You aren't going to kick me out of the park are you, Inspector?" Felicity said.

"Oh, yes, I am, Miss Carrol," Davies said.

"Very well, but you have not heard the last from me."

Davies turned back to the scene.

"Go on, there's a good girl," said the constable in a voice crushing as his physicality.

Felicity marched in front of him and walked to where Helen and Matthew waited near the carriage.

"Amateur," the constable muttered loud enough for her to hear.

Felicity had tried all her life not to let words sting, but this one clipped into her like the battle ax buried in the back of Thomas Wessex.

★   ★   ★

Felicity lay on her bed. Not bothering with breakfast or luncheon, she had been there most of the day. Guilt crushed her chest, a load heavier than the Lord Nelson statute in Trafalgar Square. Every breath had to work its way through a maze of stony organs before leaving her body. She blamed herself for driving her father to a heart attack. She blamed herself for failing to save Thomas Wessex.

And her friendship with Jackson Davies had turned as cold as the body in the garden of Belgrave Square.

Not sleeping, she stared at the ceiling, waiting for it to crash down and send her into the void.

It didn't.

After three hours, she shot up in bed. The pillows fell to the floor. Self-pity bored her worse than attending a ball with a gaggle of silly young people. As a young girl, she used to row out to the island on the lake to thrash about in self-pity over her father's neglect and her loneliness. There she sank into the grass with her misery. After an hour, she would grow bored and start skipping stones on the water or eating the gooseberries on the many bushes. It took that long to understand feeling sorry for herself would not change a thing.

Felicity got up and smoothed the coverlet. She would just have to deal with the guilt about her father and Wessex. For how long? Forever, or until she forgave herself, whichever came first. The only other way to dispatch self-pity was to take action.

She would help another human who was in peril. The next name on the list of royalty who might be in danger.

Duke Philip Chaucer.

CHAPTER 24

Felicity gazed at her reflection in the water of the Serpentine Lake. An outcast wearing a nice dress and troubled face.

She had written to Duke Philip Chaucer asking him to meet her because she had an urgent matter to discuss. She didn't want to involve the servants at the London house, so she'd thought of Hyde Park as a meeting place. She hadn't been sure he would accept the invitation, but within hours, he had.

An unsettling thought arose as she waited. She didn't want the duke to feel she was attempting to woo him into a relationship. When she had first spotted Chaucer at the Wheaton ball, other young women had talked about him as if he was a prize to be won. When they had met at William Kent's funeral reception, his allure had been unmistakable. Yes, he was handsome and dashing and all those other verbs to describe a prince in a fairy story. But a captivating intelligence smoldered within him. To be truthful, it was darn near an inferno. As important, he had appeared to accept her for who she was—a young woman who valued education—and they had talked as contemporaries. That excited her as much as she didn't want it to.

Turning around, she surveyed the scene in Hyde Park. Couples walked arm in arm. Parasols shaded women's delicate faces against the sun while their gentlemen tugged at hats to greet other passing couples. Birds tweeted out of instinct and created a cheery sound. Boaters glided along the lake, missing swimmers chopping the water with arms and legs. Old men fed pigeons with bread crumbs from a paper bag. Nannies in black dresses walked their charges about in prams, while older children skipped ahead of their harried governesses. The air was freshened with cut grass and hope.

Like many places in London, the park had had its beginnings with royalty. The land had been owned by Westminster Abbey monks. Then Henry the Eighth basically took it away so he could hunt deer in the abundant woods. For one hundred years, the park remained a private hunting ground for monarchs, until Charles the First opened it up to commoners. George the Second's wife Caroline saw to renovations, including the creation of Kensington Gardens and of the Serpentine Lake named for its snakelike form. Felicity believed it looked more like a bent ruler.

But Hyde Park had not always been filled with leisurely promenades or jolly picnics. It had also been the site of death and sorrow. Parliamentary troops had erected forts there during the civil war to defend London from royalist attacks. Noblemen dueled there. Londoners had camped out in the park to escape the Great Plague of 1665. And the pregnant wife of poet Percy Bysshe Shelley had drowned herself right in the Serpentine.

But on that bright day, the entire three hundred and fifty acres of the park appeared to be occupied with people having a good time. Even Helen, who sat a little ways away with her knitting, wore a peaceful expression. Standing on the stone Serpentine Bridge, Felicity sighed, unable to join their frivolities. Her dress weighed heavier than a sack cloth made from mortar.

Four people were dead, and she was far from a solution. She experienced an emotion she had not often felt.

Failure.

Glancing down into the lake, she clicked her tongue at the wavering reflection no longer belonging to Felicity Carrol. The face was that of the Lady of the Lake staring up and challenging her to stop her self-doubt. William Kent's stolen manuscript and other writings had portrayed Nimue as a creature who worked to aid mankind. The Lady did not hide under the water, but arose to save Arthur and other knights. With Excalibur. With guidance. With love.

Be the Lady of the Lake. Aid mankind. That meant finding the killer.

"Miss Carrol."

She jumped a little.

Duke Philip Chaucer stood a few feet away.

"Lost in thought, I was." She gave the obligatory bow to a man of his station.

"You looked very picturesque on the bridge."

"Probably more a wretched figure. Like Mrs. Shelley ready to dive into the water and float away to oblivion."

"Oh, yes, I forgot about her."

That charismatic smile sat on his lips as if placed there by the gods, if she believed in those sorts of things.

"You don't come off as the type of woman to take her own life. I suspect endurance is in your marrow." The duke took her hand and kissed it.

"The best praise I have ever received." Perhaps he saw more strength in her than she did at that moment.

"Shall we have tea?" He pointed to a nearby café.

"I would like that. First I must inform my friend; otherwise she will worry. Helen is very protective of me."

Felicity walked over to tell Helen of her plan. Helen started to rise, but Felicity touched her shoulder. "I shall be safe. He is a duke. Who wouldn't be secure in the company of royalty?"

"The people beheaded by them."

Felicity laughed, which felt good. "Helen, you are clever today."

"I got it from you, Miss."

"Shall I bring you back something from the café?"

"Just yourself, Miss. Safe and unharmed."

The café sat on the edge of the Serpentine Lake. A small place with a few outdoor tables. The tea was weak, but Felicity believed the patrons were paying more for the atmosphere than the brew in their cups.

"So kind of you to meet me, Your Grace," Felicity said. "You must be a busy man."

"My pleasure."

"What does a duke do, anyway?" The question slipped out.

He laughed. "Manage our estates and holdings, take part in the workings of the House of Lords, help with the operation of government. Those kind of dukely things."

"A stupid question; forgive me."

"Not at all."

"I am honored you even remembered me after we met at Lord Kent's funeral reception. That seems so long ago." And yet Kent's murderer had still not been caught.

His enigmatic face broke into a smile. "I have to say I find you very interesting, clever, and lovely, which is why I accepted your invitation."

Her intellect usually prevented her from fully enjoying similar compliments from men. She wondered about their motivation. But this day, she found it hard to ignore the flattery.

Felicity nodded gratitude to the young man. "Then I am truly honored." She folded her hands on the table. "As for the reason I asked you to meet me . . ."

His face feigned disappointment. "And I thought it was because you considered me appealing as well."

"I do," Felicity replied promptly, and grimaced slightly at the admission.

"Obviously, you want to discuss a serious matter. I'm sorry. I didn't mean to be so flippant."

"I would like to talk murder. Specifically, the murders of William Kent, Viscount Richard Banbury, and more recently Lord Wessex."

He sat back. "Yes, dreadful."

"What you may not be aware of is that medieval weapons were used to kill all three of them."

"What has this to do with me, Miss Carrol?"

"William was my good friend. I've been conducting my own inquiry into the murders." Her eyes scanned the nearby area to ensure no one was listening. They were alone. "Your Grace, I have reason to believe someone is killing members of the royal family. William, Lord Banbury, and Lord Wessex were in succession after the Queen's children and grandchildren. You are next in that line and could be the next victim."

He kept silent. His eyes set on her with a potent stare. No surprise, indignation, or even fright shaded his eyes, which astonished Felicity. She had just told him that a killer was targeting the Queen's family. Was he so composed a person as to not show any emotion? Or did he have any emotion to give, despite his charm? What was he hiding behind those lovely gray eyes?

He tapped his fingers against the teacup. He wore no ring that day.

"You have talked to the police about this matter?" Chaucer said.

"Of course, but Scotland Yard is convinced robbery was the motive for the killings. Treasured King Arthur relics and art were taken from William and Lord Banbury. A young woman named Elaine Charles was also slain and her painting of Guinevere taken."

His eyes stayed steady on hers. He picked up his cup and set it down without tasting the tea. "Say your suppositions are correct. The question is, why is this killer targeting the Queen's relations?"

Felicity bit one side of her lip. "I haven't determined his motive. I am confident that if I do, I will learn the identity of this murderer. I only ask that you use caution. If I am wrong"—she hated saying such a thing—"then no harm has been done, and forgive me for alarming you. But if I am right, your life might be saved." She sat back.

The duke intertwined elegant fingers. "I believe you are quite wrong."

He did say this quite politely, leaving her not so much offended as wanting to debate him. "Why do you say that, Your Grace?"

"You attended university. You must have learned that, throughout history, man has always killed to take what he wants. Be it money, a woman, land, a throne. Or including, my dear Miss Carrol, a rare and priceless manuscript, a painting, and a tapestry about a fictional king. I submit you are romanticizing these murders and thefts."

"Continue."

"Consider this. Greed might indeed be the motivation for these murders, and not because the victims were titled. The stolen pieces were worth thousands of pounds. To some men, money *is* worth killing for."

His tone was not condescending but that of one talking with an equal. Felicity appreciated this, though she disagreed with what he was saying.

"May I also point out that your theory is marred by two items, Miss Carrol. First, the deceased young woman was not a royal, and second, Wessex was not robbed of any King Arthur artifacts."

Was she so naïve? Because she had always had wealth, did she not consider that some people might kill just for gain? The crime stories she had read were chocked with such motivation.

No, there were too many questions. "I do appreciate your view, Your Grace."

He winked. "Ah, but you do not agree."

"Let's say I need more information before I make up my mind. In the meantime, I urge you to take care."

"I will. If only to please you." He was smiling.

"May I ask what is so humorous about this situation? Are you mocking me?" She couldn't keep roughness out of her voice.

"I'm not disparaging you at all, Miss Carrol. I'm smiling because I admire your bravery. That a young woman of your standing should put her reputation in jeopardy to warn me."

"This is my duty. I drew these conclusions from observations and reasoning by studying the crimes. William Kent was almost like a father to me. Because of that, I had no choice." She didn't mind being honest with Chaucer. He acted like a man who would not betray secrets.

"You have gone to great lengths for William. I have many friends, and I don't believe any would do the same for me."

"If they are true, they will. And, Your Grace, you are more fortunate than I in your number of friends."

Chaucer tilted his head. "I knew you were remarkable from our first meeting at William Kent's house."

"Persistent more than remarkable. Shall we walk?" she said.

Like other couples, they ambled along the lake banks, though not arm in arm.

"When I saw you on the bridge, you stared into the water and were in the deepest of thought," Chaucer said with empathy. "May I ask what you were thinking about?"

"The Lady of the Lake," Felicity answered. "She has been on my mind ever since the death of William Kent, along with the other tales of Arthur."

He gazed out at the placid lake. "Nimue. Such poetry in the name."

"'A mist / Of incense curled about her, and her face / Well-nigh was hidden in the minster gloom; / But there was heard among the holy hymns / A voice as of the waters, for she dwells / Down in a deep.'" Felicity saw the words in her mind and recited.

"Tennyson."

An educated man. Of course he knew the writing.

"And what were you thinking about the Lady, Miss Carrol?"

"How a character portrayed as lissome and ethereal turned out to be durable and forceful as the core of the earth. Without her, there would have been no Arthur. I wondered if she was down in the water of this lake waiting for another Arthur to appear and take Excalibur."

Chaucer smiled and glanced at the lake. "That would be something to witness."

They continued to stroll along the edge of the Serpentine Lake. Both looked out at the lake as a breeze slapped at the water, making it stir and ripple. Felicity was pleased Duke Chaucer had listened to her, though he didn't appear convinced. It also crossed her mind to wonder if she might be jailed for unduly worrying a member of the royal house.

CHAPTER 25

"So this is Scotland Yard." Felicity stood in front of the building. She had thought it might be as formidable as the Château d'If in France, where Edmond Dantès had been falsely imprisoned in *The Count of Monte Cristo*.

She didn't mind admitting she was let down. The Scotland Yard headquarters was ordinary as most London buildings. A structure of stone and shutters. The only thing setting it apart were the regular number of police officers going in and coming out of 4 Whitehall Place.

In her hand, she clutched a copy of the *Times*.

SUSPECTED KILLER OF MARQUIS
THOMAS WESSEX CAPTURED

She had to talk with Inspector Jackson Davies.

After she asked for the inspector at the front reception, he came down the hall with a grin as if the case were all tied up with the prettiest of ribbons.

"What a surprise. Well, maybe not. I was half expecting you," he told Felicity.

"You can't believe this man is to blame."

"Let's talk in my office."

He led her back down the hall. The building seemed populated only by men—if not officers, then others in suits like Davies. As she passed by them, they gave her a stern eye as if she had lifted the Crown Jewels.

Davies's office was a tiny space. Enough for a desk and chair. He had a pile of books in the corner. A window gave him a view of a wall.

"Have a seat."

She did, but before she could talk, Davies started in. "The suspect's name is Joe Crumb. Yesterday morning, he was arrested in Hyde Park. He was sleeping off a drunk under a tree on the other side of the park. The constable searched him and found these."

From his drawer, Davies took out a silver watch and two rings. "He also had Wessex's wallet. All of the money was there except for ten pounds. It'd be no stretch of the imagination to say that Joe Crumb probably spent it on drink."

"There must be another explanation," Felicity said. "Where would a drunken man get a medieval weapon to kill Lord Wessex? Surely you aren't taking this seriously."

"You bet your fortune, I am. I don't care where he got the ax; he had property from the victim. I'd call that evidence even if you don't." His voice took on a hardness of conviction.

"Did the man say anything?"

"Only that he was innocent."

"How did he explain having the wallet, rings, and watch?"

Davies grinned. "Get this. He said he woke up and the items were in his pants pockets. He thought an angel put them there."

"May I speak with him?"

"Why?"

"To see for myself."

He blinked. "I do owe you. Wait here."

After a while, two constables brought in a man with dark-blond hair who was a head shorter than Davies. The stink of stale ale and cigarette smoke emitted from his clothes. Purplish veins colored the man's otherwise wan cheeks, true signs he was a drinker. Torn, patched, and worn, his pants and shirt only barely resembled clothing. The man was as slender as a bad excuse. Perhaps in his early twenties, he had been aged beyond those years by drink. His red-lined eyes darted around the room with fear.

"I ain't done nothing, I tell you," Joe Crumb said. "Never hurt no one, sir. Never even seen that money or those trinkets before." His breath was fierce.

"Then why did you have them in your pockets?" Davies said.

Crumb batted at his head. "I can't say how they even got there."

"Do you remember killing Lord Thomas Wessex two nights ago?" Davies said.

"No, sir. But I can't remember a lot anymore."

"What were you doing in the park at Belgrave Square if not to rob and kill a rich man?"

Crumb shook his head with such force, Felicity worried he might hurt himself. "'Tweren't me. I like sleeping it off there when the weather is nice. I got a nice spot where the coppers can't see me. Like most nights, I had too much to drink and fell asleep. Then next thing, some bobby's kicking me feet and searching me pockets. I'm a drunkard, Mr. Inspector, sir. I got troubles enough without killing anyone."

"If you sleep in the park so often, you knew Lord Wessex's habit of walking there."

Crumb began to sob. The red of his nose matched his cheeks. "I'm a peaceful lad, even when I'm in my cups."

"Mr. Crumb." Felicity placed her arm on his.

"You the angel who left those treasures with me?"

"Afraid not. But maybe I can help you."

"Be most appreciative, Miss Angel."

She turned to Davies. "Were these the clothes he was wearing when you arrested him?"

"I think they're the only ones he's ever owned."

Taking out her magnifying glass, she examined the ratty shirt and pants. "Now, please, turn out your pants pockets, Mr. Crumb."

He did. In both were rips the size of a fist.

"May I also see the bottom of his shoes?" Felicity asked Davies.

The constables looked to Davies, who nodded, but with so much reluctance his head barely moved.

"Which foot?" one of the constables asked Felicity.

"Doesn't matter. I will also need a ruler, if you please."

The constable lifted the man's right leg, causing Joe Crumb to close his eyes as if ready to sleep. She measured his shoe size. On the bottom was a hole in the middle the size of a halfpenny. She dared to lean closer to Crumb and took a long sniff. Crumb lifted his head to wink at her. A heavy dose of sweat and urine made her nauseous.

"If you're quite done fitting him for a shoe, I'd like to send Crumb back to his cell." Davies pointed to the constables to remove the drunkard, who slumped and blubbered about his innocence as they took him away.

Felicity stood up. "His shoe measured nine inches. Smaller than the print we found under the tree at the park. In addition, those prints were smooth. Joe Crumb has a hole in his shoe, which would have showed up in the soft ground. He stinks, but not like the cigar butt left on the ground. There are no traces of blood on his clothing. And I doubt he could swung an ax hard enough to penetrate a piece a cheese. Inspector, this man could not have killed Lord Wessex."

"You're assuming those were the killer's prints by the tree."

"Then may I also point out that because of the sizable holes in his pockets, he would have a hard time keeping *anything* in them, much less the watch and rings."

He scowled. "The wallet, watch, and rings are evidence *he* is guilty." Davies tapped a foot. "I'm sorry this suspect didn't fit your shoe idea."

If Crumb hadn't killed Wessex, it was obvious he hadn't killed the others. She wanted to yell about Joe Crumb's innocence. *Remain calm, Felicity*, she had to remind herself.

"One other item. Thornton Rawlins and his brother Robert the art thief *were* in Paris at the time William Kent was killed. And we can't find anything at the shop to link them to the murders of Lord Banbury and Elaine Charlies. They will, however, still be going to prison for a long time for their stealing."

She had hoped for better news.

"As for the killer of Lord Thomas Wessex, we have our man."

With as much certainty as she could marshal, she looked right at Davies. "Inspector, you're making the gravest of mistakes."

★ ★ ★

As soon as she entered the shop, Felicity's eyes watered from the concentration of tobacco.

Not being a smoker, she had no idea where to start and had asked her driver Matthew for help. He knew where to go. He had seen a shop near the office of her solicitor, Martin Jameson.

Walking into Monroe Cigars was another first for her. A maiden entry into the world of men and their tobacco.

A salesman with a neat mustache lifted profuse eyebrows at her. "May I help you, Miss?"

From her bag, she produced the cigar she had found in the park where Wessex was killed.

"Can you please identify this brand?" she asked the man, and held out the cigar stub.

He reached for it, but she didn't want him to smear any fingerprints she would attempt to record later. "I will hold it, if you don't mind."

His eyebrows went even higher. "Very well." He sniffed the cigar and in an instant answered, "This brand is a Hollinger. Strawberry and oak scent and taste. Delicious."

"Expensive?"

"Very." His smile was frightening.

"Do you sell them?"

"Of course. Many cigar shops do, or should I say the exclusive shops selling the most refined brands," the salesman said.

"Can you tell me who buys this brand?"

"My dear madam. We never reveal the identity of our clientele."

Felicity placed the cigar back into her bag but pulled out a fifty-pound note. She gave an innocent smile. "Can't I persuade you?"

"No, you can't." He gasped with indignation.

"I suppose the other shops will tell me the same thing." She replaced the money in her bag.

"Only the reputable ones selling Hollingers," the salesman replied.

"I was afraid you were going to say that."

He grinned with satisfaction. "Would you like to purchase a box for your husband?"

She did buy one because the salesman had told her the brand. She would hand them out to the servants at the London house.

Felicity still visited six other shops selling expensive cigars. The salesmen there repeated what she had already learned. The cigar dropped by the killer of Thomas Wessex was a Hollinger, a costly and popular one among those who could afford them. They also refused to identify their customers.

Leaving the last shop, she dragged her feet with disappointment until she remembered the important fact she had learned. The killer had a gentleman's taste in cigars and could afford to buy one of the best.

Nearing five o'clock, she directed her driver to Landon and Son. Through the window of the shop, she saw Landon Senior shutting off the gaslights. A CLOSED sign hung on the door. She knocked and waved.

"Miss Carrol." His voice and smile were most welcoming as he unlocked the door and let her inside.

"Good to see you, too, Mr. Landon. I'm sorry to bother you at this time of the day, but I had a question about medieval battle axes."

His large face broke into another smile. "The Scotland Yard inspector has already been here to ask about them. He even produced a superb fourteenth-century battle ax."

"And what did you say, Mr. Landon?"

"That I had never seen that ax before."

Her shoulders drooped.

"You all right? Would you like a glass of water?"

"I'm fine. Tired is all."

"Do you mind if I continue closing up the shop?"

"Not at all. May I help?"

"All under control." He shut off more of the gaslights. "I asked the inspector whether I could purchase the ax, but he told me it came out of the back of a marquis of England. I changed my mind about buying it."

"Totally understandable. I will take my leave, Mr. Landon. You have been most kind." She left her card. "Please send word if you come across any information about the ax or anything else of interest related to the murders."

Landon said he would and walked her to the front. In the unlit shop, the armaments on the walls turned sinister with their sharp edges and points.

"These medieval weapons have become antiques and are meant for those people who appreciate history," she said to the older man. "Such a pity they have been used to kill again."

CHAPTER 26

Felicity had read about the Café Royal on Regent Street in *Dickens's Dictionary of London*. The book was a grand resource for activities and places within the city. Previously, she hadn't had a chance to consult the guide because her days and nights had been taken up with schooling and those silly social events her father had asked her to attend.

When she had gotten home the previous evening, she had found a note from Duke Philip Chaucer asking her to meet him there the next day.

Arriving fifteen minutes early, she asked for a seat in the corner of the opulent restaurant. Gold-colored ornamentations adorned the ceiling and pillars. The café air was fragrant with sweet pastry and mild tea. She smiled as she mentally compared the Café Royal to the simple restaurant where Inspector Jackson Davies had taken her near the coroner's office. The places were a continent apart even though they were located on the same island.

And such was the distance between Davies and Chaucer. Far apart in rank they were. One a duke, the other a police officer. One wealthy, the other decidedly not. She had no interest in the money or their station in society. More beguiling were their other differences. Such as how they wore their clothing. Chaucer engaged his costly suits with aplomb, as if they were part of his title. Davies occupied his clothes, sturdy as brick making up a building. Both fine-looking men. Davies's manner was straightforward as the law. The duke's was indefinable, which made her only want to learn more.

Felicity checked her watch. Few people sat in the café. When she had told Helen of the invitation, her friend had been horrified. The very idea that her young mistress would meet a gentleman at a public restaurant with no chaperone. But then, Felicity had expected this reaction.

"He is a duke," she had told Helen.

"I don't care if he's Prince Albert himself. What will people say?"

"Whatever it is, I don't care. He may have important information about the murders."

Before she left, Felicity kissed Helen's cheek. "The year is 1887, my dear. If this country can enjoy steam engines and electricity, England can accept a woman meeting a man for tea. And if this makes you feel any better, our discussion will be all business. Besides, Matthew will drive me."

"How do you know he wants to talk business?"

"What else could it be?" Felicity hadn't given thought to the duke courting her, nor would she.

"I will still say a prayer," Helen had replied.

The Duke arrived right on time. The sunlight through the windows cast him in an agreeable light.

She rose and bowed. "Your Grace, thank you for the invitation."

"Thank you for agreeing to meet me." He motioned for her to sit.

A young waiter in an immaculate white apron appeared with a silver tea service, which he placed down before them.

"I ordered tea, unless there was something else you wanted," Felicity said.

"Tea is fine."

The young waiter poured them each a cup and left as quickly as he had arrived.

"Do you often come here?" Chaucer asked.

"Never."

He laughed. "Miss Carrol, I don't believe I have ever met anyone like you." His smile could have been a magnet.

"I am nothing special, Your Grace."

"I must disagree with you there."

They tasted the tea, which was smooth with a trace of orange.

She placed her hands on her lap, ready to talk homicide. "May I ask why you wanted to see me?"

"Do I need a reason?"

"What?" She almost choked on her tea.

"I have thought about you quite often after our meeting at Hyde Park."

Was he courting her? No. Perhaps he just liked talking with someone other than royalty. "I don't know what to say, Your Grace." And she really didn't. Yet, there he sat across from her, and she would put the time to good use—more than romance. "Police say they have caught the man who killed Lord Wessex."

He nodded.

"However, Scotland Yard can't link that suspect to the murders of William, Lord Banbury, or Elaine Charles."

"So what does that tell you?"

Felicity paused before answering to give heft to what she was about to say. "That the murderer is still out there, and you should remain cautious."

Chaucer sat back.

"Your Grace?"

"Miss Carrol, your determination is quite extraordinary."

Now she smiled. "I believe some find it maddening." She thought about Inspector Davies. "I know you probably wanted a pleasant tea, but your safety and finding the killer is a priority to me."

"Quite extraordinary."

Felicity could accept that praise.

"I understand your father recently died. My sincere condolences." He put a hand over his heart.

"I was a disappointment to him. He desired a daughter who fit nicely into society and marriage. I didn't suit his vision." She sipped her tea and placed the cup down. "And your father? Is he still living?"

"He died when I was twelve."

His tone was similar to hers. *The duke must have had the same relationship with his father as I had with mine,* Felicity thought. "I am an orphan now. My mother died when I was less than a year old. Is your mother alive?"

"She passed three years ago. My mother was a singular person."

His voice became husky and his eyes glittery as the sun's reflection on water. Felicity's mouth widened. Until that point, Duke Chaucer had given the impression of a young man who would never allow sentiment to fracture his composure. But fracture it did at the mention of his mother. Felicity was more intrigued than ever.

"She must have been a very special woman," she said.

"My mother was passionate in her belief in me and my place in the world. She made me realize my purpose. You could say she helped mold my existence and reason for being." He turned to Felicity, his eyes blinking gently as if waking from a dream. "Too little expectations are as arduous as too many, I fear."

She shuffled her feet under the table at what she believed was a bond that had formed between them, on her part anyway. He was an orphan, too. He appeared to be holding on to great emotion but was fearful of letting anyone see it. Chaucer was like a complex mathematical formula. How different from Jackson Davies. The inspector placed all his thoughts on the table as if serving up a roast beef dinner—even those thoughts she didn't care to hear.

Chaucer's reserve returned. He took a drink of tea, sipped, and set down the cup. "Have you learned anything new in your investigation?"

"Only what I have mentioned, Your Grace. It's sad to think the tale of Arthur has been mixed up with these terrible crimes."

"Indeed."

"I loved the stories. As a young girl, I wanted to be a knight. To carry a sword and slay dragons."

"You would have made a spectacular one."

"Being related to a queen, you must also have imagined yourself a Knight of the Round Table."

"What boy didn't? One time I took my father's fusilier sword from his study, threw it into a pond, and then drew it out, pretending I was taking Excalibur from the Lady of the Lake." His voice could have been that of a youngster. "I returned it to the study but forgot to dry it, so the sword left an awful puddle. My father was very cross."

She laughed. "Do you collect any Arthurian treasures, Your Grace?"

"Only a few items, and nowhere near what my late cousin William Kent had gathered." He smiled again, pouring on charm thick as pudding.

"Small as your collection is, has anyone ever attempted to steal or buy any of your Arthurian artifacts?"

He gave his head a slight shake, and she didn't hide her disappointment.

"Not the answer you expected?" he said.

"The unexpected is common for this case," she said.

He reached out to touch her hand. "Am I just a case?"

"Much more than that. You are someone to be protected."

"Then I shall keep watch. I promise. And please call me Philip."

"Is that allowed?" She knew many things, but dealing with royalty had not topped her list of educational priorities.

"If I say it is." The duke checked his watch. His eyes shifted toward the entrance.

"I'm afraid I'm keeping you," she said.

"I have an appointment. But I do hope I may see you again."

"That would be nice." Unfortunately, she meant it.

"Let me escort you out."

The front entrance was decorated with four pillars and a crown above the Café Royal sign. The day was already hot. The sounds on Regent Street blared after the quiet of the café.

"Until we meet again." Chaucer took her hand and bent down to kiss it. When he rose, his eyes shifted fleetingly across the street and then back to Felicity. She gazed in that direction, also.

A silhouette of a man with a crossbow stood on the roof of a building across Regent Street. He aimed the weapon at them. "Watch out!" Felicity pushed Chaucer to the ground and dove down beside him.

Thwap. Thud.

"Really!" Chaucer huffed at her push.

All around them, women screamed and men scattered.

A metal bolt was imbedded in the pillar behind where they had stood. Felicity scanned the top of the building. The assailant was gone.

She stood up and pointed to the bolt, which resembled the one that had killed William Kent in the British Museum. "This is why I pushed you out of the way."

Chaucer stood and inspected the thick, arrowlike object. "I must admit I was a bit skeptical about your assertions, Felicity. But this is reality."

"Someone call a constable," a few people muttered in the crowd.

Felicity had to move and didn't have much time. "I can't stay. I must remain in the background." She feigned panic and hoped he didn't detect her falsehood. She wanted to search the building across the street for any evidence that might have been left behind by the man who had tried to kill Duke Chaucer. Certainly this was the same man who had murdered William Kent and the others.

"I shan't mention your name. Leave, and we'll talk soon." Chaucer turned back to inspect the metal object that would have ended up in his head if she hadn't pushed him out of the way.

Hurrying across the busy street, she promised herself to buy shoes more suitable for running. She slid here and there in the small-heeled boots she wore as she ducked the horse-and-carriage traffic, as well as the manure on the street.

The killer had stood on the roof of a dressmaker's shop named Madeline's. Felicity rushed in through the door. A young woman with stacks of blonde curls on her head swiveled in her direction. The clerk wore glasses and a pinched face as if her high collar had strangled all the zest out of her.

Before the woman could speak, Felicity asked, "Has anyone visited this shop in the last ten minutes?"

"No, Miss."

"Is there a back entrance?"

The clerk pointed to a door at the rear of the shop. "Would you like to see our newest fashion?"

"I would like to see the roof."

Felicity's questioning was so vigorous, the woman clerk answered, "Through the door."

Felicity ran to where the clerk pointed. The door opened to a neat room with two sewing machines, shelves of fabric, and dress-maker forms. At the back end was a wooden door flung wide open. She ran into the alley. The man was gone, but she hadn't expected he would be hanging around after attempting to kill a duke of England. The killer had vanished as if he had never been there.

Gathering up her dress, Felicity rushed up the wooden stairs two flights. Another door opened to a flat roof with a waist-high ledge around it. She bent down, seeking any clues. A cigar smoldered. She sniffed it.

"Hollinger," she said out loud. The same variety as the one she had found at the Belgrave Square garden where Thomas Wessex was slain.

Felicity peeked over the ledge. Several police officers talked with Duke Chaucer, who pointed at the shop. She replaced the cigar where she had found it. This *was* evidence, and she hoped the police would pick up the clue. Besides, she had the cigar remnant she had collected near Wessex's body to examine further.

Finding nothing else, Felicity ran down the stairs and back into the shop. Through the front window, she saw two constables dash across busy Regent Street. They were slowed by a stream of carriages. Calming her breathing, she hurried to a display of dresses and gowns on forms and ran her fingers over the fabric of one. The police officers charged into the shop.

"I am so very interested in having this gown made for me," Felicity told the clerk, whose confusion was enough that Felicity thought she might swoon.

"Has anyone come through here?" one of the officers asked the woman.

"This lady was just . . ." the clerk began.

"I simply must have it for a ball." Felicity interrupted and actually noticed the dress she was touching. An awful purple gown with frills and lace enough to stifle every woman in London. "So lovely." She tried to sound enthusiastic.

"Excuse me, Miss, but this is police business," one of the officers told Felicity, and turned back to the saleswoman. "How do we get to the roof?"

The clerk pointed the same way she had for Felicity.

The constables ran toward the door.

Felicity breathed and approached the young woman. "I am grateful you didn't tell the officers about me. An acquaintance of mine was almost killed by someone on your roof."

The saleswoman paled and swayed.

"There, there. The man did survive," Felicity said.

The girl swayed again.

"Terrible things are afoot in the world, and you should get used to them." Felicity slid a twenty-pound note from her bag and handed it to the saleswoman, who did not sway as much. "For your troubles and your silence about my visit to the roof."

"Do you still want to order the dress?" the clerk asked.

"Not really my color."

CHAPTER 27

Felicity had not returned to Carrol Manor since her father's funeral. She had been living in the London house. But she realized she had to return to make sure nothing required her attention. She doubted anything would, given the efficiency of the people who worked there. However, she was mistress of the estate now and accepted the responsibility. The house was not only her home but also home to the many servants working there. Yet the thought of Carrol Manor unsettled her, as if her father's ghost might haunt her.

Before departing London, she had stopped at the firm of Morton & Morton to ask that they also research the life of Duke Philip Chaucer. There might be a clue in his background as to why he had also been targeted for murder. While she was there, a clerk handed her a packet of information on Elaine Charles and Lord Thomas Wessex.

Felicity's arrival at the manor later in the morning allayed her dread about returning there. The atmosphere among the servants seemed light, as if a holiday had been declared. They smiled and greeted her with a "Welcome back." Fresh flowers in vases decorated the house. The men whistled while doing their chores, and the females appeared to have added a skip to their step.

Her late father's style of dealing with the servants had fluctuated from domineering to disregard. Without him there, they might be feeling a measure of freedom. Then again, she might be placing her own impressions on them.

Making a quick tour of the house, she saw that everything was in order. She complimented Horace Wilkins on the good condition of the house.

"If that is all, Miss Carrol," he replied, with indifference to her praise.

"Good to be home," she said out loud after Wilkins had left.

She was happy to chat with head groundskeeper John Ryan, who was working with builders on her new laboratory west of the manor. The plans called for a small building with many shelves and counters, as well as electricity. She had already ordered laboratory equipment, including the most up-to-date microscope she could locate. Ryan approved of the plan and even suggested expanding the ventilation system. Felicity had not taken that feature into account and grinned at the idea.

"Maybe I will invent something of worth one day," she told Ryan while they studied the plans.

"I'm sure of it," he replied, "if you don't blow up the place first."

While eating dinner, she read the financial reports of the family's holdings sent on by Martin Jameson. As she did, the food became tasteless. She had no idea of the breadth of her father's business. She should have asked, but he wouldn't have told her.

Tired of those papers, she went to the library and started in on the reports from Morton & Morton about Elaine Charles and Lord Wessex. Each of the victims had led an exemplary life with no suggestion of scandal. Although Elaine's heart condition had been worrisome, she had done well with the ailment. She had headed a few charities but mostly remained close to her home, probably because of her heart. Neither she nor Lord Wessex had had any enemies the firm's investigators could uncover, nor had they attended the King Arthur exhibit reception before William Kent's murder. Aside from the painting in Elaine's bedroom, neither was a collector of King Arthur relics.

Wessex had been in excellent health and was dedicated to his wife and young son. In addition to his spot in the House of Lords, Wessex was one of the architects of the Queen's Golden Jubilee celebrations, which Felicity did know. From the reports, both of the victims appeared to be fine people, and it upset her that they had been so cruelly dispatched.

Placing down the reports, she dismissed robbery as the primary motive. Three of the victims were royalty. Duke Chaucer might have been the fourth if she had not pushed him out of the way of the crossbow's bolt.

Royalty.

England and the royal family did have plenty of enemies both outside and within the country's borders.

Between 1881 and 1885, supporters of an independent Irish Republic had protested British rule in an explosive way. They had set off a campaign of dynamite explosions at sites around London, including one at the House of Commons and Tower of London. Yet the Irish Republic group had directed the blasts against government buildings and not necessarily against people with regal blood. Only William Kent and Thomas Wessex had been members of the House of Lords, which was part of Parliament. So, the killer's motivation did not smack of politics.

Her Majesty had also been marked for assassination. Seven attempts had been made on Queen Victoria's life since 1840. Men had taken gunshots at her and Prince Albert, mostly when they were on their way to and from their palaces. In a majority of those cases, the would-be shooters were described as having mental problems or being on a crazed quest for infamy by killing the monarch.

This recent spate of murders was not the work of a madman.

The murderer had been clever enough to elude Scotland Yard and her. The killings had been carried out by someone with single-minded resolve.

Murder was a violent act, no matter the form it took, be it from poisons or pistols. Considering the pitiless methods he used, this killer also wanted to punish his victims. A crossbow. A flail. Suffocation. A battle ax. Cruel and unusual methods. As if the murderer had practiced his own horrible execution of those people. But why? She felt the answer was so close, which was exasperating.

Felicity headed to her favorite place to quiet her mind, which zipped along faster than a horse at Ascot. She was frustrated that the reports revealed nothing new. On her way to the lake, she gathered wildflowers and took a detour to the family cemetery, enclosed by black wrought iron. Her grandparents' headstones stood polished and white. The lawn was trimmed around them.

The crypt her father had constructed for her mother and brother was a temple to his grief. Created out of pink-tinged marble, the crypt resembled a miniature cathedral with spires. Now he had joined them there. Felicity had not visited the grave site since he was buried. She stayed away because she imagined his soul would accuse her of failure. Failure to find William Kent's killer. Failure to find her purpose in life. Whispery accusations from the grave.

Tree branches above her swayed with the same indictment as she placed the flowers before the crypt.

She reached the lake. In the falling sunset, the water took on the purple and orange colors of the sky as she rowed out to the pavilion on the island. The boat skidded through water inky in the evening light. Nocturnal birds began their serenades.

She sat on the bench where she had rested many times as a girl enjoying novels. The water lapped against the shores of the island with a soothing rhythm. The flowers growing wild around the pavilion enticed her with fragrance, as did the sweetness of the gooseberries on the plentiful bushes. She hoped the familiar place might placate her anxieties. But her mind bubbled with misgiving.

She had been sheltered all her years, either at the manor, with tutors, or at the university. Life had been something she learned out of a book. Was she so prideful she wouldn't listen to or accept the views of others? Had she been blinded to all else because she was so sure of her deductions? Had she become as inflexible as Inspector Jackson Davies? Despite the discrepancies in this case, was money and greed the cause of it all?

The breeze whooshing over the water raised goosebumps on her arms. Not from the chill, but reservations about her own observations and conclusions. Worse, she had been arrogant to believe she could solve these murders. Jackson Davies was accurate in his accusations. She had no proof to take to a magistrate.

She *was* an amateur. She *was* playing detective.

Placing her head in her hands, Felicity slumped forward.

A stick crunched behind her and she jerked upright. Another crunch. Too loud for a bird or animal to make. They were footsteps. She was not alone.

It was too late to row back to shore for an escape. She had to face what was there with her on the island. She didn't want the intruder to realize she had been alerted to his presence. Surprise could be a weapon. That and a big rock. With as much casualness as she could fake, she walked out of the pavilion and bent down to pick up one of the stones encompassing the flower bed.

Another crunch, then more. The footsteps quickened behind her. She heard sharp breaths. She spun toward the man, whose left hand went around her neck. Because of the night, she had no clear view of her attacker.

"For my sovereign." His words were powerful as his grip. He began to squeeze. She began to gasp.

How could she stop this man with the stone in her hand?

Seeking a vulnerable spot, her mind sped through the pages of medical books she had read. Fueled by terror and incensed at the attack, she slammed the rock down on the bridge of the attacker's nose. He yelled and his eyes watered. He put his hands to his face from the pain that was probably spearing through his head.

Good.

He staggered back. With both arms aimed at his chest, she ran at him and pushed. He flew into one of the thick gooseberry bushes on the island and yelled from the spines. Picking up her skirt, she bolted to the boat, pushed off, jumped in, and rowed as she never had. She heard a splash in the water. He was coming.

His left hand clamped on to the right side of the boat, making it rock. Felicity brought down the flat end of an oar on that hand. The man cried out and let go. She continued her frantic rowing. Daring to turn around, she saw she was near the shore. At once, two hands grabbed the back of the boat. The man was pulling himself up. Swinging another oar with both hands, Felicity clipped him hard on the side of the head. He yelled again and splashed back into the water.

Reaching the shore, she leapt out of the boat and onto the ground, ready to run for help. Skidding to a stop, she spun around. The man floated in the water faceup, arms out in an unanswered prayer.

She did not normally curse, but this appeared to be a proper time to start. "Damnation!" she said.

Sprinting back to the shore, she sprang into the water. With caution, she swam out to the man. He didn't react when she poked him in his bleeding face. Sure he was unconscious, she put one arm around his neck and swam back to the shore. Tugging on his clothing, she dragged him onto the shore, though water kicked at his legs. She placed her fingers on his jugular vein. The pulse was robust. He might not remain out for long.

Yanking the laces off his shoes, she tied his feet together with sturdy knots. Pulling off his belt, she used it to bind his hands behind his back. Her job complete, she sat back on the grass, her breathing reckless. Her heart clapped like a grateful audience.

She was alive.

She also had time to think. This man was not the killer. He was left-handed, whereas all the evidence pointed to a right-handed villain. She was elated, however. If someone wanted her dead, she must be on the right path to solving this case.

After dashing back to Carrol Manor, Felicity asked the servants to rouse John Ryan. Ryan and three male servants rushed to the lake and dragged the man to the house, where they placed him in a wagon, hands still bound. Her assailant said nothing but glared at Felicity.

They drove the attacker to the nearby town of Guildford. Felicity and Helen followed in the carriage. On the way, Felicity comforted her friend, who cried after seeing her. Felicity *was* a mess, which she noticed after passing a mirror in the foyer of the manor before they left. Hair wet and stringy. Torn blouse and skirt, muddy hems, and red marks popping up on the left side of her throat. Her eyes resembled wild insects that had misplaced the light.

"Why did he try to hurt you, Miss?" Helen's voice trembled with the question.

"That, my dear, is what I'm hoping to find out." Since her attacker was not the killer, that meant he was still out there. But Felicity didn't want to tell this to Helen, who was already upset.

Once in Guildford, Felicity asked the constables to telegraph Inspector Davies about the incident.

The constable in charge at Guildford was stout as strong ale. His white hair contrasted with his uniform, but he appeared capable of tearing down the constabulary building brick by red brick. His nightshirt hung out from under his jacket.

A blanket wrapped around her, Felicity remained in her damp clothes. In another room, she provided details of the assault to the constable in charge. He wrote down the information on a piece of paper. Helen, meanwhile, stood a few steps from her young mistress. Her hands balled in fists. Felicity sipped a cup of tea offered by another constable.

"Did he say anything to you, Miss Carrol?" asked the constable in charge.

"He said, 'For my sovereign.'"

"What does that mean?"

"Haven't a clue." Felicity didn't tell the constable her theories about the murders, especially the reason she believed the man had tried to choke her to death. She would save the explanation for Inspector Davies when he arrived. If he arrived.

The constable stood and pulled up his sagging trousers. "Time to have a talk with the man."

"Please, may I be in the room?" Felicity said.

"No, Miss!" Helen said.

"I am perfectly safe. I am protected by these fine officers."

"And so you will be," the constable said.

The officers had removed the belt Felicity used to bind the assailant's hands and replaced it with metal handcuffs.

"Who are you?" the constable asked the man who sat in the middle of a claustrophobic interrogation room.

The attacker said nothing. Felicity assessed him under the gaslight. This was no ordinary criminal.

He was in his late twenties and slim. Clean-shaven with a muted blond mustache, the same color as on his head. From the clip of his hair, he had been to the barber lately. His clothes were simple, but not torn or patched, and his shoes were new, although wet and muddy from the lake. His shoe size appeared to be smaller than the prints she had found near the body of Thomas Wessex.

The observation supported her conclusion. This was not the killer, but he knew who the killer was.

The man sat on the chair with a straight back. His eyes were steady, his mouth a smirk. His expression held arrogance, as if he was superior to the predicament in which he found himself. Not exactly the picture of a crazed man who strangled women. His left hand had gone blue from where she had smacked it with the oar. From the slant of his nose, she had broken it with the stone. A horizontal gash running the full length of his cheek marked the right side of his face. The wound had been stitched by the Guildford doctor. Felicity's cheeks heated at the violence she had inflicted on the man sitting a little ways from her. Then she thought of how he had meant to murder her. The hand marks on her throat throbbed as a reminder.

"Why'd you try to kill this young woman?" the constable asked the man.

Again, no answer.

"Did he have anything on him?" the constable asked another officer who stood near the door.

"Nothing at all, sir. No identification. Not even a farthing in his pocket."

The constable confronted the man. "Don't matter to me if you don't speak, mister. You don't have to say a word either when the judge sends you to prison for trying to choke the life out of this nice young woman."

The attacker moved his head to look at Felicity and smiled.

"Don't you dare put your eyes on that lady." The constable pushed him back against the chair.

"I am thirsty. May I have a glass of water?" the man asked.

From his accent, he had an education, Felicity concluded.

"Polite, aren't you?" the constable said.

Another officer brought him a glass. The assailant picked it up with his left hand and drank.

"Well, mister?" said the constable. "You've quenched your thirst. Time to quench ours."

"I have nothing to say." The attacker smirked again.

The constable turned to another officer in the room. "Lock him up good and tight."

"My pleasure, sir." The officer yanked the man to his feet and took him away.

"That is one peculiar fellow," the constable said to Felicity.

"Constable, you would make a fine detective."

"And you, Miss Carrol, a fine scrapper." He blushed at using such a word. "I must say, you are the bravest woman I've ever met. Few females would battle back."

"Females are among the fiercest fighters in the animal kingdom. So why not humans?"

"Never thought about that, but you got a point," he said, and tucked his nightshirt into his pants.

"One thing. May I have his glass?" Felicity asked.

"But he drank from that one."

"Call it a trophy."

He shrugged his shoulders. "All yours."

Felicity asked Helen for her handkerchief and picked up the glass carefully so as not to smear his fingerprints.

Fatigue settled on Felicity as she and Helen rode home to Carrol Manor near midnight. Helen dozed and startled herself awake, as if to make sure her young friend was safe in the carriage.

Back at the manor, Felicity bathed and went to bed. She did not sleep well. She dreamed she was on the boat on the lake. The Lady of the Lake rose out of the water wearing white, her hair waved over her shoulders like the leaves of a water plant. The Lady held a mighty sword in her right hand and skimmed over the water toward Felicity in the boat. As the Lady neared, a man with large hands grabbed Felicity and jerked her down into the dim waters of the lake. There, Felicity sucked in water instead of air. She reached out to the Lady of the Lake for help, but the woman sank deeper and then out of sight, taking the sword with her.

Felicity bolted up and wondered if she would be able to have a good night's sleep ever again.

★　★　★

Inspector Jackson Davies appeared at Carrol Manor at eight the next morning. His eyes went to the marks on Felicity's neck, which had turned a nice shade of blue in the shape of a clear handprint.

"What have you gotten yourself into?" he asked with a mix of anger and worry.

"Good morning to you, Jackson," she said. "It was a long night. Join me for breakfast."

He stayed quiet and followed her into a smaller dining room. Since her father's passing, Felicity had asked for the food to be set out on a side table from which she would serve herself. She had always disliked being served like a tyrant over the servants. She had imagined Horace Wilkins might explode like her homemade dynamite at the idea, but he had only swallowed and remarked, "As you wish."

Felicity asked Wilkins and the servants to leave her alone with the inspector.

"Don't be shy, Jackson." She filled her plate with eggs, sausages, and toast. "I am famished." She told herself she shouldn't be in such good spirits after the previous night.

Davies remained standing. "What is going on?"

"Have a cup of coffee." She poured one for him and one for herself. She stirred in two teaspoons of sugar.

"Jackson, I have much to tell you. I realize this is terribly rude, but may I eat as I talk?"

"Go ahead."

"Promise me one thing," she asked with a smile.

"What?"

"You won't get upset."

He sat down. "I'm already upset."

Felicity took a bite of toast, followed by a sip of coffee. "Good, then it won't matter."

She told him about what had happened, starting with the near murder of Duke Philip Chaucer at teatime and ending with her attack at the lake.

"What's all this mean, then?" he said when she wrapped up her narrative.

"I had begun to doubt my conclusions in this case. But the assault on me was the clearest of signals. I am headed in the right direction."

"I read the report about what took place in front of the Café Royal. I had no idea you were the woman involved. On my way here, I stopped at the Guildford constabulary for its report on the incident last night. I tried to interrogate the suspect, but he wasn't talking. Why did he attack you? Did he . . . ?"

"It was not that type of assault." She picked up a forkful of eggs. "But I am convinced the man who tried to kill me last night did not murder William Kent and the others."

Davies said nothing. She chewed and swallowed.

"Jackson, my attacker is left-handed. The murderer who swung the flail at Lord Banbury and the ax at Lord Wessex was right-handed based on the wounds we both saw. My assailant also was only a bit taller than me. The man who shot the crossbow at William Kent at the British Museum was much taller. So if he didn't kill those two, then he didn't kill Elaine Charles or Lord Wessex, because the same man murdered them all."

"You're making my head hurt. We have the drunkard Joe Crumb in custody for Wessex's murder."

"Oh my God. He's just a diversion." She had been too scattered to see that possibility despite the facts glaring straight at her. She slapped her fist down on table.

"What in the bloody hell are you talking about?"

"Joe Crumb was meant to divert Scotland Yard's attention away from what really happened. It's only logical."

Davies finally sat.

"The real killer must have placed Lord Wessex's watch, rings, and money into the pockets of Joe Crumb to give the police a scapegoat. And why not do the same with Elaine Charles?"

"What do you mean?"

"The death of Elaine Charles was the only flaw in my theory that this killer is after royalty. She didn't have any royal blood. But she was murdered to direct investigators away from his other victims."

"So why kill her at all?"

"The murderer still wanted Elaine's painting. What the crimes have demonstrated is that this villain does have a perverted passion for King Arthur. In addition, he must have known Elaine Charles and about the painting."

She used her fork to emphasize her next point. "Before my attacker tried to choke the life out of me, he said, 'For my sovereign.'"

"He must be crazy. Why would Queen Victoria want you killed?" Davies spoke each word with emphasis.

"There's no reason Her Majesty would want me dead. Neither would she order the deaths of her own cousins. So my assailant must have been referring to someone else."

"I hate to admit it, but I agree with you."

"You interviewed the man. Did he appear insane to you?" Felicity cut up a piece of sausage.

"No. Then, he didn't say much."

"I was hoping you might, what you call, 'get it' out of him."

"Want me to put him on the rack?" Sarcasm thickened his voice.

"How absurd." She lifted her eyebrows. "Is that even allowed anymore?"

Davies emitted a low growl. "All right, I'll give you that the suspect may not be a lunatic, but why in heaven's name did he try to strangle you?"

She placed down her fork. "Because he thinks I can name the killer."

"Can you?"

"I wish I could." She dabbed a napkin to her lips. "I have formulated a new theory, however."

"God help us."

"When he proclaimed 'For my sovereign,' he meant an allegiance to *his* king. This so-called king was the person who killed William Kent and the rest. Though why he is going after royalty still eludes me." She took a breath.

"I'm sorry what you went through. But to enforce the law, I must have evidence to take before a judge. Without it, we have no case against anyone. That means we have nothing, barely a vague notion of a motive. We are no closer to finding the murderer than the day we first met."

"Jackson . . ."

"The man who tried to kill you at the lake will face a judge for the crime. There will be justice." He stood up and left.

Felicity pushed away her plate. Her reservations had evaporated. She was right; otherwise, why would someone want her dead?

She poured herself another cup of coffee but didn't concentrate. The coffee overran her cup, spilling onto the cloth. How did her attacker even know she was investigating the murders? In her mind, she listed all who knew and blew out a breath at the number of people. She had accompanied Davies on several interviews and shown up at the scenes of the crimes, including Belgrave Square, where the body of Lord Wessex had been discovered. In a public café, she had had tea with Duke Chaucer, another intended victim.

Martin Jameson had had her followed at her father's behest. She must have been observed again. This time at the request of a killer.

CHAPTER 28

Felicity stared at the glass on her desk. Her disposition was as miserable as her recurring nightmares about drowning in the lake.

Her mood hadn't improved when it came to the man who had tried to kill her. Scotland Yard could find no information about him, the Guildford constable had told her. The suspect had no criminal record they could locate, mostly because he refused to give them his name. His description didn't match that of any wanted criminal. The attacker remained in jail in Guildford, which was the seat of the Borough of Guildford, the local government district in Surrey County. He would face an attempted homicide charge in front of magistrates and a jury in the fall when a court session met.

She had removed the man's fingerprints from the glass he drank from at the constabulary. From the cigar stub she had found near Wessex's body, she had lifted more prints and compared them with a magnifying glass. They did not match. She had been sure they wouldn't anyway, but it depressed her nevertheless.

She had no evidence, but logic told her that the man who had tried to kill her was a pawn and not the chess master. What worried her more—the master might make yet another attempt on Chaucer's life unless she could solve this case. And yes, he might try to kill her too.

When she returned to the London house, she found the report from Morton & Morton on Duke Philip Chaucer.

Educated at Oxford, Chaucer had earned a history degree, which was no surprise, and also a degree in chemistry, which was unexpected. He didn't appear to be the scientific type like the ones she had met at the University of London. A fencing master, hunter, and philanthropist, Chaucer had no apparent vices the Morton & Morton investigators could unearth. Neither could they report any gossip or taint of shame about the man. In his late twenties, he had never been married, nor did he have any romantic attachment, although he was regularly seen in the company of beautiful women. Along with Lord Wessex, Chaucer was one of the organizers of the Golden Jubilee celebrations for Queen Victoria.

The report did become more interesting. Chaucer's beloved mother Marianne had gone mad, but the firm could not find out what form the madness had taken or the cause. To keep her out of public view, which was typical with insane relatives of the rich, Lady Chaucer had been housed in a private cottage on the grounds of Garbutt's Asylum at Dunston for six years. The woman had died there three years ago.

No wonder Chaucer had become emotional when he had spoken to Felicity about his mother and how her influence on him had been profound.

Helen's knock startled her.

"You have received an invitation to a ball, Miss Felicity," Helen announced.

"I'm in no temperament to attend, my dear." How true. Felicity picked up a book to read. "I may never dance again, Hellie. Then again, I didn't like dancing very much."

Helen's eyes were puffy and she moved slower than usual. Felicity was ashamed she hadn't noticed until then. Too preoccupied with murder.

"Have you been sleeping well, my friend? You look weary, and it's been so ever since the attack."

Helen's cheeks reddened to match her eyes. "I'm fine, Miss."

Felicity took her hand. "Hellie, I'm truly sorry to have caused you so much worry." Helen placed her hand on top, and Felicity enjoyed the affection.

"Part of my job, and my pleasure."

"So about this ball I will not be attending."

"Thought you might interested in this particular event, Miss Felicity. An invitation to Queen Victoria's Golden Jubilee ball."

"Why would anyone invite me to that?"

Helen moved the printed invitation closer to her eyes. "Duke Philip Chaucer himself."

"Really?"

Helen held out the invitation, which was embossed with gold-colored lettering. "He also sent a gift." She handed her a wooden box decorated with hand-painted flowers on the front and sides.

Felicity opened the box. Inside was a small volume. She read the title. "*The Tale of Arthur and his Love, Poems*, by Roderick Fellows."

"Love poems, eh? Shall I begin to address you as Duchess Felicity?"

"Helen, I never appreciated your sense of humor." Felicity rubbed her neck, which still ached, though the handprints of her attacker had faded into a light purple. Inscribed on the inside of the book in stylish handwriting was a message: "To the woman who saved my life, Philip."

"Are you being wooed, Miss Felicity?"

She ran her fingers over the writing. "I'm not sure."

"Forgive me, Miss, but sometimes I can't understand what the blazes you're talking about."

Felicity let out a laugh. "So where is this ball being held?"

"Chaucer Hall."

Felicity wanted to see Chaucer's collection of King Arthur relics, no matter its size. The ball would be the perfect opportunity to examine them. And truth was, she wouldn't mind meeting Chaucer again. "Hellie, I might have to attend this one."

"May I ask how you first met this gentleman?" Helen sounded like a mother asking why her daughter had stayed out late the night before.

"Our meeting was very respectful. I met Duke Chaucer at William Kent's funeral reception."

"Why did he thank you for saving his life?"

Felicity smiled. "I suspect he's being romantic." She had spared Helen the details of the murder attempt in front of the Café Royal. She didn't want to cause her friend more concern.

"And what does all this have to do with the murder of your friend Lord Kent?"

Felicity's body sagged as if gravity had finally won out. The anxious look on Helen's face made Felicity want to cry, and Felicity hated to cry.

"Please sit and I shall tell you. You deserve an explanation, since you have been so understanding of such odd behavior for a proper young lady of London. Well, *young* at any rate."

Helen sat with a *harrumph* on the settee. Felicity placed a pillow behind her back.

"Hellie, the Duke owns a few Arthur relics. I want to look at them. They might hold a clue about why members of royalty are being killed. More importantly, the Duke could be the next victim, and I'd like to prevent that."

"I see, Miss Felicity. Is your detective work the reason why you and your father had the disagreement?"

"My father thought I was a scandal." Felicity's voice lowered.

"He wanted you to be a grand lady like your mother."

"You always see the best in people, Hellie. That's why I love you. But you're also realistic enough to know that the best in some people may be buried deep as a mine."

"I won't argue with you." Helen stood up. "I do have a thought, Miss Felicity."

"What?"

"When we're at Chaucer Hall, I'll chat up the servants. They might have the information you need to find those King Arthur things. Servants will probably talk easier to me than to my young mistress."

Felicity smiled and picked up the invitation. "Please ready your best silk, my dear. We are going to a ball."

CHAPTER 29

Inside Felicity's elegant silk bag, she carried a handkerchief, a magnifying glass, a skeleton key, and tools to open locked doors.

Quite the accessories for a ball, she mused on the way to Chaucer Hall.

Felicity wore a black satin dress with short puffed sleeves. Because the gown was low in the front, Helen had sewn a black lace collar to hide Felicity's bruised neck. Felicity wanted no questions about her injury. The gown was not new, but Felicity doubted anyone would care. She didn't.

As she and Helen rode in the carriage, Felicity pressed the pearls on her bracelet, the only piece of jewelry she wore. The bracelet had belonged to her mother. She knew so little of her mother's character, only what Helen had told her. Specifically, Margaret Carrol had been a smart, thoughtful, and generous woman. Felicity hoped her mother would understand what she was about to do that night.

After Matthew stopped the carriage, a servant in regal red opened the door. He extended a big hand, as if Felicity would break like crystal. She sighed, took his hand, and got out of the carriage. Her eyes skimmed the initial obstacle.

Chaucer's home resembled a castle more than a hall, albeit a small castle compared to others in England. She stared at a square structure of light-gray stone enhanced with carvings of red limestone and four towers. Each light gleamed with opulence and rank.

Inside the grand double doors, twinkling candelabras and twittering attendees created an atmosphere of gaiety and pageantry. Felicity and Helen entered the gigantic ballroom, which was enclosed by golden-colored walls. Above were borders of carved grapes, vines, and dancing nymphs. Gaslights blazed, giving the scene a yellow glow. Dazzling chandeliers hung like jewels over the wooden floor. At one end of the rectangular-shaped ballroom, an orchestra played on a stand. An overlay of women's perfumes, burning gaslights, and wax candles infused the large room with a sweet acid scent.

Felicity was impressed, and that didn't happen easily.

She had attended many a ball, but this one boasted more beautiful women in more expensive gowns. The men looked richer and of nobility, and the rank of the military officers soared higher than lieutenant and captain. A newspaper article had reported that four hundred people would attend the event to honor the fifty-year reign of Victoria. And Chaucer Hall was large enough to give everyone room to have a pleasant time.

While other young women waved their fans in flirty swiftness, Felicity waved hers in front of her face to remain in the background. Several men still smiled, bowed, and asked her for a dance. She refused. She did make one observation about Chaucer Hall right away. Nowhere did she see any King Arthur artifacts. The walls of the ballroom and other rooms in the house displayed tasteful artwork, but there was not one of a knight or the mythical king among them.

Helen winked at Felicity and then joined a group of older women who must have been chaperones, governesses, or other servants in a room off the ballroom.

Felicity started her exploration of the house to find Chaucer's Arthurian collection. The side sitting rooms off the ballroom and foyer were as luxurious as any she had ever seen, but held swarms of chatting people. Tables of punches, bowls of fruit, and platters of dainty biscuits, tortes, and cakes were offered in the grand dining room.

This was going to be more difficult than she had imagined.

She headed up to the mezzanine, where more rooms held yet more people. Felicity passed an open door to what appeared to be a drawing room, a big one like a majority of the rooms in the hall. Elaborate chairs and sofas sat in front of a fireplace of Italian marble so tall she could probably stand underneath it. A long mirror on one wall expanded the room within its reflection. Mounted heads of deer on the walls stalked the proceedings with their dead black eyes. In golden frames were paintings of what could have been Chaucer's male ancestors. They all had the same fine-looking face and enigmatic expression. In the drawing room, a lake of men in costly clothing smoked cigars and held glasses of whiskey. Such a familiar sight at the Carrols' London house with her father and his friends.

Taking a few steps deeper into the drawing room, she smelled a fruity wood scent from the cigars the male guests were smoking. She picked up a cigar from one of several open boxes on tables around the room. Putting the cigar up to her nose, she drew in the scent. Strawberry and oak.

A Hollinger.

The same cigar as the one she had found on the roof of the dressmaker's shop, the one dropped by the man with the crossbow. The same cigar she had found in the park where Thomas Wessex was killed.

Her arms prickled. She recalled the lines in Charles Dickens's *Bleak House.* "What connection can there have been between many people in the innumerable histories of this world, who, from opposite sides of great gulfs, have, nevertheless, been very curiously brought together!"

"Only the best," said an older man with a white mustache, its pomaded tips pointing upward. He held a glass of whiskey and a smoking cigar in his right hand.

"Beg your pardon?" she said, studying the cigar she was holding.

"The duke's favorite cigar."

"Hollinger."

"Why, yes."

"Distinctive."

"As a queen from a commoner. And Duke Chaucer does love for his guests to be comfortable at his home." The man put the cigar in his mouth and puffed.

The cigar store clerks had told her that Hollingers were the best, and why wouldn't a duke want the best? The killer smoked the same brand. The odds on such an occurrence were astounding. Her chest stung and it wasn't from the smoke.

Walking out of the room, Felicity looked over the mezzanine railing and down on the dance floor. An outstanding place for reconnaissance. Below, people crowded the floor waltzing, talking, and sipping wine. She spotted the host. With his poise and assurance, Chaucer glided among the guests. Really, the guests cleared a way for him as if he were both the arrow aimed at a target and the bowman who had fired it. Women flirted with him, and men bowed deeper to him than to others. He stood out from them not only because of his height but also for his self-possession.

Helen waved her handkerchief at her young mistress, and Felicity made her way down and through the crowd.

"Miss, I have a clue where you might look," Helen whispered in her ear.

"Let's find a quiet place and you can tell me," Felicity replied, and took Helen's hand.

They had to go outside, where the activity was downright peaceful compared to inside Chaucer Hall.

"What did you learn?" Felicity asked.

"I mentioned to one of Duke Chaucer's servants that my master loved medieval objects. I kept your name out of it."

"Brilliant!"

"If I do say so, it was. Anyway, the servant told me the Duke has a whole floor of what she called 'King Arthur trappings.' Swords, suits of armor, weapons, and the like."

"A whole floor?" Chaucer had told her he had only a few items in his collection.

He had lied.

"The servant called it his personal museum. Then, eight months ago or so, Duke Chaucer ordered all the servants to stop cleaning in there."

"That *is* interesting."

"Several times the servant brought him his dinner while he was in the room. He wouldn't let her in. But here is the peculiar thing. When he opened the door, the servant smelled almonds."

"What's odd about that?" Felicity asked.

"The servant said Duke Chaucer never ate almonds, Miss, nor did he ever ask for any."

"Where is this collection?"

"First floor, east wing. The servant told me you can't miss the place. The doors are carved with some crazy lion creatures."

A chimera. The supposed crest of King Arthur.

"Helen, you are wonderful."

"One other bizarre thing happened, the servant said. A week before the ball, Duke Chaucer ordered all the servants in the hall to take a two-day holiday."

"That is even more remarkable. What reason did he give them?"

"The duke told all the servants they had been working hard and he wanted to reward them."

Which meant Chaucer had not wanted the servants to see what he was up to. And what exactly was that? The answer must lie with his Arthurian collection. Based on what she had discovered at the house of the deceased Elaine Charles, Felicity presumed there were also servants' stairs near the kitchen leading to the first floor.

"How will you get in there if the door is locked?" Helen asked.

"I have my methods."

Helen turned around. "When will you get away?"

"The Queen will give me the opportunity."

"Whenever you go and whatever you do, be careful, Miss."

"I will, Hellie."

Helen's eyes became sparkling as the chandeliers. "I must confess, there is something exciting about this detective business, Miss Felicity."

"Yes, there is." Felicity headed off and Helen returned inside.

Felicity walked around, checking on where to make her exit at the right moment. She drifted to the back of the ground floor of the hall. Servants entered and exited out a set of double doors off a hallway. The passage was quite utilitarian and plain compared to the opulence of the rest of the house.

Felicity rejoined the crowd. The hour neared seven. The Queen should be arriving soon.

Tightening her hand on her bag, Felicity readied herself for the search. She might never have another chance.

At the top of the hour, people began shifting their feet and lifting up on toes, anticipating Her Majesty's entrance.

"The Queen is coming," several guests shouted throughout. The announcement made its way around the hall.

Men straightened. Women fluffed their hair back into place. Soldiers checked their buttons and swords. With the declaration, however, Felicity walked to the servants' hallway, where she hoped to find the stairs leading to the first floor.

A trill of trumpets sounded near the entrance to the ballroom.

"Her Serene Majesty, Queen Victoria," rang out a male voice. The whole room of people took a breath and cheered as the monarch entered the room. The musicians began to play "God Save the Queen," and the guests began to sing.

This was Felicity's cue to leave. Watching for Duke Chaucer, or anyone else, for that matter, she made her way to the kitchen. She heard the clanging of pans and hurried voices of servants and took in a whiff of the sugary punch they were serving. She hustled past a line of rooms on both sides of the hallway. At the end of the hallway were the stairs leading to the first floor. Felicity dashed up them and hoped no one was coming down the other way. With all the activity downstairs, particularly with the appearance of the Queen, the servants and Philip Chaucer would have no reason to visit the upstairs.

Constructed of gray stone, the hallway was twice as long as Carrol Manor and twice as splendorous with its carpeting, artwork, and refined furnishings. In spite of the decorations, she had the sensation of being led into a trap.

Gaslights lit the gallery, making the way a little easier. At the end of the hall, she came upon two doors double her height in length. On them, carved chimeras faced each other with paws upturned as if to protect the interior.

She tried the doors. Locked.

Predicting she would run into secured doors during her investigation, both literally and figuratively, Felicity had obtained door-opening tools from a grizzled locksmith in Guildford. She had told him she persistently lost her keys and asked for lessons on how to get past a lock. The locksmith told her she proved a topnotch student. In fact, if she had not been a lady, she could have earned a proficient living as a thief, he said. That was the best compliment she had ever received, she replied, much to his mystification.

From her evening bag, Felicity drew out a skeleton key and inserted it into the lock, but the door did not budge. Withdrawing the key, she used a file to shave off bits. She kept filing and trying the key until it turned. Getting down on her hands and knees, she lifted the rug and blew the filings underneath to hide her trail.

She opened one of the heavy oak doors. The room felt immense as the inside of a whale. Without lights, she could not see to the other end. Her slippers made no sound on the wooden floor, while the noise from the ball below faded to nothing when she shut the door behind her and locked it so no one would know she was inside. She took a sniff. Almonds. Faint but unmistakable. A bank of sizable windows on one wall provided vague light. She dared not ignite the gaslights on the wall.

The servant had been correct in her description of the room. A place to rival any museum. On the walls hung tapestries and paintings of figures and scenes from medieval times. Grand ladies dancing, knights upon steeds with swords drawn. Jousting tournaments. From what she saw, a majority of the artwork depicted King Arthur in various stages of his life, from young boy to glorious ruler to dying king. Other paintings were of Guinevere, Merlin, Lancelot, and other knights. Medieval swords, javelins, spears, and daggers hung on another wall. Under them were shelves of books. As at William Kent's home, they were stories about King Arthur, from what she could tell.

Felicity was awestruck at the Arthur treasures Duke Chaucer had gathered, especially since he had told her he had only a few items. From the magnitude, this man truly loved the legendary king. But the size of the collection also attested to someone obsessed.

Slowly turning around, she let her shoulders droop. She would need hours to comb through the pieces to find clues about why Chaucer and the others had been targeted for murder. Why had he lied to her about the scope of his collection?

She walked toward the marble fireplace at one end of the room. A few feet in front, the floorboards imitated the squeak of mice. She stepped on them again. More squeaking. If she had time, she would investigate further.

Above the fireplace was a large carving of the chimera wearing a crown. Below the carving was a mounted sword, luminescent, magnificent, and deadly even in dim light. She estimated the double-edged blade to be forty inches long and four inches at the base near the golden hilt. Set on a field of purple velvet, the sword was exhibited in a reverential way. On the grip was the same chimera motif.

"Excalibur?" she whispered to herself. Her mind set on Lord Tennyson's description of the famous sword in his *Morte d'Arthur* poem. The mortally wounded Arthur ordering Sir Bedivere to throw Excalibur into the water. From water was how Arthur had first received the renowned sword from the Lady of the Lake:

> *Thou therefore take my brand Excalibur,*
> *Which was my pride: for thou rememberest how*
> *In those old days, one summer noon, an arm*
> *Rose up from out the bosom of the lake,*
> *Clothed in white samite, mystic, wonderful,*
> *Holding the sword—and how I row'd across*
> *And took it, and have worn it, like a king*

Her fingertips tingled. There was something unsettling about this sword. As if the chimeras depicted on the handle, carved above the fireplace and into the doors, would be set free—and not for good. Did Philip Chaucer actually believe he owned the sword given to Arthur by the Lady of the Lake? No, he was much too intelligent for such a notion. But the displayed sword said otherwise, and that made her even more worried.

She guessed she had a half hour left before the Queen would take her leave. She had to hurry and examine what she could. Her attention was drawn to two large desks shoved together in the middle of the room near the windows. The desk drawers were unlocked but empty. There, the almond odor was strongest. Removing her gloves, she ran her hands over the tops of the wooden desks. Lengthwise scratches covered them, as if something had been dragged along. Besides the scent of almonds, there was something else.

Click.

Someone was opening the door. Dropping down behind the large desk, she scooted underneath. She cursed all the fabric in her gown, which created a racket in her ears. She gnashed her teeth. Perspiration formed on her forehead, and she was furious at herself for the panic. *Be strong, Felicity Carrol, be brave. For the moment, at any rate*, she added as a postscript. She did congratulate herself on not wearing any perfume to give away her presence.

She tried not to breathe but did listen. It had to be Duke Chaucer, since he didn't even allow servants in there. Chaucer walked around for a bit. From the clack of his footsteps, he stopped in the middle of the room, turned, and walked out, closing the door behind him.

Whoosh. Felicity breathed out.

She got up, but her hands were coated in grit from hiding under the desk. She put her palms up to her nose. Almonds and acid. What was this substance? She cursed herself for not bringing any envelopes, but then she hadn't known she would find anything to collect.

She had an idea. Getting back on her knees, she took off one of her gloves and brushed the coarse material into it. Patting the floor, she came across something else wedged in one corner of the desk. She pinched the material between her fingers and took a whiff. No scent, but rougher than the other substance. Removing her other glove, she brushed the specimen into that one. She rolled up her gloves and placed them in her bag. She had to get back downstairs soon, but swiveled in a circle in case she had missed something.

On the far back wall was a display of crossbows. She walked closer for a better look in the muted light. Among them was a crossbow with a pull lever—the same type used by the man on the roof. Alongside the crossbows was a framed set of identical bolts on velvet. The bolts were similar to the one shot at Chaucer in front of the Café Royal. From the indentation in the velvet, one of the bolts was gone. Her mouth parched. Was Chaucer involved? And to what end? She became dazed and nauseous. She felt betrayed and deceived by a man she had come to admire.

Stumbling, she reached the door and peeped out. The gallery was clear and she left the way she had come, by the servants' stairway. Throughout the ground floor of the hall, the ball continued. She saw Helen looking for her, and when their eyes connected, relief emanated from Helen's face.

"I'm so glad you're back and in one piece, Miss. But you look quite pale."

"Where is the Queen?"

"She left a mere five minutes ago. Shall we go, too?"

"I don't want to call attention to myself by leaving so soon after breaking into a private room. So we'll relax and have some wine. I need it."

Felicity sipped the wine, which did little to give her any peace. She looked up. Duke Philip Chaucer stared at her, his eyes wide as if amazed to see her.

Turning around, she placed the glass on a table. "Blast," Felicity mouthed, and then turned around, putting on a smile. She headed to meet him. To do otherwise would ignite suspicion about why she had attended the ball or what she had discovered upstairs.

"Felicity, how kind of you to accept my invitation. Why did you not come and find me sooner?" His charm was abundant this evening, as always.

"You appeared engaged with all your guests. I didn't want to bother you."

He took up her hand. "I hope you might reserve a dance for me."

The music started in the ballroom. "Shall we?" He put out his hand.

She took it. He glanced at her bare hands, which stood out among the other women who wore gloves. "I spilled wine on my gloves and took them off."

"No matter. You look beautiful tonight," he said.

"And you very dashing."

He held her and they danced.

"Thank you for the lovely book of poetry." She gazed right at his face, hoping for an explanation of what she had seen upstairs. "It wasn't necessary."

He smiled. That captivating smile. "So little reward for saving my life. Without your intervention, I would have died most horribly." His voice trembled a bit from emotion.

"I didn't mean to push you to the ground."

"I was a bit surprised at your strength."

"It arises when needed. Have the police found a suspect?"

"I'm afraid they couldn't find their headquarters without a sign." He swirled her around.

"Well, the book you sent was most appreciated."

He brought her closer to him. "The first tales of Arthur were love stories." Raising her hand to his lips, he kept it there. His breath warming her fingers. "They were stories about ladies yearning for knights and suffering from broken hearts when their attentions were not returned."

"Or betraying love, as did Guinevere."

"Tish, tish. Are you so harsh toward your own gender?"

"Do I strike you as a yearning woman? A woman who would do anything for love? Even destroy a kingdom like Arthur's wife?" With more feeling than thinking, she stepped closer to him.

"I would love to discuss this topic more, Felicity. In depth."

They glided among the landscape of black coats and twirling gowns. "In spite of the frivolity tonight, there is also a tragedy. The death of Lord Thomas Wessex, who helped organize the Jubilee events," she said.

"There is always tragedy in the world." Despite the sympathetic words, Chaucer's bearing was the depth of arctic waters.

"Were you and Lord Wessex friends?" It couldn't hurt to find out.

"A woman's question."

"I am still curious."

"Not close, although we were related."

His pressure on her hands tightened slightly, as if he feared she might run away. His lips firmed. His posture aligned so fast, she could have sworn his vertebrae clicked. She recalled what Sir Francis Bacon had stated on the subject—the body would reveal what the mind was thinking. From his posture, she inferred that Chaucer and Wessex did not get along.

"How thoughtless of me to discuss such a sad event at this joyous occasion," she said.

The song ended, but he did not release her.

"Thank you for the dance, Felicity."

"And you for a remarkable evening."

He kissed her hand and took his leave. Felicity watched him blend back into the crowd. Turning around, he eyed her as if she might disappear.

She didn't disappear. She didn't want to appear too conspicuous. Amid the crowd, he often caught her eye and smiled. She returned it. But she was anxious to get back to Carrol Manor to analyze the materials she had found. When the fire had broken out in the east wing, she had managed to save much of her equipment, which she had stored in her room at the manor until her new laboratory could be completed. Since her father died, she had left the wooden boxes stacked in a corner. She needed to unpack the equipment.

After twenty minutes, Felicity signaled Helen it was time to leave.

"What did you find up there, Miss?" Helen whispered as they waited for their carriage in a hallway off the main doors.

Felicity rubbed her head. "Enough to give me another nightmare."

CHAPTER 30

Felicity leaned back from her microscope. During the examination, her breathing had quickened, and now she forced herself to take slower breaths at the evidence coming into focus under the lens.

She had identified the material acquired from under Chaucer's desk as dried wood pulp. But there was another coarse white material mingled with the wood pulp, which she meticulously separated out. Suspecting its nature after also studying it under the microscope, she placed a tiny bit of both substances into a ceramic bowl and threw in a lit match.

Whoof.

The material flashed a lilac color. The particular shade indicated the white grains were potassium nitrate, more commonly called saltpeter.

Potassium nitrate and wood pulp. The two ingredients, mixed with guncotton liquefied in nitroglycerin, all went into the making of blasting gelatin.

Duke Philip Chaucer had created a bomb.

She was positive about the ingredients because she had made her own version of dynamite several weeks ago to stop the spreading fire at Carrol Manor. Unlike its cousin dynamite, blasting gelatin was supposed to be safer to handle and could be formed into shapes but did require a detonator to set off its destruction. Gelatin explosive had been invented by Swedish chemist Alfred Nobel, who had also given the world dynamite.

The gelatin explosive had the odor of almonds, which is what she and the servant had smelled in the room.

The other material Felicity had discovered under the desk turned out to be a dried ceramic the color of stone.

"My God." She stood up.

Chaucer, who had earned a chemistry degree from Oxford, had made the explosive gelatin and placed it in some type of ceramic for concealment. No wonder he didn't allow the servants to clean the room. Thank goodness aristocrats were not efficient at cleaning up after themselves and she had been able to find traces of the ingredients left behind.

But why and where would he set off the device? This case had developed more limbs than the mythical kraken sea monster.

Felicity stared out the window of her room. Outside, summer had created a masterpiece of green and gold. The servants working under the sun had a fine sheen of perspiration. The sky was the bluest color imaginable above Carrol Manor. Birds flitted in nature's dance. But inside, the day was gloomy and ruined by her discovery and the realization that she had been very much fooled by Duke Philip Chaucer.

In her mind, she replayed the actions in front of the Café Royal. She slowed down the movements as if watching a stage play in the slowest of motion in hopes of detecting a motive.

The would-be assassin standing on the roof of the building across Regent Street.

The assailant bringing up the crossbow to aim.

Pushing down Duke Chaucer.

The bolt striking the pillar behind them.

Her flight to the dressmaker's shop.

The expensive cigar smoldering on the roof.

Again and again, she rewound the events. For one run-through, she focused on the man who had stood on the roof of the dress-maker's shop. She wanted to remember every detail.

He was slim. A bowler hat low on his head. Wearing a suit. The crossbow had a pull lever to stretch back the bow. The bolt was iron. Thick and deadly. The same as the weapons she had spotted at Chaucer's house.

One more time, she thought through what had happened. This time, her mind only on Duke Philip Chaucer. His eyes. His flawless gray eyes. Seconds before the bolt struck the pillar, he had glanced up and across the street as if looking for something. Or someone. She had noticed the direction of his eyes, and that's why she had looked up in time to see the assassin and pushed him out of the way.

Chaucer must have seen the man on the roof, but hadn't said anything. She chewed on her lower lip, but stopped. The biting of one's lip was a bad habit. Instead, she placed her hands on the table and pressed down with an alarming conclusion. The assassination attempt on Chaucer had been a farce, one to lead her and anyone else to believe that he was the intended victim. His bomb-making told her otherwise.

She had been so intent on saving Chaucer in front of the café, she hadn't grasped the discrepancies under his lies. Seen him as potential prey rather than a predator. She had been blinded by her attraction to him. He *was* the chess master behind everything.

And that made him the killer. But what was his motive? What did he have against others who shared the same royal blood?

Felicity sat on her bed and shook her head at the terrible, ter-rible likelihood.

"No, no, no."

The validation might be found at a madhouse.

★ ★ ★

The administrator tapped bony fingers together. His straight red-dish hair was acutely parted in the middle of his head. The sun coming through a window reflected in his glasses, so he appeared to have no eyes.

"We at Garbutt's Asylum are most discreet, Miss Holland." His voice was soothing as a toothache.

"How comforting," Felicity replied in a high-pitched voice. All part of her disguise. She didn't want to reveal her identity in case word got back to Duke Chaucer.

Along with providing a phony name, she had pulled her wavy hair to the back of her neck. She wore round spectacles she had bor-rowed from one of the servants, promising him a new pair when she returned. Her dress was as quaint as she could find at a shop near the station where she had caught the train to Dunston, some 280 miles from London. She had chosen a brimless toque hat of blue satin with a ribbon at the back. More importantly, a patterned blue netting covered her face, to which she had added extra face powder and a beauty mark on her right cheek.

"I don't want anyone to find out about Uncle Otto's peculiari-ties." The fictitious relative went along with the disguise. Felicity had made up a mental illness for him. "His alternating fits of scream-ing and laughing. Hallucinations of the strangest kind."

"I'm sure he would be very comfortable here," the administra-tor said.

"I understand that for families with means, you can house rela-tives in small cottages on the asylum grounds," she said. At such a house, Lady Chaucer had lived for many years, according to a report from Morton & Morton.

"We have several such cottages."

"Well, you do come with high recommendations. I heard you even cared for Lady Chaucer during her stay at the asylum."

His face barely broke a smile. "We never discuss our clients."

"I hoped you might say that. But a friend of a friend of a friend says her caretaker was exceptional. May I hire the same person for Uncle Otto?"

The administrator swallowed. His Adam's apple rolled up and down in his thin neck. "She is available."

"May I interview her to see if she would be a right fit for my beloved relative?"

"I shall go and find her. Why don't you wait in the physician's office? He is gone this week on holiday."

He led her down a long hallway in the brick building. The asylum consisted of the larger rectangular structure and several smaller square buildings. They were set down in a complex surrounded by a brick fence in the middle of a hay field. From afar, the asylum had the look of a large farm, except for the screams coming from elsewhere in the buildings. The place reeked of cooking potatoes.

While Felicity had waited to meet with the administrator, a woman in a plain gray dress had walked by hitting her head with both fists. Her eyes spoke of an inner hell. Behind the inmate walked a nurse in a black dress and white apron, Spartan as her demeanor.

A nurse entered the room. "The administrator said you had questions for me, Miss." She smiled.

"Jane Holland," Felicity said, and asked the woman to take a seat.

She was daunting even sitting down. Big and durable. She held dry hands on her lap. But her eyes were not what Felicity had predicted. Instead of being hardened by the madness she had seen, the nurse's eyes were sympathetic and gentle. Felicity estimated her to be in her forties. On her black dress was pinned a small cameo. The nurse's mouth was a straight line in a face more masculine than feminine. But her hair was stylish under her nurse's cap and smelled of lavender. She used nail varnish, her eyebrows were plucked, and her lips were glossy with beeswax. She wore no wedding ring. Clearly, the nurse wanted more than her lot. She was an ugly duckling who dreamed of being a swan. And although she knew she never would be, she never stopped trying.

"I am investigating places for my Uncle Otto, who has lost his mind. I understand that until three years ago, you tended Lady Chaucer."

"We are told not to give names."

"I understand and applaud your prudence," Felicity said. "How long have you worked here?"

"Ten years, Miss."

"Do you like it?"

"I like helping people who have lost their way." She pointed to her head. "In here. Most times, they never find their way home."

"Excuse me for saying this, but you are no ordinary nurse."

Her expression transformed into mistrust.

"I meant that as a compliment."

The woman shifted her head as if not used to hearing one.

"You care about your appearance in a place where no one else does, especially your male coworkers. Not born a beauty, you did not become embittered or surrender to sour envy. You see more in yourself than what your mirror reflects," Felicity said. "Although this is a demanding place, I see no cynicism in your eyes. You are kind to those in your charge. You're proud of your work, for it is your life. That makes your life noble."

The nurse's eyes watered. "It's like you read what's carved in me soul, Miss."

"I only report what I observe."

She smiled. "I did care for Lady Chaucer for the years she spent at the asylum."

"I understand she was a remarkable woman."

"She was that. She was also angry."

"May I ask about Lady Chaucer's malady? I will tell no one."

"Don't know the medical name for it. Most of the time, she would read or knit in her chair. Then she'd head into her nasty moods. She paced, shook her fists, and ranted on about how she should have been queen. How her family was the true heir to the kingdom. How they were cheated."

"How curious."

"During her rages, Lady Chaucer would yell that Albert's affections were stolen from her. He ended up marrying his first cousin, Victoria." The nurse raised her eyebrows up and down. "And you know the Victoria I mean."

Felicity put a handkerchief to her mouth to feign distress. "That is shocking."

"I felt like a traitor even listening to Lady Chaucer's rages, but it was part of my job." The nurse leaned in and lowered her voice. "She even had photos of the late Prince Albert all about her room."

"Did her son the duke come often to visit?"

"Twice a month like clockwork. Handsome he is, but never a good-morning or hello to me," the nurse said. "He'd only ask me to wait in the other room while they visited."

"What did they talk about, I wonder?" Felicity said.

She shook her large head. "The duke always closed the door. Then, after a bit, his mother started up her regular shouting and carrying on. About his legacy and destiny. Then all would go quiet. I heard her talking to him but couldn't make out the words. She was like a bee buzzing in his mind."

"How did he look when he left his mother?"

"As if his face had been whittled out of oak, firm and set. Now, about your uncle."

"You would be a fine caretaker for Uncle Otto. But I'm wondering whether it might be best if he stayed closer to home."

"I understand, Miss." She stood.

Felicity handed the woman a fifty-pound note. "For your kindness and time, and your silence if anyone inquires about our visit."

The nurse blinked in awe and gratitude.

Traveling back to London, Felicity clutched her hands together, the sound in her ears whirring like the wheels of the train. She was right about Duke Philip Chaucer. She had probably realized it when she stepped into his room full of King Arthur antiquities.

He wanted to be king and was killing everyone in his path to the throne.

He had slain those ahead of him one by one, but more relations stood between him and the crown. The explosive he made was meant for a larger number of victims in one location. Where was he going to set it off?

According to the report by Morton & Morton on Chaucer's life, the duke and Lord Thomas Wessex were among the architects of the Queen's Golden Jubilee celebration. Several of the jubilee events had already taken place, such as the parade and the gala ball Felicity had attended the previous night at Chaucer Hall. The final event of the year was going to be a service at Westminster Abbey. Before that was an official family photograph taken at Glastonbury Castle in Somerset. The photograph would be taken in three days' time. The entire royal family would be there. The Queen would be there. Her children, grandchildren, and great-grandchildren.

Glastonbury.

In the 1100s, monks at Glastonbury Abbey had claimed to have found the remains of King Arthur and Guinevere. The tale was considered a lie, supposedly told to garner fame and revenue for the abbey. Folklore also had it that Joseph of Arimathea, the keeper of the cup of Christ, had requested the abbey be built to house the Holy Grail. The grail that Arthur and his knights had sought for many years.

Since the duke had helped scheduled the Jubilee events, she imagined he had probably suggested the site. Like many castles in England, the one at Glastonbury was constructed of stone. Stone, she would bet, that was the same color as the ceramic she had found in Chaucer's room full of Arthurian artifacts. Chaucer's servant had told Helen that the duke had given a two-day holiday to all his servants just weeks before the Jubilee ball. That was probably when he had moved the explosive to Glastonbury. He must have had help from the man who had shot the crossbow bolt in front of the café. The man who had later tried to strangle her at the lake. Chaucer had wanted her out of the way because she was asking too many questions, perhaps getting too close to naming him as the killer.

She closed her eyes to see again the painting in the National Gallery. The painting of the mighty tree with the names of the royal members written upon its branches. In nature, a tree was as strong as its trunk and its roots. In the case of the British monarchy, this represented Queen Victoria. And Chaucer was attempting to topple the tree. Not topple, *slaughter* his way to the crown.

Felicity opened her eyes. The Queen and her family would go to Glastonbury Castle. They would be photographed for posterity and perhaps for the last time. He was going to kill them all.

CHAPTER 31

The effect was a good one. In the mirror, she resembled a nondescript young man. Albeit, a lad with a trace of apprehension in his green eyes. Her braided hair went up inside the boy's cap. She had obtained pants, a shirt, jacket, and suspenders from one of the young male servants at Carrol Manor. Offering a nice amount of money for the outfit, she had paid the young man extra not to tell anyone she had bought them. She wore her own riding boots but scuffed them up with a rock so they didn't appear new.

Sitting on the bed, she appreciated the comfort of her room at Carrol Manor. She would soon be leaving it to stop a killer from killing again. Yes, she was frightened down to her soles that she might never return. But her biggest fear was what would happen if she didn't make the journey.

No rail lines connected Guildford to Glastonbury, so she would have to ride there on horseback. She didn't want Matthew to drive her because she wanted no questions about the trip, especially from Helen, who watched her closely after the incident at the lake. Felicity prepared to slip away.

Before dawn, she rode off from Carrol Manor. The trip would take two days, and she would stay at an inn that night. She needed to be at the castle before the royal family arrived for the official photograph. She needed to be there to find the bomb Duke Philip Chaucer had hidden.

In a leather hunting bag she had borrowed from one of the cooks, she included an oil lantern and her lock-opening tools, as well as enough money to pay her way on her journey. She placed a box of matches in her pockets. Her father's pistols were at the London house and John Ryan and his groundskeepers carried only rifles, so she had no weapon. If she had one, would she shoot Philip Chaucer to stop him? She hesitated in her answer. Anyway, it was all academic, since she didn't have a gun. She would just have to find a different way to contain him. But first, she had to locate the bomb and disarm it to save the royalty. Then, hopefully, the police would take care of the duke.

As she rode to Glastonbury, her mind moved as swiftly as her horse clopping on the dirt road. She had thought—though not for too long—about informing Inspector Jackson Davies of her plan to foil the duke. Yet, the Scotland Yard inspector had failed to believe her three times before. She was certain he wouldn't this time either. Even if she supplied him the evidence of the bomb-making, she had found it by breaking into the duke's room. She suspected the Metropolitan Police might discount her proof because of how she had obtained it.

Must not fail. Must not fail. Must not fail. Her thoughts echoed the clomping of her horse on the road.

Back at Carrol Manor, Felicity had left a note for Helen telling her she had wanted to get away from recent events and set off on a trip. Felicity had sent another letter to the firm of Morton & Morton to be opened in the event of her death, which might be likely. With no family except Helen, she left a generous bequest to her, as well as to all the servants who had helped raise her. The will also called for Carrol Manor to be turned into a school for girls. Any girl of any class or station who wanted to learn would be admitted.

She had also named Joshua Morton as the executor since his firm had performed so well for her in the past.

In the parcel with her will, she had placed her notes on the case, the evidence she had collected during her investigation, the name of the suspect, and his inspiration for murder. If she died, the solicitor firm would deliver the package to Davies so he could bring the killer to justice if she was unsuccessful.

Must not fail. Must not fail.

Uncertainty in her chances at success clung to her like mud to the horse's legs. The duke might not even be the one to detonate the bomb. He might have other associates working for him. She forced down her doubts. She needed resolve and concentration. Nighttime was coming. She clicked her tongue for the horse to speed up.

Helen had once asked her what she would do if she did find the murderer. At last, Felicity had a reply. An answer to her father's question about what she would do with her life. An answer to her own question about her future. And it all waited for her at Glastonbury Castle.

Up ahead were the lights of Salisbury, where she would stay for the night. Felicity rode on, relaxed compared to when she had started out with the emerging sun. All her life, she had been heading to this destination.

★   ★   ★

The sunset softened the outline of Glastonbury Castle on the horizon. Thanks to a book she had found at the London Library about English castles, she had memorized the layout of Glastonbury's historic stronghold before her trip. The castle had been built in the 1200s as a protection for the region and Glastonbury Abbey, in those days one of the richest and most controlling in the country. Minor compared to the infamous Tower of London and other fortresses still standing in Great Britain, Glastonbury Castle did provide an impressive picture of majesty and power.

Jutting out of the tranquil plains, the walls of gray sandstone were seventy feet high and more than ten feet thick. Rounded towers were set at each corner. The walls of the rectangular-shaped fortress surrounded a courtyard of stone and grass.

A number of the castles in England had descended into ruin, while others had been protected, restored, and opened to visitors fascinated with the country's past. Glastonbury Castle was among the latter. But the place had been closed to visitors in preparation for the Queen and her progeny and their official photograph scheduled for the following day. That gave Felicity plenty of time to find the bomb. She hoped, anyway.

After tying her horse to a tree a few feet away, she walked to the castle. She flung the hunting bag across her shoulder. In the compelling light of the full moon, her shadow appeared tiny as a child's. Felicity threw back her shoulders to give the silhouette substance and herself courage.

Since the royal family was not scheduled to arrive until the next day, there were no guards stationed at the sturdy metal gate at the front entrance. From what she had ascertained from her research, only a gatekeeper resided in a small house off the entrance. Her watch read ten thirty, which meant the gatekeeper was probably asleep. No lights shone in his house.

Felicity peeped through the front iron gates. In the courtyard, workers had built a wooden stage where the royal family would sit for the photograph. The stage was built at the foot of the castle keep. The central tower stood more than ninety feet high and was located in the middle of the wall on the right side of the castle. That's where she would start her search for the explosive.

She would enter through a door at the back of the castle. The door was twice her size and secured. Using her tools, she went to work on the lock, lucky to be hidden in the shadow of the massive door sunken into the wall. With a rusty click, the lock opened, though she had to push hard on the door to get through. She closed it behind her. The place was clammy with condensation and age. With the matches in her pocket, she lit the oil lantern she had packed in the hunting bag.

From the drawings of the castle she had reviewed, she had to take a few right turns to find a door leading to the courtyard. Caution made her perspire, and she mopped her brow with her sleeve. In the shadowy, narrow halls, she could have been walking through a netherworld forged by a murderer. The light from the lantern formed specters on both sides of her. She was fairly confident that Chaucer, or whoever he would send to set off the bomb, would not arrive until the morning. Although she moved quickly, time slowed as if her feet were heavier than the rock walls engulfing her.

She came to a great hall. Windows high above the room let in slices of moonlight. Once lords and ladies of the castle had feasted and danced there, above them banners of their houses hung with grandeur. Her boots snapped in the emptiness. Set against one wall were two cameras, tripods, and a box of flat magnesium ribbons to light the flash lamp for the photograph of the royal family. Stacked against another wall were lines of golden chairs on which the royals would probably sit for the photograph.

A door off the hall led out to the courtyard, but it was locked. She went to work on opening it, which it did with a moan. She stepped outside.

On the grass, the stage had been built four feet tall and fifty feet long and wide, from her estimate. On top were rows of wooden risers upon which the chairs would be set. Red carpeting had been laid on top, at the front, and on two sides. Carpeted stairs led to the top. The stage had been built four feet from the castle keep. The back section of the stage was open. Felicity checked her watch.

Eleven. In case she was incorrect about where Chaucer had placed the bomb, she had time to explore.

Felicity crawled underneath the wooden structure and started her search using the lantern to light her way. She saw nothing but wood and nails. She grimaced and clamped a hand over her mouth as an exposed nail dug into her right calf.

She crawled back out and stood up. The castle keep rose above the stage like a round mountain. The duke had used gray ceramic. He must have concealed the bomb among the stones of the castle walls. The blast would cause the wall of the keep to crash down on the people below. She searched the outside wall for any indication the explosives had been placed there. With a metal tool used to open locks, she rapped at the stones. They had not been disturbed.

She returned through the door, which locked behind her, and retraced her steps back into the castle. By her estimation, she had reached the point in the keep directly in back of where the royal family would sit on the stage. She had expected to see Chaucer standing there gloating and wringing his hands in triumph like the villain in a bad play. He was not there, nor was there any sign of his bomb. If he was going to set one off, that would be the spot. From her study of the castle plans, the wall was less than two feet thick at that point.

"It has to be here," she whispered. She removed the hunting bag from her shoulder and dropped to her knees, feeling the wall with her hands.

Beneath her knees were crumbles of mortar. In the light of the lantern, she examined the grit. The material was much like what she had found at Chaucer Hall. This was not dry ancient grout, however, but damp. She used the skeleton key and dug the mortar from around one stone near the bottom of the wall. Pulling out the stone, she turned it over. One side was hollow and filled with the molded gelatin explosive.

He was going to topple the whole keep down on them all.

She moved her hands around the floor in search of the fuse. The lantern light was not that bright.

"You must be here," she whispered. Her fingers turned raw, scraping against the stone.

There it was. Tucked into the crevasse between the floor and false wall.

Then she smelled it. The scent of the Hollinger cigar.

Thunk.

A fist came down at the back of her neck, and she fell forward. Her instinct fired up. Her hands shot out to protect her head, which still hit the wall. Sparks of light blasted in her vision from the blow.

Conscious but stunned, she was yanked up by her jacket to a sitting position against the wall of explosives. In the light of her lantern stood Duke Philip Chaucer holding a gun in his right hand. An Enfield service revolver, official sidearm of the British Army. Eighteen-rounds-per-minute rate of fire. He pointed the barrel at her head. On his finger was a large ring with golden chimera. The supposed symbol of Arthur.

She attempted to get up.

"Please stay where you are," he ordered. He was dressed as a humble worker.

"Your disguise is a smart choice. As you were constructing your wall of destruction, you probably didn't stand out among the other workers around the castle as they prepared for the visit of the royal family." With her sleeve, she wiped at the blood trickling down from where her head had hit the wall.

At his side, Chaucer wore a sheathed sword with a chimera handle. The same one she had seen as his home.

"That sword doesn't go with your disguise, however," Felicity said. She rubbed her head, which ached from the bash.

"I apologize. I did find it difficult striking a woman."

She touched the back of her neck, which also pulsated with pain. "You didn't seem to mind suffocating Elaine Charles."

One side of his mouth lifted. "She was pathetically boring and so frail. I did her a service really. With that heart of hers, she probably wouldn't have lasted more than a few years anyway. But she did serve a purpose."

"To distract Scotland Yard away from your real objective. Oh yes, you did covet her painting. And incriminating Joe Crumb in Lord Wessex's murder. That was clever, planting the stolen goods on him as he slept. I suspect you also alerted the constables about a drunk in the park."

"The ploy did work on the police, but unfortunately not on you."

"And the others you killed. William." Felicity started to rise in anger. He wiggled the barrel of the gun at her. "In his own blood, he called you traitor. Medraut. Like Mordred who betrayed his king."

"William always had a dramatic flair."

"It was all you, Philip. Out of a twisted sense of honor, you couldn't let any commoner dispatch other royals. No, the deed had to be done by your hand and not the henchman you sent to kill me. Besides, the murder scenes were as perfect as they were brutal. I even suspect you took pleasure in the killings."

His head slanted to one side as if assessing Felicity's situation. "I don't take you as a screamer, so I won't gag you. But if you yell, I will hit you again."

"Such a gentleman," she said.

He bowed.

"And you should have been an actor. Your performance at the Café Royal was seamless. But you made a mistake when you looked up at the roof across the street. You expected the attack. On the roof I found a high-priced cigar. The same brand I found at the park where Thomas Wessex was slain. The same cigar you offered to your guests during the ball."

"Ah, the Hollinger. I am allowed some vices."

She sat up, albeit with effort. "That bolt *was* meant for me in front of the Café Royal. If your compatriot had killed me, I couldn't ask any more questions, and you'd never be a suspect. But I lived and you sent him to my home for another try. Well, he got the worst of it. Your only loyal subject is in jail."

"So I heard. But my man will never talk. I trust him completely." He said this very slowly, as if she didn't comprehend her predicament.

"What did you do? Promise to make him an earl if you succeeded?"

"I must have struck you too hard."

"You're going to have to kill me if you want me to stop."

He grinned with admiration, crouched down, and placed his hand on her cheek. The other held the gun. "You are quite the survivor, Felicity Carrol. Rising out of the water like the Lady of the Lake. I did regret sending him after you, and when you turned up at the ball, I was delighted. Of course, our relationship would have been short-lived because you knew too much. If you only had been accepting of my calling, what a queen you might have made."

"Not the best circumstances in which to romance a girl."

"See, no understanding." He stood up.

"Well, I'm not your Nimue, Guinevere, or even Alice in Wonderland." She pointed to the sword at his side. "And that is not Excalibur, because there was no Arthur. Because of what you've done, you're not even fit to wear the crown."

"You are a stupid girl." He slapped his chest. "You carry nothing but blood in your veins. I have the blood of Arthur in mine, of every king who has ruled England. It is my destiny, and no one will get in my way."

She was more furious than frightened. Enraged at the carnage this man had left in his wake. "All those people you killed because of this insane plan to steal the throne of England. Did you tire of getting rid of them one by one?"

"It *was* tiresome but necessary. And yes, I did want the antiquities they owned. This scheduled photograph was a godsend. Otherwise my ascension would take forever. I would have been an old man. Now there is only this last task."

"They're your family. Are you going to kill women and children? The Queen? Please, Philip, I beg you not to do this. For the sake of your soul."

"A king is anointed by God, and so am I." He quickly looked at his watch. "Soon, my relatives will start to gather behind this very wall. And it will become their crypt."

"I *am* going to scream." She hated women who yelled like the damsels of old, but she hoped someone might hear and stop this madman.

"The wall is too thick, and the workers don't arrive until six in the morning."

"You're right. Yelling is a waste of time." She guessed the hour to be near one in the morning.

"No one will even hear the bullet go through your head. Someday your body might be found amid the rubble. Someday." In the lantern light, his handsome face distorted into malignancy. "I did enjoy knowing you."

She had to move or she would never move again. She didn't fear death as much as failing to stop this man. Grabbing her leather bag, Felicity kicked at the lantern, sending it crashing against the wall. The room sank into blackness.

"No!" he shouted, and her skin shrank with the venom in his voice.

She heard a bullet whiz by her head. She jumped up, aimed her body at where Chaucer last stood, and crashed into his legs. There was an *umph* from where he landed on the rocky floor. Then a *clank* when the handgun hit the ground. Scrambling to her feet, she ran through the unlit corridor and headed to the great hall. She expected a bullet to slam into her back at any moment, that is, if he had found the gun in the blackness. As she ran, all she could hear was the sound of her footsteps and breathing.

When she reached the great hall, she swiveled around. Chaucer was not behind her. But he would be coming. She had no weapon, while he had that damnable sword and perhaps the revolver, if he had located it. She was betting he hadn't taken time to look for the gun. A risky bet, but she believed his fury would drive him on. Her lock-opening tools were in the leather bag, but she had no time to work on the locked door leading out to the courtyard and possibly escape. He was coming.

Reason it out, she urged herself.

The room was empty except for the chairs and photography equipment. She needed a weapon. She could break one of the golden chairs and use a leg as a stout sword.

No, there was a better option of escape, and she grinned as much as she could manage. Dashing to the stack of photographic equipment, she picked up three of the flat magnesium ribbons that would be used to illuminate the flash lamp. She also patted her pockets to make sure the matches were there.

Recalling the setup of the castle, she headed straight to a set of stairs leading up to the battlements on top of the walls. From there she would yell and try to summon help from the groundskeeper. Small windows in the high walls allowed in moonlight to show her the way.

Taking the stairs, she headed to the battlement. Once there, she yelled for help. Stillness answered her. The stone parapets were waist high. She dared to look down at the long way to the court-yard below.

Footsteps behind her declared Chaucer's approach.

"Help!" she called again. She spun around. Philip Chaucer ran up the stairs to the battlement. She moved the magnesium ribbons behind her back.

Chaucer had no revolver but carried the sword in front of him. The blade flashed in the moonlight and the point was aimed at her heart.

"You have caused me enough trouble." He breathed as though his chest might burst with spite. "Every king has to fight for what is his."

"How dare you even contemplate that you might be the new King Arthur. Real or not, he stood for good and truth. You have none of those qualities."

"How dare you speak to your king in such a manner!"

She stepped back to keep her distance from him and give her time to use her own impromptu defense. "A sword doesn't make a king, Philip. A mighty heart makes a sovereign."

Despite his rage, his eyes teared like a boy lost forever.

"For years, your mother poisoned your mind with this terrible ambition as her mind had been poisoned. She hated the Queen and passed on that hate to you over the years."

Behind her back, Felicity pulled a match from her pocket.

"Do not speak of my mother. She gave me purpose." His breathing increased as he spoke. "Every dynasty requires a sacrifice." He charged her.

Felicity scraped the match against the stone. It flared up. She lit the end of one of the magnesium ribbons, threw it at Chaucer's face, and hid her eyes with her hands.

The flash strobed the night sky. Chaucer screamed and backed against the parapet. Eyes red from the flash, he gritted his teeth with hate and again raised the sword to strike. Felicity lit the other ribbon and threw it at his head, and then another.

Dropping the sword to shield his eyes, he took more steps back, hit the parapet ledge, and toppled back and downward over the wall. His yells faded into the night and ended with an awful thud below.

Felicity ran back down to the great hall and opened the locked door leading out into the courtyard. She stood over the shattered body of Philip Chaucer on the stones. She was as shattered. She threw her arms around herself to steady her shivering. If she hadn't fought him, her body would be lying on the parapet above or slashed with the sword he thought was Excalibur. But his death was no victory.

Holding a lantern, an old man in a white nightshirt ran up to her. "What in heaven's name is going on here?" He panted with age and fright when he saw the body. "What are you doing here?"

"Foiling a plan to kill the Queen of England and her family," she said flatly.

He had no answer to that.

"Is there a constabulary?" Her voice was peaceful as the night.

The old man nodded his head in affirmation.

"You must send for them."

The groundskeeper placed his lantern close to the body. "So this man was going to harm the Queen?"

"And her family."

"Maybe it's good he's dead." The old man glanced up from the body to Felicity. "And who are you?"

"No one really. A loyal subject."

He ran off, his nightshirt flapping like a bird's wings. Felicity gazed down at the remains of the man who had wanted to be king and sat down beside the body. His corrupt dream, like his body, crushed on the stones. Another quote by Alfred, Lord Tennyson, pierced her mind.

"'Better not be at all than not be noble,'" she recited, and began to cry.

CHAPTER 32

Inspector Jackson Davies rushed to her. "My God, are you all right, Felicity?"

"Only a few bumps." She didn't want to sound flippant. A man was dead.

In the middle of the courtyard at Glastonbury, Davies engulfed her in his arms. She was taken aback at his action, as if he were a gallant knight ready to save the damsel, albeit one who had saved herself from the dragon. She didn't move away, however. She liked the feel of his embrace and allowed herself to remain there for a while.

"I'm happy you're here, Jackson. I was worried you wouldn't come."

"I will always be there. Maybe late, but I will come."

"I believe you will."

"So why are you dressed up like a boy?"

"It's a rather long story." At that point, Felicity had already lost track of the number of times she had recounted the events of the previous evening. Really, she was too tired to count.

Upon their arrival to Glastonbury Castle, two local constables had first listened to her account. One of them had rushed back to the constabulary in Glastonbury to wire for directions from the

Queen's Guard and Scotland Yard on how to proceed. That's what another constable had told Felicity while they waited in the great hall.

As the morning came, so did Jackson Davies. With him was the Queen's Guard commander to prepare for the visit of Her Majesty and the royal family later that morning *and* to investigate the happenings of the previous night. Felicity showed everyone the sample of the explosives Duke Philip Chaucer had placed in the wall of the castle keep.

"Lord in heaven," pronounced one of the constables. "It would have brought down perdition on them all."

The Queen's Guard commander reached down to touch the faux stone containing the blasting gelatin, but he stopped.

"It's quite safe, sir," Felicity said, and picked it up. "The gelatin has to be detonated." She proceeded to show them the fuse.

The men removed eighty bricks containing explosive material.

Near the stone wall was the gun Chaucer had dropped when she rammed her body into his. Up on the parapet, she showed them the sword with which he had tried to kill her, as well as the burned magnesium ribbons that had saved her life.

The mouths of the men stayed open while she explained what had happened and how she had escaped from the murderous duke. Chaucer's fist had created quite an egg of a bump on the back of her neck, and she had a cut on the front of her head from where he had knocked her into the wall. She held out her hands which had been burned from igniting the flash ribbons. The gatekeeper, who had since put on his pants, cleaned her wounds.

Everyone stood in the great hall of Glastonbury Castle, which had been lit with candles and lanterns. There Felicity outlined to the Queen's Guard commander and the constables how she had unearthed Duke Philip Chaucer's plot to murder his way to the crown. She left out the fact that she had broken into the duke's room at his house. She didn't want to go to jail. Later in the day, she repeated the case specifics for a finely dressed representative of the prime minister.

"Gentleman, I am sure if you search Chaucer Hall, you will find traces of the explosives he made and intended to use here today." She had talked so much her throat had begun to burn, and she asked for water. "I am also convinced you will discover the *Le Morte d'Arthur* manuscript belonging to the late William Kent as well as the tapestry owned by late Viscount Banbury and Elaine Charles's Guinevere painting."

"Why didn't you report all this beforehand to Scotland Yard?" the guard commander asked. His hands were big enough to crush her head if he so desired.

Felicity did not look at Davies. She didn't want to get him in trouble. She smiled. "Because no one would have believed me, sir. Who would believe an amateur sleuth with a story about a duke killing his way to the throne of England?"

The commander grinned through a thicket of a mustache. "You're probably right, Miss. To tell you the truth, I didn't believe you either until we found the explosives."

Davies cleared his throat. "Miss Carrol did mention her suspicions to me, but I did not believe her, either. To my shame." He kept his head down. "I apologize for my doubts."

She bowed her head at him, though he still didn't look at her.

The questioning continued for another two hours.

"May I go home? I am quite exhausted," she said.

"I can understand why," the prime minister's representative said with courtesy in his otherwise bureaucratic voice.

She rubbed her aching neck. "I would not be lying if I called this the most extraordinary day of my life."

"Extraordinary for any day, Miss Carrol," the representative said.

"I am going home to Carrol Manor in Surrey. I don't intend to leave the country or go anywhere except to bed. I believe Inspector Davies will vouch for me," Felicity said.

The guard commander looked at the prime minister's representative, who looked at the constables, and they all turned to Davies. They dipped their heads one by one.

"We'll check out your suspicions, Miss Carrol," Davies said.

"I am sure you will, Inspector."

Before Felicity left Glastonbury Castle, the royal family began filing in for the photograph. She asked Davies if she could stay and watch for a moment.

"I thought you were exhausted," he said.

"I am, but I want to see the fruits of my labors, so to speak."

The women wore impeccable dresses and jewel earrings. The men had on their most elegant suits and top hats. Medals, golden braiding, and sashes bedecked the uniforms on other royalty. Boys messed with their kilts, while the curls of the young girls bounded with each of their steps up to the stage.

The Queen was the last to arrive and be seated. She was clothed in her familiar black silk and crown atop a white veil down her back. While she didn't smile in any of the photographs Felicity had seen of her, Victoria smiled as her family was arranged about her on the stage to commemorate her fifty years as head of England.

The photographer stood at the end of the stage. Duke Philip Chaucer had selected Glastonbury Castle for a nefarious reason, but the grand and historic setting did befit the monarch and her kin. When ready, the photographer's assistant asked for the royal family to pose. The flash ignited and the photograph was taken. Felicity grinned so hard the sides of her cheeks smarted.

Afterward, the constables escorted Felicity to Carrol Manor in their carriage with her horse tied behind. She slept all the way there.

CHAPTER 33

At the Café Royal on Regent Street, Felicity sat at the exact table where she and Duke Philip Chaucer had talked. Two days before, she had written a message to Inspector Davies and asked him to lunch. She wondered if he would show up, but at precisely noon, he came up the stairs.

He moved his eyes about the café. "I can't believe you chose this place, Felicity."

"I thought it might be amusing."

"Amusing to visit a place where you almost got killed?"

"Yes, but it makes one appreciate one's survival. Please, sit."

He did.

"I ordered lunch, if that's all right." She winked. "I made it nice and expensive, but I'm buying."

"I wouldn't have expected anything less."

Once the waiter poured tea for them, he vanished, as was his custom. The same waiter who had served her and Chaucer.

"How have you been? Injuries healing?" he asked.

"Yes, except one. I still feel terrible for not catching on sooner to Duke Philip Chaucer and his murderous plan. Like others, I had been swayed by his charm and charisma. That, and my own desire to protect what I thought was another victim."

"He was a clever man. We were all duped."

"Well, it was my first time meeting an actual murderer." She winked and sipped her tea.

Davies did not pick up his cup. He stared at his hands, knotted in his lap.

"What is it, Jackson?"

He looked up at her. "I'm glad you invited me to lunch, Felicity. I was going to write you a letter when I got up the nerve." He tugged at his collar. "You know, I can face cold-blooded thieves and scoundrels, but the thought of that letter gave me the sweats."

"What were you going to say?" She placed down her cup.

"That I was sorry you lost faith in me, Felicity. I was going to write that I should have trusted you and your methods and deductions. And because I didn't, you placed yourself in harm's way to save the Queen and the royal family. You got hurt because of my lack of trust in your conclusions."

"A nice sentiment, Jackson."

"And much harder to say to your face than send in a letter, although it is a very nice face."

She normally would have taken offense at such compliments but didn't on this occasion. "We can try at being friends again, at trusting each other."

"I'd like that."

"Did you get into trouble with your superiors because of what happened at Glastonbury Castle?"

"No, but they did say that if you had any more opinions about a case in the future, I should take heed of them," he said.

"So will you?" She threw him a devilish grin.

"Maybe." He returned one just as devilish.

"How would you have ended your letter to me, Jackson?"

He cleared his throat. "I would have written that I shall never doubt you again. And if you ever get back to town, please look me up. I would buy you luncheon and you could talk about all the crime you wanted."

"I couldn't ask for a nicer apology."

"I do have a gift for you."

She made a significant act of looking about. "Where are the flowers and perfume, eh?"

"Couldn't afford them. I have something better, but after."

The waiter served them the salmon pâté she had ordered. But she didn't eat right away.

"Jackson, as long as we are being honest, I have to admit I didn't want to believe Duke Philip Chaucer was the murderer."

"Why?"

"Why do you think?"

"Oh." He placed his hands on his lap. "I guess he was dashing and intelligent. A prince charming in the flesh."

"Yes, he was. Not to mention homicidal."

He grinned. They dug into their lunch and chatted about the unsolved murders in London. Felicity hadn't spent such a pleasant time in years.

After they finished eating, Davies led her to a black carriage of the Metropolitan Police outside the café.

"You're not going to arrest me, are you?" she asked as a joke, though she was not completely sure she wasn't going to be taken into custody for meddling in a murder investigation.

"Part of the surprise. Get in, please." He held out his hand, which was rough and comforting simultaneously. "And no questions until we get there. I know it will be torture for you."

"I didn't realize you had a sense of humor, Jackson."

Within a mile or so, she realized they were heading to Chaucer Hall.

"Why are we going there, Jackson?"

"I believe I owe you a look, a real look, at Chaucer's Arthur collection. No more sneaking about this time."

As part of her narrative about the events leading up to

Glastonbury, she had confessed to Davies how she had examined the room during the Jubilee ball. He informed her it was breaking and entering, and she replied that, since she had been invited to Chaucer Hall, the law might not apply. Besides, the only items she had removed were evidence of Chaucer's bomb-making.

She followed Davies into Chaucer's room of antiquities. Behind them were six constables. Everyone stood motionless because of the number of relics in the room, as well as their beauty and history.

"They are very exquisite," Felicity said at last. "Especially to see them in the day."

She showed the inspector the desk where she had found the ingredients the duke had used to mix the explosive gelatin.

"We should also look under the floor by the fireplace," she added.

"Because?" Davies said.

"When I visited before, I heard the floorboards squeak but didn't have time to investigate more than that."

Under a rug, Davies located a door in the floor and opened it. Underneath was a small chamber and sacks of materials. Davies jumped down into the chamber and handed out the sacks to a constable, while Felicity checked out the ingredients.

"Saltpeter, potassium nitrate, wood pulp, and nitroglycerin, everything needed for a bomb."

"It is safe, Felicity?" Davies said, pulling himself out of the chamber under the floor and slapping dust off his hands.

"We won't all blow up, if that's what you mean."

The find also included bags of gray mortar. "Chaucer used this material to form those stones at the castle, didn't he?" he asked Felicity.

"Right on all counts."

A constable called to them from the back of the gigantic room.

"Look what we found, Inspector." The officer showed a chamber hidden behind a large tapestry. "We had to break a lock to get in."

With Felicity following, Davies lit a gaslight that shone upon the property stolen from the murder victims. Elaine Charles's Guinevere painting hung on one wall, alongside the King Arthur tapestry owned by the late Viscount Richard Banbury. Set on a superb silk cloth surrounded by candles, Sir Thomas Malory's *Le Morte d'Arthur* manuscript was displayed with a kind of reverence. Felicity's fingers brushed one of the pages. The book was open to the section about the Lady of the Lake.

"Look at this," Davies said.

He had opened a wooden box sitting in the corner. She bent down for a closer view of a flail. "The spikes on this weapon match those on the wounds of Richard Banbury," she said.

The air in the smaller chamber seemed to have dissipated. She returned to the larger room, where constables were busy removing the evidence of the crimes.

Davies came up to her. "Why in blazes did he keep all this?" He scratched his head.

"You don't understand, Jackson; he really did believe in the story of Arthur. He wanted it to be true. Philip Chaucer had no spirit in the water to guide him to his imagined kingdom. Only a mad ambition."

"And what a terrible thing that was."

Davies and the constables busied themselves with the evidence left by Chaucer. Felicity watched but thought of Tennyson's epic poem *Idylls of the King*. The part where Arthur struck down his nephew Mordred with Excalibur, but not before Mordred had dealt the king a mortal blow.

Then spake the King: "My house hath been my doom.
But call not thou this traitor of my house
Who hath but dwelt beneath one roof with me."

CHAPTER 34

Sucking in air, Felicity approached 10 Downing Street. Though she disliked shopping, she had bought a new outfit for the appointment. A purple skirt and jacket the color of a splendid sunset as well as black silk gloves and a hat from Paris. If she was going to be imprisoned for inserting herself inside such an important case, she was going to make sure to dress oh-so-stylishly when imprisoned in the Tower of London. Anne Boleyn had probably had the same idea as she was led away for an engagement with the man wearing a black hood.

The country's prime minister had summoned her there with a note on the best stationery. The note was polite and a good sign she probably wouldn't end up in a cell of stone and metal, Felicity had told Helen.

"You're right, Miss; otherwise, the invitation might have been delivered by an armed guard," the ever truthful Helen had replied.

Glancing at her watch, Felicity arrived a little before her appointment at the building on Downing Street in Westminster, London. With its unpretentious brick demeanor, Number 10 did not even look like what it was—the seat of the British Government. In 1732, Number 10 had started out as three houses awarded by King George the Second to the first lord of the treasury, a job presently held by the prime minister. The three houses were later joined into the larger one. If that wasn't enough to hold Number 10's place in English power, nearby was Westminster Palace.

Felicity had read up on the history of 10 Downing Street before her visit. She might be tested later, she thought with amusement. Her favorite fact about the property was that one of the early residents had been Thomas Knyvet, the keeper of Whitehall Palace. Knyvet had captured the notorious Guy Fawkes in 1605 and stopped Fawkes's plot to kill King James the First. She and Knyvet could have commiserated about the foiling of plots.

The black oak door with the number 10 on it was bounded by cream-colored casting with a fan-shaped window above. She took a breath and reached out to the knocker shaped like a lion's head, but an ancient clerk in a neat black suit opened the door for her before she could knock.

"Miss Felicity Carrol?" he said.

"I am."

With the wave of a gloved hand, he showed her in. He moved with such decorum, she hoped he wouldn't break into tiny pieces if he tripped. Then again, he would probably never trip. The black-and-white-checkered marble floor of the entrance hall reminded her of an ongoing chess game. A stunning white fireplace dominated the room.

"The prime minister would like to see you out on the terrace," the clerk said. "Please come this way."

She followed him to another part of the building. They walked past a stone and wrought-iron staircase with mahogany handrails and a decorative scroll design. The staircase had been installed when the interior was reworked in the 1730s. On the walls were photographs or paintings of the past prime ministers. All those eyes staring down at her. She smoothed her skirt, though it didn't need it. She did relish the atmosphere, which was thick with history.

The terrace ran across the back of the building with a view of Number 10's enclosed lovely garden of flowers, lawn, and trees in a large courtyard below.

The man himself stood contemplating the garden, as if it was a reprieve from the business of running the British Empire. In his photographs, the prime minister was a foreboding, serious, and imposing figure. Then again, all government officials wore that same expression in official photographs. Must have been a requirement of the job.

The clerk coughed to call the prime minister's attention to Felicity's presence. When he had it, the clerk introduced her.

"Your Excellency." She hoped this was the correct greeting.

"My dear Miss Carrol. Good to meet you at last. I have heard so much about you."

She wasn't sure if that was a good thing.

The prime minister nodded to the clerk. "Thank you, Merriweather."

The clerk left with all his decorum intact.

"I thought this might be more pleasant than one of the meeting rooms in Number 10. I am inside so often with the government's work, I find it refreshing to take a break outside. I do appreciate nature," he told her. His voice was deep and genuine.

"I understand, Mr. Prime Minister. I love the outdoors, also." She breathed in the morning air, which was clean and fresh. The day had already warmed up, but she contended with icy toes and fingers that had plagued her ever since the events at Glastonbury Castle. Fortunately, the chill dissipated a little each day.

The prime minister placed large hands behind his back. "You might wonder why I have called you here."

"Not at all. You want to talk about what transpired at Glastonbury Castle."

"I have read all the reports from the constables, the Queen's

Guard commander, and a Scotland Yard inspector. Quite an exploit. My word, it read like a novel."

"You really had to be there to appreciate it, sir."

"And your wounds?"

"I am quite well, thank you for asking."

He put a hand to his mouth. His posture aligned, and she swore he even grew an inch. He was about to say something important.

The prime minister took one of her hands and kissed it. "May I say the Queen extends her utmost thanks for your intervention in this astonishing and troubling affair. She wanted me to thank you for saving her family and her life, and at great risk to your own."

"I am grateful I could help, and I am overwhelmed at the Queen's gratitude."

"Miss Carrol, you have done a tremendous service not only to Her Majesty but to this country, this nation." His voice took on an oratory ring. "There is one matter . . ."

Here comes the rest, Felicity thought.

"Queen Victoria and I agree, along with top advisers of this government, that the appalling plot of Duke Philip Chaucer to seize the crown must never be revealed to the public. Such information might cause instability in the monarchy. The scheme of one royal killing another to obtain the crown would shake the entire empire."

Felicity probably didn't have to remind the prime minister that one monarch murdering another to gain or keep a throne was not unusual. Uncommon certainly, but it did occur, including in England. Queen Elizabeth herself had ordered the execution of her half sister, Mary Queen of Scots. Richard the Third had been responsible for the death of Henry the Fifth and his brother the Duke of York after he disappeared into the bowels of the Tower of London, though historians continued to debate who was to blame. At any rate, though, this was probably not the right time to talk history with the prime minister.

"Are you astonished by our request for secrecy?" he asked.

"Not at all. I had seen no stories in *The Times* about the true events that took place at Glastonbury Castle. There was only the short notice about the death of Duke Philip Chaucer. I assumed something was going on behind the newsprint."

"We will release a statement later this week but wanted to speak with you first."

"How will you account for Duke Chaucer's demise, Mr. Prime Minister?" she asked.

"We shall say Duke Chaucer was under extreme stress and accidentally fell from the parapet to his death at Glastonbury Castle."

"It *was* accidental. I didn't mean for him to fall."

"If he had not died that day, *you* would have, along with the Queen and the royal family." He took out a handkerchief and patted perspiration from his head. "We all believe keeping this secret is the best for all concerned."

"And what about the constables, the guards, and Scotland Yard? They were there and know the truth."

"They have been sworn to secrecy as well. Do you mind if I sit? My lumbago aches me leg."

"Please."

He took a seat at a wrought-iron chair and asked her to sit as well. "Miss Carrol, may we count on your silence in this dreadful episode?"

"Although I believe the truth is always best, in this case I understand and agree, sir. You have my word," she said.

His big head bowed in appreciation. "The crown does owe you a service, even though it may be a secretive one." He again mopped his large brow with a handkerchief. "Is there any reward you seek?"

She didn't need any money or lands. "How about a knighthood?"

"What?" The prime minister coughed with confusion.

"A jest, Your Excellency."

"I heard you had a sense of humor. But really, what can the crown do for you?"

Felicity thought of what she had gone through. The doubts, the pain, the humiliation. The possibility of death twice over.

She could only smile. "I do have something in mind."

★ ★ ★

Felicity walked around the manor and chatted with each of the servants—from those in the kitchen to those in the stables and in between. She asked about their families, their health, and their work. Many of them had been in her family's employ since she was a girl, and she knew them well because she had ignored her father's attitude that servants should be seen but not acknowledged unless needed. For the last month, Felicity had swept through the manor while on her investigation and had spoken very little to any of them with the exception of Helen. There was a crime in that neglect, and she hoped now to make it right.

Felicity had not told Helen about what had happened at Glastonbury Castle or about the plot of Duke Philip Chaucer. She had merely told her friend that the murders of William Kent and the others had been solved.

"I cannot tell you anything else, my dear," she told Helen after her visit with the prime minister in London. "You must trust me, Hellie."

"I trust you. Always have."

"Let me assure you, the culprit has already been severely penalized for his crimes."

"As it should be," Helen said.

The manor had gone through other changes while Felicity worked on the murder cases. Helen's brother Horace Wilkins had left one week earlier to work for her late father's friend, solicitor Martin Jameson.

"I hope you are not too saddened that your brother has joined Mr. Jameson's household," Felicity told Helen.

"Miss, I truly believe those two deserve each other."

After Wilkins's departure, Felicity had asked Abraham Stephens to take his place as head butler in charge of the household staff. In his thirties, Stephens's affability was demonstrated by the household staff's respect and admiration for him. His wife, Molly, who worked as a cook at the manor, was just as cheery and kind. Stephens had accepted the position with appreciation and grace. Felicity had also selected him because he was excited about her plan to install electric lights throughout the manor and in her new laboratory.

"Those electric things will save us having to light all those candles and gaslights at night. Not to mention cutting down on wicks and replacing candles," Stephens had remarked. "And consider the money you will save on matches, Miss Felicity." He grinned.

"Exactly," she had replied.

Felicity was most pleased at her first decision as the legal head of Carrol Manor. She had decided to increase the wages of the staff there and at the house in London as well. They deserved the boost for their generous treatment of her through the years. They had been her family.

She had read the latest financial reports on her family's businesses and investments that Martin Jameson's firm had delivered. Her monetary future was guaranteed, and she would do her best to ensure that the companies continued to run efficiently. The many workers in the mills and shipping lines depended on them, and her. She would also move forward with studies to modernize the operations and guarantee a safe environment for the employees. She had already written the managers of both companies asking them to increase the wages of the people who worked there. They wrote back saying that it was about time.

A week had gone by since the incident at Glastonbury. One afternoon Felicity had tea in the library. Never had she been so weary. The earth's gravity seemed to yank her soul down through the covering of crust and rock. In the days since the murder of her friend William Kent, her whole existence had been engrossed in finding his murderer, and she had. Her life had forever been altered by her experiences during the last few weeks. She had transformed into a person who wanted justice not only for William Kent, but for the victims of one man's avarice for the crown. From that, she had gained a tremendous amount of satisfaction. She had also settled on her own goal in life.

She would seek justice for the murdered and damaged. She would direct her head, heart, and vast resources to this goal. The thought revived her.

Her father would have been quite scandalized by such a decision.

"I have finally realized my purpose, Father," she said out loud in the empty library. "I hope you would be proud of this accomplishment."

She remembered herself as a young girl sitting in her mother's chair and reading, lonely and unhappy. As an adult, she now sat in the same chair. This time, smiling, happy, and comfortable in her own house. As Duke Philip Chaucer had called her, she was a survivor.

She had come home at last.

CHAPTER 35

At six in the evening, Inspector Jackson Davies appeared at the front door of Carrol Manor. Felicity was there to greet him.

"Thank you for coming all the way out here, Jackson."

"My pleasure."

Helen stood behind her young mistress and curtsied at the Scotland Yard inspector. He bowed his head. Helen smiled and hugged him. Davies gave a clear sigh of relief at her greeting.

Felicity and Davies ate in one of the smaller dining rooms. She had planned a good dinner of venison, which had come from the woods on the estate. Alongside the meat were red potatoes, asparagus, and bread so fresh it was warm in the middle.

"I neglected to ask about Joe Crumb, the drunkard you arrested for murdering Thomas Wessex at Belgrave Square," she said. "What happened?"

"We let him go."

"Good for you."

"And the man who attacked me at the lake, did he ever say anything?" Felicity asked during the soup course.

"His name is Simon Manley," Davies said.

"Who is he?"

"When Manley learned about the duke's death, we couldn't

stop him from talking. Manley was a childhood friend of Chaucer who had tumbled into financial hardships. The duke hired him to attack you, Felicity. Though Manley claimed he was only trying to scare you."

"He did a good job." She placed down her soup spoon.

"Manley says the duke promised him thousands of pounds for the assault but never told him why, and he didn't ask questions." He wiped his mouth with a napkin. "Trouble is, Manley won't confess to shooting the crossbow at you in front of the Café Royal. No one could identify him as the culprit. Even you."

"Since English courts don't admit fingerprints as evidence, it would be no use matching his to the crossbows at Chaucer's home."

"We took Manley to Chaucer Hall. The duke's head butler did recognize him and said he had visited the duke several times during the last six months. The butler didn't know the man's name, only that the duke had ordered Manley to have access to the hall at any time."

"Nice detective work."

He narrowed eyes at her. "Are you being sarcastic?"

"Not at all. Simon Manley probably helped the duke move the explosives to the castle at Glastonbury," Felicity said.

"Good assumption, but we have no evidence to connect Simon Manley with Chaucer's plot to become king. If we did, we could hang him for treason. The only consolation is that Manley will be in prison a long time for attempting to murder you."

"That will do." She raised her wine glass. "And there is justice for all the victims of Duke Philip Chaucer."

He saluted with his glass.

"To William, Richard, Elaine, and Thomas," she said.

"Aye."

After dinner, Felicity suggested to Davies that they walk to the lake. Sunset began to kiss the landscape with evening color as they strolled.

"And you will be happy to hear this," Davies said. "The tapestry Duke Chaucer stole was returned to the estate of the Viscount Richard Banbury, and the Guinevere painting went to the family of Elaine Charles."

"Well done, Inspector. And what of William Kent's manuscript?"

"That book and Kent's sizable collection of King Arthur artifacts were all donated to the British Museum, as noted in his will."

She took his arm. "There is a lovely completeness in that."

When they reached the lake, the water twinkled in the sunset. Felicity and Jackson Davies rowed out to the island, stood by the edge, and let the cool water tease their bare feet.

"It is beautiful here," he said.

"Yes, beautiful. When I used to come out here, I felt very lonely."

"Now?"

Leaning her head back, she filled her lungs with as much air as they could hold. She swore the delicious evening breeze had entered her body, her being. "That lonely girl has vanished, and good riddance."

"I should be starting back to London," he said.

"I have one more thing to do to wrap up this case, and I wanted you with me."

From under the bench in the pavilion, she retrieved a burlap bag she had placed there that morning. She took out the sword.

"Is that?"

"The prime minister asked if I wanted a reward for saving the Queen and her family, and this is what I requested."

The sword flashed in the full moon. The sword Duke Philip

Chaucer had thought he deserved for his kingdom. His perverted idea of Excalibur. Not acquired from the hand of the Lady of the Lake with the promise to do good, but procured with money. Chaucer's sword symbolized murder and greed for a crown.

The sword was heavy in her hands. She ran her fingers over the gold chimera carved into the handle.

"Go on then," Davies said.

With all her might, Felicity flung the sword into the water.

Acknowledgments

I could not have stepped back in time without the aid of many resources, including help from the House of Parliament Parliamentary Archives and the British Railroad Museum as well as information from the websites of the Royal Parks, the Digital Library of Villanova University, the University of London, the City of London, the Victoria and Albert Museum, the Metropolitan Police, the BBC, Wikipedia, Express.co.uk, Nationalarchives.gov.uk, Britishnewspaperarchive.org, Historic UK, Smithsonianmag.com, and Nationalgallery.org.

I am most grateful to my writing friend Bonnie Dodge for her insights; to my terrific agent, Elizabeth Kracht, who helped me become a better writer; and to editor Faith Black Ross, who helped this become a better book. Ongoing love to my family who support me in all that I do.